Advance Praise for

EVERYTHING I NEED TO KNOW
I LEARNED FROM DUNGEONS & DRAGONS

"Mazzanoble is one brave she-warrior. In *Everything I Need to Know I Learned from Dungeons & Dragons*, she delightfully bares the mundane details of a 21st century woman's life—from religion to love, domesticity to dietary habits—refracting her vision through the 20-sided prism of D&D. All the while, she battles and playfully defeats her most fearsome foe, her mother. Huzzah!"
　　　　　—Ethan Gilsdorf, author of *Fantasy Freaks and Gaming Geeks*

"Looking at life as one big (adventuring) party, Shelly Mazzanoble shows us 'how she rolls,' by meeting her every day encounters with self-effacing charisma and plucky fortitude. If Carrie Bradshaw were a bard, this might be her tale. The characters we create in D&D must work harmoniously in a group and open themselves to unique philosophies, principles and strategies in order to help them overcome their obstacles. Applying that same open-mindedness to her daily life, Shelly shares with good humor her attempt to become 'Master of her own Dungeon,' as she goes outside her comfort zone to earn real-life experience and reach new levels of potential."
　　　　　—Dan Milano, writer of TV series *Robot Chicken*

"I love this book, especially the mother."
　　　　　　　　　　　　　　—Judy Mazzanoble

ALSO BY
SHELLY MAZZANOBLE:

Confessions of a Part-Time Sorceress:

A Girl's Guide to the Dungeons & Dragons Game

EVERYTHING
I NEED TO KNOW
I LEARNED FROM
DUNGEONS & DRAGONS

One Woman's Quest to Turn Self-Help into Elf-Help

SHELLY MAZZANOBLE

Everything I Need to Know I Learned from Dungeons & Dragons

©2011 Wizards of the Coast LLC

Printed in the U.S.A.

Cover photo by: Allison Shinkle

First Printing: September 2011

9 8 7 6 5 4 3 2 1

ISBN: 978-0-7869-5775-0
ISBN: 978-0-7869-5936-5 (ebook)
620-30694000-001-EN

Library of Congress Cataloging-in-Publication Data

Mazzanoble, Shelly, 1972-
  Everything I need to know I learned from Dungeons & Dragons / Shelly Mazzanoble.
    p. cm.
  Summary: "With tongue-in-cheek humor, the creator of the award-winning Confessions of a Part-Time Sorceress takes on the self-help section, proving that the benefits of the Dungeons & Dragons? game goes far beyond simple entertainment"-- Provided by publisher.
  ISBN 978-0-7869-5775-0 (pbk.)
  1. Dungeons and dragons (Game)--Humor. 2. Dungeons and dragons (Game)--Social aspects--Humor. 3. Women fantasy gamers--Humor. I. Title.
  GV1469.62.D84M4 2011
  793.93--dc22
                        2011015518

U.S., CANADA,
ASIA, PACIFIC, & LATIN AMERICA
Wizards of the Coast LLC
P.O. Box 707
Renton, WA 98057-0707
+1-800-324-6496

EUROPEAN HEADQUARTERS
Hasbro UK Ltd
Caswell Way
Newport, Gwent NP9 0YH
GREAT BRITAIN
Save this address for your records.

Visit our web site at www.dungeonsanddragons.com

DEDICATION

To Dungeons & Dragons players—past, present, and future.

And to Bart—best adventuring buddy a girl could have.

CHAPTER 1

DUNGEON MOTHER

Mothers are like dungeons. Some really stink and you'll do anything to avoid them. And some are lush sanctuaries filled with gold, jewels, and butter-scotch schnapps-spiked Nestlé Nesquik.

That's Judy, my mom and epic-level dungeon. Moms like Judy are few and far between, so when you find one, you should sit and relish their charms for hours. Though I suppose sitting in a dungeon is a little weird and potentially dangerous—because no matter how lush or treasure-filled, the bottom line is that all dungeons are filled with crap you best run away from.

This, too, is true of my mother.

Oh, come on. What did you think this was? A memoir of a 1980s sitcom family? I mean, even Elyse Keaton must have had her freak-outs, despite how maternally perfect she seemed to be. Bet you anything that as soon as the last of the craft service table had been packed away, she and Mallory had those kinds of unbridled fights only mothers and daughters can have. If you're a woman who grew up with a mother or a man who grew up with a sister, you know what I'm talking about. Screeching, tear-down-the-walls, full-on Animal Planet brawls. What did we fight about? Oh, I don't know. Forgetting to call when Mrs. Hopper got us to the mall safely. That time she crashed Chuck E. Cheese on Teen Night because my brother Mike told her his friend Mark's sister Pam's best friend Missy said she saw me smoking. (I wasn't. I didn't start smoking for at least eight months after this incident.)

"If I wanted your advice, I would have asked!" I shouted at least 1,483 times a day.

"Fine," she said, barely raising a brow even though I was yelling at a decibel even the neighbors' Australian Cattle Dog found inappropriate. "But you should really stop hanging out with Kim and Lisa. You're going to get a reputation as a pothead."

A pothead? "What do you mean by that?" I asked.

"I hear things."

She "heard" lots of things, and often well before I heard them. Kim and Lisa *were* potheads. I thought they had allergies. So she got lucky on that one, but she didn't always know what's what. Like who was worthy of friendship, what was worthy of wearing, what shows were worthy of watching.

"Mommy knows best," she always said. And when she wasn't saying it, she was showing it by sending me tiny satin embroidered pillows, coasters, even shot glasses with that saying on them.

"Someday, when you're a mother—God willing—you'll know what I mean."

I know having a mother who bombards her daughter with unsolicited advice isn't exactly worthy of a *Dateline* investigation. But still, even at twelve I wanted to be in control of my own destiny. What did Judy know about perms and two-toned jeans?

But for all her buttinsky tendencies and amateur-shrink psychologies, my friends sure loved her. Growing up, our house was the house everyone went to after school, and I couldn't have been prouder.

Not only was our kitchen always stocked with Lender's bagels and Ring Dings, but we also had a pool table and my mom wasn't afraid to use it. When the guys came over before lacrosse practice to carb up, my mom would be slathering bagels with strawberry cream cheese one minute and then staring into the eyes of my future prom date the next, commanding him to "Rack 'em up." We knew what that meant. Down to the basement we went to watch my forty-something mom banking and cutting and putting a little English on the "stripes." The guys tried to win, knowing the worst thing you could do to Judy was show a little respect for your elders and let her beat you. She didn't need anyone to let her win. She was *really* good. And she was a horrible sport, which is by far the worst combination. Judy had this obnoxious march she'd do around the table, pumping her pool cue into the air and making *rum pum pum* noises. That's always been my mom. Always kicking someone's ass.

"Let me give you some advice," she would tell the boys. "Never underestimate a woman's rack."

That's also my mommy. Not just making high school kids blush but hustling anyone within earshot with unsolicited advice. My friends didn't seem to mind. She was the keeper of their deepest, darkest problems, and they all turned to her for help. Her advice was like a splotch of red juice and they were like a Bounty paper towel. She spoke. They absorbed.

Right around the time I moved to Seattle, Judy's love affair with advice kicked it up a notch. Self-help, in the form of television talk shows, satellite radio, and online book retailers that, like Judy, love giving you tips on what to read next based on a recent purchase for your friend's four-year-old boy, were all the rage. (Really, Amazon? You're sure I'll enjoy *Thomas and the Naughty Diesel*? Wait. Maybe that was based on a different purchase.)

No matter. The point is, all this technology meant Judy barely needed to lift a manicured fingernail to discover the next great bit of wisdom that would surely turn my life around. Why did I ever teach her how to bookmark Web sites?

But did my life need turning around? I didn't think so. I was a fairly typical twenty-something doing twenty-something things. I had a bitchin' apartment in Seattle's Capitol Hill neighborhood that I shared with a roommate. Between us we had six part-time jobs. My four were to support an unpaid internship at Sub Pop records. I lived off Taco del Mar burritos and pints of Ben and Jerry's. I never exercised. I took writing classes and started drinking coffee. I developed a love affair with the Space Needle and discontentment with camping, socks with sandals, and Tibetan prayer flags.

Overall, I was happy. Even the old journals I kept are embarrassingly angst-free. If anything was causing me anxiety, it was the lack of anxiety I was experiencing.

And let me tell you, I'm the first one to give Judy credit for this. She's a great mom, even if most of her sentences start with, "Why don't you …" But could she leave well enough alone? Noooooooo. She was hell-bent on guiding me down the self-help path.

"You can thank Stephen Covey for your new job," she told me shortly after I was hired at Wizards of the Coast.

"Oh, I will," I said. "Right after my thank-you lunch with Deepak Chopra for giving me the courage to wake up this morning."

Judy was so big on Stephen Covey's *Seven Habits of Highly Effective People*, my dad and I thought Stephen had her wrapped up in some pyramid scheme where he was offering her toaster ovens and Maui time-shares in exchange for getting people to buy into his teachings. I probably would have been more amendable if that was the case. Sadly, for me Stephen and his habits made a better coaster than a coach.

"Here's some advice for you," I said to Judy after receiving yet another self-help tome from Amazon.com. "If it ain't broke, don't fix it."

"Consider this a preemptive strike," she answered back. "I'm sure you'll have to make a tough decision in the next few decades. Now you'll know what to do."

"In just thirteen easy steps," I said. "Gee, I hope my big decision isn't a time-sensitive one."

I had to admit Wizards was a dream job. Health insurance, neon Post-It Notes, and a rumored-to-be chocolate fondue fountain at the annual holiday party. This was a major coup and one I'd like to think my résumé filled with unpaid internships in marketing and promotions (not to mention an embarrassing story about having to dress up like a chicken for an Easter Seals event with children while the open bar loosened up their parents' purse strings) was what landed me the job.

Just a few weeks into my employ, I was in the R&D department trying to understand what exactly a Trading Card Game was ("You mean these cards attack one other? With magic?") when my boss came to find me.

"How do you feel about College Station?" he asked.

"Like KEXP?" I asked. "I love it."

He laughed. "Not that college station. I mean College Station, Texas. We need to send you there for a very special assignment."

Well, check out the new girl! I barely had time to figure out how to program my out-of-office message on my voicemail and I was already heading out on a business trip.

"Sure! When do I leave?" I sounded like Julie McCoy responding to an order from Captain Steubing. But Julie certainly would have remembered to ask Captain Steubing why she was going to College Station and what she was expected to do there.

A few days later my boss gave me the details. "It's really exciting," he said in such a manner I could tell he thought I wouldn't find this exciting at all. If it were really exciting, *he'd* probably go, right?

Later that night, on the phone, I told Judy about the Silver Anniversary Tour.

"Whose anniversary is it?" she asked. "Wizards?"

"Umm, no," I answered carefully. "One of the games. Dungeons & Dragons." The way I said it sounded more like "Durgin and Dooggins."

"Did you say 'Dungeons & Dragons'?" she asked. Curse her and her ability to decode secret information. Just like that time in seventh grade when she knew I didn't pay for those tie-dyed lace Madonna gloves and in eighth grade when she knew that wasn't a tin full of colored pencils in my LeSportsac purse for an art project but rather a can of Genesee Cream Ale. And let's not forget ninth grade when I told her I was going on the chaperoned class trip to Darien Lake for the day when really I was in Rochester with Cindy in her uncle's "borrowed" Cadillac trying to sneak into a Bon Jovi concert. Jeez. Maybe I should have been playing D&D.

I tried explaining to Judy that I was the new girl, this was a big initiative for the company, and I should be flattered they trusted me enough to send me on one of the tour stops.

"But *can they make you*?" she asked.

"I think so," I answered. "I mean, they pay me to, you know, do stuff for the company." Besides, I hadn't even had my ninety-day review. I wasn't going to ask. "Wait a minute," I continued. "Are you crying?"

"This is hazing!" she shouted. "Oprah was just talking about this. It's a growing problem in the U.S.!"

"In universities and on Lifetime Television for Women movies maybe," I said. "Not in suburban office parks!"

"Well, I'm going to call The Wizards and tell them they can't make you do that," she insisted. "And then I'm going to tell your father."

Clearly Judy thought "The Wizards" was a collective body of nine-year-old girls who make the rest of us do horrible, dangerous, and embarrassing things. Next I'll be forced to sing Kenny Loggins songs during company karaoke.

"Don't walk out to your car alone," she told me. "Have the security guard escort you."

"But Mom, the security guard is a Minotaur!"

Days later, Jason from shipping dropped by. Jason and I had gotten to be good friends, seeing as how he was at my desk nearly every week with another package. Inside would be a computer-generated note from Mommy explaining how she thought of me when she saw *this* or *O Magazine* called *this* essential reading for women in their 30s and, oh, how she just read *this* and loved it so naturally she got a copy for me, too. These were books like *What You Say Is What You Get*; *The Key*; *The Laws of Attraction*; *Act Like a Lady, Think Like a Man*; and the one I blame for triggering Judy's quest for betterment: *The Secret*. (If you haven't read it yet, I'll save you the time and let you in on *The Secret*: Get cozy with the Universe. It can make you or break you.) It was like I'd been enrolled in the mental-health rehab-of-the-month club.

At first Judy denied sending me these books.

"Maybe one of your magazine subscriptions sold your name to a book club."

"Or maybe you're trying to tell me something?"

"Me?" she'd ask innocently. "*Or the Universe.*"

Don't get me wrong. I love helping myself. To a second helping of mashed potatoes. To a handful of M&Ms. To another pair of shoes. But self-help is a whole other story. I always thought therapy would be a hoot if I weren't so terrified doctors would unearth something and discover

I really am nuts. But Judy was adamant about the self-help movement and clearly thought I might benefit from a little paperback guidance. So I indulged her by not putting "Return to Sender" on her packages. I wouldn't read her books, but I'd keep them stacked by the side of my bed. At least until I could afford to buy those bedside tables I'd been eyeing. Maybe by then I'd figure out a way to convince her that prepacked psychobabble isn't the key to self-betterment. If only I knew what was.

"You sure do a lot of online shopping," Jason said as he dropped off yet another box at my desk, noting the all-too-familiar black logo from Amazon. I'd been working at Wizards thirty-nine days and had already received so many self-help books from Judy that I caught the attention of the shipping manager?

I sighed, taking the box. "My mom does a lot of shopping," I corrected. "I'm really sorry. I can just come by and pick these things up."

"Or you could just stop by Amazon's warehouse on your way home," he said. "They're just down the street."

Ah, great. More advice.

The contents of that box were by far some of Judy's finest work.

I called Judy at lunch from my car. "*Nice Girl Syndrome?*" This was definitely not a conversation I could have with my co-workers eavesdropping. "*Ten Steps to Empowering Yourself and Ending Abuse*? Abuse?"

"What?" she said, sounding genuinely confused. "You're a young woman just starting her career. I don't want anyone to take advantage of my Moo Moo."

"Your Moo Moo's professional career does not involve abuse!" I shouted.

"They're sending you to Texas against your will!" She shouted. "To play Dungeons & Dragons!"

"You do know they pay me to be here, right? There are a few things I have to do in return, like W.O.R.K. That hardly constitutes abuse!"

Besides, I thought. Who said it was against my will. I admit, I was curious. A little bit about D&D but mostly about how an expense account worked.

Much to her dismay, none of the ten steps promising to make me less of a nice girl could save—I mean—stop me. Oh, I went to College Station, all right. I even waited an hour after we landed to call her.

"Where have you been?" she shouted. "According to American Airlines your plane landed one hour and twelve minutes ago!"

"What's that, Judy? It's hard to hear with my new elf ears."

My tour duty was managing logistics—making sure the game designer and celebrity author woke up in time for the event. Put tablecloths on the tables. Take pictures. It was eye-opening, to say the least. At Hastings, a bookstore in College Station, Texas, D&D and I had our first real encounter. Dare I say I found the little bugger to be rather charming? I mean, here were all these people standing in line before the store opened just to wish D&D a Happy Anniversary. The real shocker? They were *adults*. And not adults with children. They were (mostly) men who were here for their own purposes. I tried to imagine what could get me up at 8:30 on a Saturday morning to stand in line with a bunch of strangers. Anniversary Sale at Nordstrom Rack? Nothing I can't get online. Ben & Jerry's Free Ice Cream Cone Day? Small servings prove to be not worth the wait in line. The chance to win a makeover by Stacy and Clinton from *What Not to Wear*? Heck, no. Well, maybe.

When the store opened and the festivities began, it was less "silver anniversary party" and more "brother's birthday party." Tables were filled with dice and miniatures and eraser shavings. The authors and designers held court. There was lots of laughter—the kind of eruptive, collective laughter that succeeds a story that's going to be told for years to come. Most of these guys didn't know each other when they showed up that morning, but within the hour it was like a regular old family reunion. Except this was a reunion everyone wanted to be at and not one your mother blackmailed you into attending. These people had clearly connected over a common love: my strange, reclusive co-worker, Dungeons & Dragons.

That was the first time I saw a sampling of the people outside of work play D&D. They were disappointingly normal in jeans and T-shirts. Not a speck of armor or chain mail in the whole joint. No weird accents (unless they had one naturally; this was Texas, after all). Just a bunch of happy people, spending the afternoon at a bookstore, celebrating the anniversary of a game they obviously loved. What would Judy say about this little scene?

Although I wasn't exactly ready to join them at the table, I developed a protective feeling for D&D, mostly because the people I met were so passionate and thoughtful and grateful. And their stories. Some of them had been playing for all of twenty-five years. They regaled each other with tales of their first characters. Every story started with "And then there was this one time ... " and ended with "It was awesome.... "

Suddenly D&D had a face, a personality, and I found myself telling my friends to "shut up!" when they asked me how much it cost to dry-clean all of my black capes.

"Is that frankincense you're wearing?" my friend Dan asked one day.

Those were fighting words. It was Coco Mademoiselle, thank you very much.

Unlike most of my co-workers, I was no expert on D&D, but I was instantly drawn to the way it was played. The inside jokes, the character backstories, the moments of greatness. The lack of competition. If you've read *Confessions of a Part-Time Sorceress* you know what happens next. If you haven't read it, go on and do that now.

It's okay.

I'll wait.

Weird, right? A nice girl like me started playing D&D! And the kicker? We fell in love. It hit me as soon as my Dungeon Master, Teddy, handed me my freshly penciled-in character sheet and a beautiful miniature elf with flowing blonde hair and bubble gum-pink robes. I named her Astrid.

"The other elves are going to call her *Ass*," Judy warned.

"No, they're not. Elves are very refined creatures. Only someone with barbaric tendencies and the couth of an eight-year-old boy would be so cruel."

"Well, her Grandma's going to call her *Ass*."

Oh yes, this was a much different game than I'd ever known. Much different than those basement billiards games with Judy. There wasn't a clear winner or loser. You and your party worked together. You shared the victories and the failures. You knew your role and supported one another. Sometimes you even faced the occasional loss. Some hurt more than others. (I still miss you, Freya—the best Dragonborn BFF an elf could have!)

Even Judy came around once I started recapping my weekly games with her.

"You tell stories and make up characters? You're pretending to be little magical monsters? Oh honey! You found your people! I always knew they'd come for you!"

A few years later, I was staring at my computer screen, willing an idea for my *Dragon* column to appear on the blank Word doc. It was due in three days. Why wouldn't Judy send me a book about procrastination? That's one I'd probably read. Eventually.

While I was waiting for the creative engine to rev up, I started unloading my poor, overworked DVR. It was 99% full and much of it was a backlog of *The Real Housewives* episodes. No sense in keeping my DVR *and* my creativity blocked, so I gave in to the comfort of the couch. You never know when inspiration can strike. Besides, Judy couldn't wait forever for me to catch up. Apparently last week's episode was a doozy.

The housewives were fighting. Surprise! And they were in public. And they were wearing heels and dresses that made their cleavage look like age-spotted sacks of jellyfish. They have an uncanny ability to move their necks and wag a boldly painted acrylic finger in the faces of their "friends" without an ounce of champagne sloshing over the sides of their crystal flutes. I can't even hold a conversation *and* a drink without leaving a liquid trail down my pant leg. Don't stand next to me at cocktail parties. There. You've been warned.

Maybe it was the looming deadline, or maybe it was the pressure to free up some space on the DVR before quality programming like *Gossip Girl* and *Fashion Police* started up again, but I started imagining *The Real Housewives* as a D&D party.

Those crazy hens would fail before they even accepted their first mission. For one thing, they wouldn't go anywhere they could potentially ruin their manicures, and they wouldn't dream of venturing out without caravans of nannies and house managers. And really, even I wouldn't wear heels in a dungeon. *The Real Housewives of Beverly Hills* would probably have the best shot at making it through an encounter. Some of those women actually get along for at least part of an episode, and two of them are related so they're kind of used to fighting and making up. And another two even have jobs. Well, three if you count Camille, the jilted ex-wife of Kelsey Grammer, better known as "an A-list television star," like she refers to him. *Several times an hour.* Her job is managing the two house managers that manage everything else and "keeping Kelsey sober." The woman who has more nannies than children and still can't find time to pack for Hawaii. Oh Camille, I feel your pain.

The next morning, I call Judy. We talk every day on my way to work even if it's been approximately ten hours and sixteen minutes since our last conversation. Chances are a reality show meltdown occurred while we were sleeping or *Barefoot Contessa* came up with an even better way to roast red peppers, so there's always something to talk about.

"You're late," she said instead of hello. "I've been waiting for you to call so I can get my nails done."

It was 8:12 am. Approximately four minutes later than when I usually call.

"I hear at some point in the distant future, we'll all have these crazy things called cell phones," I told her. "We'll be able to roam freely, without being tethered to cords in our kitchen. Imagine that—you can get your nails done anytime, anywhere, while talking to me!"

"Dare to dream," she sighed. "What could possibly be new?"

Judy loves to act put out by my incessant phone calls, but truthfully, if we should miss a morning call due to unforeseen circumstances like emergency root canals or spontaneous Gin Rummy games with the neighbor, I'll be plagued with lovelorn e-mails starting at around 2:00 p.m.

TO: Shelly
FROM: Judy

MOMMY MISSES YOU.
CALL ME.
HELLO??????

"Lots is new!" I told her. "After catching up on my *Real Housewives* drama, I may have come up with an interesting idea."

"Does it involve a way to siphon collagen from lips?"

"No, but wow. Great idea. What is with Taylor's face? She'd be pretty if not for the giant pink football she wears under her nose."

"It looks like a baboon's ass, if you ask me."

"Ugh. Why did I ask? But back to my idea."

Judy said something but it was muffled.

"Did you just call me Camille?"

"Maybe."

"Fine. Tell me what you think. Let's get them all in a room with a Dungeon Master so they can work out their problems."

"Oh, wouldn't the housewives love a Dungeon Master," Judy said. "Especially that dopey housewife who's desperate to find a husband. You know who she looks like? Ralphie, your Aunt Elly's old beagle. Remember Ralphie?"

"Seriously, Judy?" I've been working at Wizards for more than a decade and still her mind reverts to ball gags and cat-o'-nine tails when I mention Dungeon Master? Kim does kind of look like Ralphie, though. "I'm talking about the very innocent game called Dungeons & Dragons, where a Dungeon Master helps tell you a story."

"Oh. Well, I think you'd have better luck selling the idea to Bravo if you used my idea."

I continued with my plan. "Playing D&D would force them to work out their issues. Taking on different roles would foster respect for each other and encourage them to band together to solve a common problem. It's way better than the old exercise of falling backward into your so-called friend's waiting arms."

"Or they could pick up a copy of *When Friendship Hurts,*" she said. "Did you read that yet?"

"Aw, come on! Why are you sending me that?"

"Remember when your so-called friend Trisha deliberately threw a party on the same day as your birthday? And she didn't invite you?"

"Yes, in sixth grade!" I argued. "And I'm 99% over it!"

"And I spent all that money renting out Skate Estate for what turned out to be your brother, his weird friend Petey, and you. And none of you skated!"

Oh, I see. The reason she's still pissed is because she wasted money on the skating party. "Look, Mommy," I explained. "Trisha was offering to teach kids how to French inhale with the cigarettes she stole from the lunch monitor! Unlimited pitchers of orange juice and couples-skate with my brother can't compete with that. Even I didn't want to go to my own party!"

"Well, read the book," she said. "Now you'll know what to do next time someone abandons, betrays, or wounds you."

"I already know what to do," I told her. "Hang up. Or hit 'em with a *magic missile.*"

"I think you have some work to do on your pitch."

"Just arrived at work. Call you on the way home!"

I thought about those batty housewives the next time my group and I got together to play D&D. What's crazy is that playing D&D at work *is* work for a lot of my co-workers. And it's no accident they ended up at Wizards. In fact, it's their dream job. The company is filled with lifelong gamers. Men and women who have fond memories of discovering D&D in their older cousins' closets, under Christmas trees, at the game and comic book shops their older siblings brought them to when they were supposed to be baby-sitting. Seems everyone has a how-I-discovered-D&D story around here.

In fact, some of those stories rival those found between the covers of Judy's favorite self-help tomes. I'm not the only one who finds inspiration with D&D. And that's when it hit me.

"Are you out of your tree?" Judy asked when I called from my commute home to expand on my new idea. "You think D&D can make you and the Housewives better people than Oprah could?"

"Well, maybe not Oprah," I said. "But certainly Dr. Phil."

"Prove it," she said.

"For starters, D&D players are the nicest people I've ever met."

It is a lame argument but one she has to agree with because she's met some of them. She still refers to the co-workers she met while visiting the office one day as "Nice Chris," "Charming Bertrand," and "Why aren't you dating that guy, Bart? He's just as weird as you are." (Okay, she was right about that one.)

"So?" Judy fired back. "They could have been born that way."

I can tell this is going to be a tough sell so I rattle off a list of things D&D can do: foster creativity, strengthen relationships, provide creative problem-solving alternatives, make you a better public speaker.

"First grade does that, too," she said. "What else you got?"

"It lets you tap into different facets of your personality you might not be in touch with otherwise," I said.

"Take an improv class."

"It gives you an outlet for all that pent up anger you might be toting around. Anger you might take out on your poor mother's living conditions when she no longer has the faculties to take care of herself."

She was silent for a beat. "Go on."

"Don't tell me you haven't thought of casting spells on drivers who cut you off or cashiers who are rude to you," I challenged.

Or lazy shoe salesmen who you just know aren't looking for a pair of eights in the back room. Or the supertall woman with the bad perm who sits in front of you in an almost empty movie theater. Or first dates who don't think you're worthy of a second date. As if you wanted one! Grrrr ... ! Tyler from Walla Walla, if you're reading this, I knew it wasn't going anywhere before the salads even arrived. I was just hungry, okay?

"I do cast spells," she argued. "My favorite is called *flipping the birdie*."

"Yeah, you really need to stop doing that. Drivers have been shot for less."

Judy and I digressed to all sorts of other things that make us mad, but the more we talked, the more confidence I had in what started as a funny little thought bubble.

* ⚝ ✳ ☆ ✱

Maybe you don't need all of these self-help books or nagging mothers or guru-like talk show hosts smiling at you from the covers of their eponymous magazines. If you want to be enlightened; popular; fabulously fit; a better lover; a great friend; an influential speaker; a wealthy raiser of happy, healthy, spiritually enlightened children with nice muscle tone and good teeth, then you, my friend, need to do nothing else than play Dungeons & Dragons.

Right?

Possibly?

Worth a shot?

If this little thought nugget were to blossom into, say, oh, I don't know, a book, then I obviously needed evidence to back up my claim. And I would need to get familiar with my competition. As soon as I got home I went in search of all the books Judy sent me—the ones I used for end tables, the ones under the bed. The ones I recently wrapped up to re-gift for friends with less "thoughtful" mothers. And I got to reading. For real this time. Not just the funny parts out loud to my friends at dinner parties. Okay, maybe "read" is a bit misleading. I read book jackets and cover copy. I read reviews on Amazon. I scanned Wikipedia pages. I read the authors' blogs and the blogs of people who gave the books glowing reviews. If Dan S. from Macon, Georgia, can break free from emotional eating and Glenda D. from Valencia, California, can finally conquer her emotional clutter and Stephanie T. from Santa Fe, New Mexico, has finally found her soul mate (can your soul mate be an inanimate object like, say, a turquoise ring? Hmm... I may have to read this one), then who's to say a little quality time in your cousin's crawl space with some oddly shaped dice and your seventh-grade imagination couldn't do the same years and years later?

For once, Judy and I agreed on the topic of self-help. You can improve your well-being by reading a book: *The Player's Handbook, The Dungeon Master's Guide,* maybe even *Tomb of Horrors.* That's the thing about D&D. It changes lives. And it was about to change mine.

Roll for initiative, Universe.

CHAPTER 2

LOSING MY RELIGION

JUDY: WHAT'S the MATTER? YOU SOUND SAD.

ME: I'm not sad, just busy. There's a lot going on right now.

JUDY: YOU'RE telling me. TABATHA'S SALON TAKEOVER AND MILLIONAIRE MATCHMAKER ARE BOTH ON. WHO CAN keep up with thAt stuff?

ME: You have a DVR, you know. You can record that stuff and watch it anytime.

JUDY: You sound like A COMMERCIAL. A SAD COMMERCIAL, BUT A COMMERCIAL nonetheless.

ME: I'm not sad!

JUDY: BAD MOOD, WHAtever.

me: I'm not in a bad mood! I'm just … introspective. I told you, there's a lot going on.

judy: You were always like that when you were in a bad mood, even as a child.

me: I'm not in a bad mood! At least I wasn't until you just put me in one.

judy: You'd get upset about something—a girl made fun of your jacket, your brother threw up on your teddy bear, we ran out of liverwurst—you would get real quiet and moody and sulk around for days. You never knew how to just let it go.

me: I don't remember that at all. I thought I was a happy child.

judy: When you were on the Phenobarbital, yes.

me: Seriously? You really doped me? I thought that was just a funny story you told on holidays.

judy: Nope. Doctor's orders. You were such a crybaby. Turns out you were just gassy.

me: Well, that and I was *a baby*.

judy: All you did was cry. And then your dad would come home and you'd shut right up. Ooh, that made me mad. I'm getting mad just thinking about it.

me: But kids get upset about things. Someone puking on your favorite teddy bear is on par with losing your job or finding out your spouse is cheating on you. I wasn't abnormal. I was just reacting to things.

judy: *Overreacting.*

me: What?

judy: Nothing. Do you remember what I always used to tell you?

me: Ugh. Yes. *Everything happens for a reason.* You still say that. All the time.

judy: It's true. I tried so hard to teach you not to get worked up over little things. Whatever happened happens because it was meant to. Once you accept that, there's very little to worry about.

me: Yeah, except nine out of ten times you never find out what the reason was.

judy: And you'd get upset about that, too.

me: Of course I did! I was promised a lesson!

judy: If you were more in touch with the universe, maybe you would have figured it out.

me: Here we go.

judy: You know what would have made you happier? Getting in touch with your spiritual side.

me: I tried. Didn't work.

judy: Maybe what you tried didn't work. But you can't just quit because one of seventeen billion avenues isn't for you. You just need to keep trying until you find one that feels like the right path. Religion and spirituality for you were just like Brownies or dance or gymnastics.

me: Things my mother forced me to do instead of letting me take naps and watch soap operas like other normal four-year-olds?

judy: I never should have let you quit any of those things.

me: Well, I can absolutely see how gymnastics would have helped me to become a better person, what with my secret life as a superhero. But how could finding my spiritual side help?

judy: Less time stewing and more time being happy.

me: Maybe I could refill that Phenobarbital prescription....

judy: Look at your brother! He's all about the Universe these days and can't stop making money. Ever since he *put it out to the Universe*. He even got a $1.84 credit from McDonald's. Can you believe that? They overcharged him for something and gave him the credit without him even having to ask for it.

me: If the Universe is giving out $1.84 credits then it's going to take a while for me to get those end tables.

judy: And he won $30 on a lottery ticket.

me: Since when does he buy lottery tickets?

judy: He doesn't. He found that ticket.

me: Let me guess. On a homeless person?

judy: See? That's your problem. You're too cynical to let the good stuff in. You keep up that negative attitude and you'll reap negativity twofold.

me: Come on! There's a difference between being cynical and down-right delusional. You're telling me that if I eat a pan of brownies for dinner every night for a week, all the while telling myself how thin I am, I'd actually lose weight?

judy: You try it and let me know.

me: What about manifesting my own destiny? Purveying my own happiness? Didn't you always tell me not to rely on anyone else to give me what I want?

judy: The universe isn't just anyone.

me: What would Deepak say?

judy: To listen to your mother.

Everything I Need to Know I learned from D&D

I was six years old when I had my first existential crisis. In my mind, God was a cowboy. I don't know why I saw him this way as I didn't know any cowboys, didn't grow up on a farm, and, other than the clothing worn by my Western Barbie, I wasn't particularly fond of big hats and pointy boots. Yet the God I believed in was a giant, bandana-wearing wrangler in a ten-gallon hat. I remember lying in the grass in the backyard and looking up at the clouds.

"God," I said. "Show me your cowboy boot."

Yes, even six-year-olds need proof of existence. And to be fair, I wasn't asking for miracles. I just wanted to see the tip of his boot or a shiny spur poke through the gauzy whiteness of the clouds.

I waited, maybe an hour. Maybe ten minutes. To a six-year-old it felt like a lifetime willing that giant in brown leather to wink down at me. But alas, not so much as a sunbeam poked through the clouds. I was highly disappointed. I mean, I knew God was busy and all, but I was always told he had time enough for all of us. No doubt there were people asking him to cure cancers or snuff out house fires or find loved ones who were lost at sea. As far as I was concerned, my request was an easy one.

"Well, I guess you don't really exist," I sighed. Then I called Woofie, my imaginary German shepherd over and went inside for a Ring Ding.

"What's the matter?" Judy asked when she came into the kitchen and saw me face down in plastic wrap and white cream.

Yes, even at six years old, I turned to chocolate when I was having a bad day. Good thing I didn't have a credit card.

"God ignored me," I said. "And now I'm going to ignore him. Forever."

The following Sunday, my brother Mike and I were enrolled in Sunday school.

We went to church at 10:00 a.m. (got to respect a parish that doesn't open its doors before double digits) and Sunday school at 11:00. If there is a hell I'm sure that whole pushing Heather Hoffman in the slush on picture day in fourth grade and playing Mommie Dearest with my seven-year-old cousin (I was Joan, of course) had already granted me a one-way ticket there, so I'm just going to say this: I hated it. There's not enough Chips Ahoy and Hawaiian Punch that could have made those sixty minutes bearable. The only saving grace was that Mike and I were in the same class. Together we were a Bible-studying Heckle and Jeckle. We were like Statler and Waldorf from the Muppets, questioning the teacher's teachings. Laughing inappropriately. Mike used me as his mouthpiece when he wanted more cookies or answers to things like, "Were apples the only thing to eat in the garden? Apples? Really?" (Mike's not a fruit guy.) Or, "Didn't Noah have any human friends? Why did he just save the animals?"

(Noah was my favorite Bible character, by the way. I could totally relate to only saving animals.)

From 11:00 a.m. to 12:00 p.m., Judy and the rest of the moms who had kids in Sunday school met in the back room of the Tally Ho diner across the street. There they could be found smoking cigarettes and drinking black coffee. I know this because Mike and I left class one Sunday under the guise of having the stomach flu, claiming we needed to use the facilities. Mike was really good at faking the heaves. We walked across the street to the Tally Ho.

"What are you doing here?" Judy asked when she saw Mike and me meander around the tables and chairs strewn with peacoats and purses. "You're supposed to be in class."

Mike took a slab of bacon from her plate.

"It's booooooooooooring!" I told her. "Can I have a cigarette?"

We did the whole Sunday school thing every week for about five years. (Give or take a few Sundays when I was excused because I "passed out" in church. It was a phase and about forty thousand CT scans said as much, but once I learned it would get me out of Sunday school, I staged a few episodes. See? Going to hell.)

A few years later we took our first communion (wine!) and a couple years after that we were confirmed (cash!). I'm sure the official meaning of "confirmation" isn't "stop going to church now," but that's what it meant for us. Perhaps Judy was hoping we wouldn't need her throwing the covers off our sleeping bodies every Sunday to get up and go. Or maybe it had something to do with the Tally Ho burning down. I'm just saying . . .

Back then I dreaded Sundays, but now I look back with some gratitude. I'm glad Judy tried to instill a sense of religion in us. Other than the fact that we were kids and therefore couldn't say no to her, Judy never forced it on us. It was more of a canvas for us to expand (or not) upon.

I chose to expand. In high school I went through a phase where I got really into crystals. I wore an amethyst around my neck and a tiger stone bundle in my pocket at all times. Later I learned one of the properties of amethyst was "inhibits drunkenness," so I left it home on Fridays and Saturdays. No point in taking in all those empty calories if you're not even going to get a buzz off it. My love of crystals was a portal into a whole New Age world. I was an honest-to-god tree hugger in every sense of the world, mixing concoctions of oatmeal and cornmeal and ham into a paste and spreading it at the roots of the grand oaks in our backyard. This was supposedly an offering in exchange for the lead in my school's play or to get Skid Row to come to town for a concert. (And maybe a backstage pass for my friend Cindy and myself. *And* if possible, maybe for Sebastian Bach to fall in love with me. Just asking. . . .)

When the full moon rolled around, I concocted an offering to the tree spirits made of oatmeal, corn meal, maple syrup, and birdseed (generously donated by my parakeet Bogie) and gathered up all my beloved gems and brought them outside in a bath of cool water and set them under the moonlight to recharge and clean them of my teenage karma. My parents saw me doing these things. I left the house armed with the only flashlight we had in the house, Judy's spatulas, and a Tupperware bowl, yet they never commented. At least not verbally. Judy's stamp of spiritual exploration approval came in the form of a ribbon-wrapped bundle of brand-new commercial-grade spatulas she left on my bed. They were the perfect size for spreading goo on the roots of old oak trees. My friends were making cash offerings to the college-aged potheads who lived across the street from the high school. I guess there were worse things I could be doing.

Judy was all too happy to drop me off at The Spirit Hut on Main Street to stock up on my crystals and dream catchers and bundles of sage.

"Better than dropping you off at Planned Parenthood," she said.

She even got in on the action, plying me with more rose quartz than what was available in all the mines in Brazil. Rose quartz earrings, rose quartz pendants, rose quartz elephants and teddy bears. Apparently rose quartz is effective in "opening the fourth chakra"—yes, of course, the one that deals with "matters of the heart." Rose quartz, among others, was said to help get in touch with our spirit guides—the divine forces I sought when faced with all the difficult challenges of being a teenager in upstate New York.

Alone in my hot-pink bedroom, I imagined myself surrounded by white light. Once engulfed in the light (divine light, not manufactured by GE) I took a deep breath and asked, "Spirit guides, please touch me."

I used my voice to ask the spirit guides. Not telepathy or sign language or a smear of oatmeal on my forehead. Oh sure, there were lots of girls my age mumbling that same prayer. Only *their* spirit guides were senior class presidents and football players.

My books instructed me to determine how many guides I have. Apparently some girls have more than others.

"Is there at least one of you?" I asked.

Wait for an answer and then ask Number 1 to touch you.

I'm not sure how many guides I had or if the sensations I felt were real or just my subconscious blushing in embarrassment, but the first sign of a chill freaked me out. I turned on all my lights and ran downstairs to the

TV room to join my parents for an hour of *Murder, She Wrote*. I wanted to believe. But perhaps fourteen was too young to be fully enlightened.

Moving to Seattle catapulted me knee-deep into the throes of "finding myself." Unfettered from life as I knew it and the people who knew me, I now had the freedom to be whoever I wanted. Who I wanted to be was a cast member from *Singles*. I lived mere blocks from the apartment complex in the movie and fully expected life to imitate art. I (like Bridget Fonda) didn't know anyone in Seattle, but it was a Mecca for flannel-loving twenty-somethings from all over the country. Meeting people was easy, thanks to my four part-time jobs and cool, indie record label internship.

One of my new friends was an earthy hippy artist named Phoebe. She was beautiful in an I-just-danced-all-the-way-here-from-Eureka, California-barefoot-and-razorless way. I was all too familiar with these patchouli-soaked hippy wannabes thanks to my four years at a liberal arts college in upstate New York, but Phoebe, with her anklet-jangling, toe-ring-wearing, yin–yang-tattoo-sporting style really pulled it off. She, too, was from New York and that, along with our appreciation for essential oils, birthdays in February, and abilities to consume vast quantities of red wine, bonded us. She was deeply spiritual, and I envied her that. Phoebe seemed to float through life in a lavender-infused cloud of mysticism. What religion she aligned herself with I couldn't tell. Part Buddhist, part Wiccan, part stoner, Phoebe was always bathed in incense and good intentions. She appeared grounded and even-keeled and all kinds of motherly, even if she was four days younger than me. Her à la carte approach to religion inspired me. (She was also a receptionist at a massage school, so that air of calm about her wasn't a façade. She got massages nearly every day.)

Phoebe was (of course) an artist—a painter and a poet—and as talented as she was, she suffered from delusions of other people's grandeur. In an effort to channel the frustrated artist who allegedly lived inside all of us, she guided me through a series of meditative exercises guaranteed to free him.

"How do you know my frustrated artist is a he?" I asked her.

"It's so obvious," she answered. "You can't feel that?"

Yeah, seems weird that I wouldn't feel that, but no. My frustrated artist was more hands-off than I was.

"Close your eyes," she whispered.

"Is this where you steal my kidneys and leave me in an ice bath?"

"Shh.... Feel the air moving through your mind, taking your thoughts with it."

The emptying-my-mind part worked. Her voice was as soft and soothing as a corduroy pillowcase. How could I not fall asleep? When I woke up a few hours later, Phoebe had finished two paintings. One a portrait of Frida Kahlo and one of a frustrated artist breaking free from the confines of a stiff-armed skeptic who will always be picked last in Pictionary.

"That happened while I was asleep? Damn. Looks painful." I checked myself for puncture wounds.

A few months later Phoebe and I were walking around Capitol Hill, dreaming about a vacation in Belize—or maybe Portland—when we came across a nondescript white house turned into a place of worship. The only sign of the holiness that lurked within was a tiny cross painted on the mailbox and a small sign planted in the grass proclaiming this the New Aquarian Church.

Still open to filling the spiritual void my perverted spiritual guides left when I was fourteen, I got excited. Phoebe and I were both Aquarians. It was meant to be.

We attended a service the following Sunday. (And like the church of my youth, these Aquarians didn't get things started until double digits.) Phoebe and I were two of seven people total. Perhaps the later services were better attended?

A woman dressed in a colorful muumuu stepped up to the podium.

"Thank you for coming," she said as she smiled. "And welcome to our new guests."

All five regulars turned around to delight in our company. Aquarians are very friendly. We waved back.

"Today's sermon is a special one. Reverend Joe is going to talk about forgiveness."

"Oh good," I said, leaning over to Phoebe. "Maybe I'll learn to forgive you for putting that Free Mumia bumper sticker on my car."

We stifled giggles, not wanting to make a bad first impression. While we waited for Reverend Joe to enter, Miss Muumuu brought out an old-school cassette player and placed it, along with a microphone, near the speaker.

"What's going on?" Phoebe whispered. "Is this like the opening act?"

"They must be recording the sermon," I said. "Maybe you can buy a cassette tape for a souvenir? I'm so getting one for Judy."

Miss Muumuu clasped her hands in front of her. "Enjoy," she said, winking at us.

Phoebe's giggles were snuffed out by sounds of muffled chanting coming from the tape recorder. Where the heck was Reverend Joe?

Perhaps he should get out here and clean the tape heads. Didn't Miss Muumuu lady say enjoy? Enjoy what? Ear strain by electronics circa 1978? And then it hit me.

"Oh no, that's Reverend Joe!" I whispered. "Or, at least, his voice."

"Maybe he's sick today?" Phoebe, ever optimistic, suggested.

"I'm in this dude's house of worship and he can't bother to come out and say hello?"

I felt the giggles coming on and fully expected Phoebe and me to be asked to leave. I tried to focus on the sermon and the rest of the parishioners but I could only make out every seventh word or so. Miss Muumuu was bobbing her head in the corner. Our fellow parishioners were smiling along. Not only could they understand this drivel but they agreed with it. When I turned to Phoebe to point this out, I was stunned by what I saw: tears.

Noticing the tears (from laughter) streaming down my own face, she mouthed, "I know. So beautiful."

What had I missed?

On the walk home, she touted the absentee reverend's wisdom after reading the brochure Miss Muumuu handed us on the way out.

"He receives his sermons from another plane and channels them into the tape recorder. Isn't that amazing? He's so wise."

Wise? Great. Now I'll find a Free Reverend Joe from the Tape Recorder bumper sticker on my car.

Phoebe was deeply moved by Reverend Joe. She went back to the Aquarian Church every Sunday and bawled her face off during our coffee dates later that day.

"You should come back," she begged me. "I've never felt more in touch with the Universe."

Once again, spirituality had leapfrogged me.

These days I know all too well who my spiritual guide is. Her name is Judy and enlightenment can be yours, too, with the right amount of postage. Judy is open to all forms of illumination, including New Age philosophy. Obviously she loves the universe as much as if she were its mother, too. In return the universe finds her premier parking spots and the eight of clubs during Gin Rummy games. My one-year gift subscription to Netflix can hardly compete with *that*.

I already have tons of books about spiritual enlightenment from Judy and even a couple from Mike who used those $1.84 refund checks to spread the good word of the universe.

"You need to set aside seventeen or sixty-eight seconds every day to close your eyes and visualize your goals."

Don't ask. I already did. Apparently those times have been proven to be most efficient.

Mike claims it was *The Secret* that helped him sell his overpriced, almost sinking townhouse by the river (and subsequently not get sued by the buyers when he decided to *not* sell it at the last minute). Personally, I think the sale should be credited to the St. Joseph statue I buried headfirst in his front lawn, but whatever. Joseph and I don't need the credit. The universe knows the truth and the universe will have to live with it.

I pick up the copy of Deepak's *Ultimate Happiness Prescription*. Yep. I still have this book. It's one of the few on Judy's recommended reading list that isn't residing on my secret bookshelf. (And by "secret bookshelf" I mean the one at Half-Price Books.) Admittedly, my favorite part of this book is the cover. The color goes with my living room décor quite nicely.

Even Deepak can't inspire me. Judy and Mike could have him. I have James Wyatt.

As is Deepak, James is a nice guy with a sage-like air. He also happens to be the creative manager for Dungeons & Dragons. I know what you're thinking. *Creative manager* for a product that's all about boundless imagination and inspired originality? If I didn't know better I'd think he spent all day modeling his feelings out of clay and watching PBS.

"I do a lot, thank you," James said when I asked him. "I'm in charge of story and innovation. I manage a think tank!"

And they're all geniuses, too, according to James.

"But please don't tell them I said that," he urged. "I don't want it going to their heads."

"I won't." Well, sort of.

I kind of glossed over the pages on religion and alignment in the D&D rule books. Although I loved creating characters who were the anti-me— fearless, rugged, totally fine with living out of a suitcase for months on end—no one ever explained to me how religion factors into D&D, or at least to your character. And I guess I never asked. Until now.

James is the right guy to answer all of my burning questions. In addition to being a nice and sage-like person, he's got a background as a minister. He studied religion at Oberlin College and then went on to receive a master's of divinity from Union Theological Seminary in New York City that prepared him, or rather, promised to, for the two and a half years he spent as a parish minister. And yes, he was playing D&D the whole time he was a practicing minister.

Just as Judy tried to instill her spiritual side into my brother and me by forcing us to attend Sunday service and school, I felt like I was doing just the opposite in my D&D game.

"I'm afraid my characters are suffering due to my lack of faith," I told James. "Or rather lack of any clear religious influence. Why do I keep rolling up these spiritually ambivalent characters?"

"Who's to say that's a bad thing?" James asked.

"Judy."

"Judy?"

"My mom," I said realizing I probably need to give James a little backstory. An hour later we're back on topic.

"Well, the beauty of D&D is that you have an avenue to explore religion in a nonthreatening, nonconformist atmosphere. You should try out lots of gods and see who fits with your—I mean your characters'—ideals. Overall, religion can be as important as you want it to be and as comfortable as your group is comfortable with it being."

"Just like in real life?"

"Just like in real life."

The beauty of religion in D&D, according to James, is "that we have all of these different gods you can choose from, so you can find a set of commandments that are already in line with how you want to play your character."

Oh yeah, I should explain: In D&D, it's common to worship more than one deity and to pray to a different god at different times. For instance, there's a god for protection, a god for knowledge, and a god for arcane magic. Depending on the god(s) you choose to worship, you'll be expected to act a certain way.

"Well, that's easy," I noted. "Now if I could just find a god that supported consumerism, sleeping in, and reality television, I'd never be in a spiritual conflict. If only D&D gods were real gods."

"Who's to say they're not?" James asked.

"Um, probably Judy?"

"I'm sure even Judy would agree that you should follow in life whatever makes you happy, right? As long as you're not harming anyone," he added when he noticed the huge grin spread across my face. "You won't harm anyone, will you?"

"Well, I *am* unaligned."

James gave me a fabulous idea. The following Sunday, my quest for divine guidance began. With *The Real Housewives of Beverly Hills* in the background, I cozied up on the couch with a copy of *The Player's Handbook*. There are twenty deities listed, and each lists three commandments you'll be expected to follow if you choose to worship that particular god. *Three*. Not ten. And I can worship as many gods as it makes sense to. I shall have a menagerie of deities. A sort of Panda Express combo platter

SHELLY'S INTERVIEW WITH JAMES WYATT IN WHICH SHE MAKES HIM CRY. SORT OF. WELL, MAYBE ON THE INSIDE

So James, who was an actual pastor and all, must have some insights into D&D's "shady lady" reputation. It must have affected the work he was doing, right?

"Were you preaching to the same people who believe the spells in those books of yours were real?" I asked.

"I didn't preach about it," James said. "I didn't bring it up anywhere near the pulpit or anywhere else on church grounds."

"Because?" I prodded, getting all Barbara Walters on him.

"I was afraid of a negative reaction."

Oops. Now I might cry. I feel for all those other people who are closeting the D&D-playing part of themselves for fear of how their community would receive them.

But back to my mad interrogation skillz. I had done my research. I dug up an old interview with James in which he said, "I found that my D&D work was a source of freedom and energy when ministry was more life-draining for me."

It seems pretty obvious as to why that is. Ministers aren't all weddings and baptisms and leading the choir in a candlelit serenade of "Silent Night." It's funerals and heartfelt confessions and counseling parish members who are in bad, dark places. That's a lot to take on for even the most seasoned veteran, let alone a twenty-five-year-old fresh out of seminary school. Even Roma Downey's angel needed to take a chill pill and recharge before she could resume touching all of those forlorn souls. And she had Della Reece to give her a few temporary hit points. Needless to say, James's work was "very demanding and very draining."

But his silver lining? Surprise! Dungeons & Dragons.

"Can I get that in writing?" I asked him, thinking of sending a very special card to Judy.

"Umm, isn't that what you're doing?" he asked.

Yes. Right. The book.

James continued. "I would come home and work on D&D adventures."

Adventures that would eventually be published by *Dungeon* magazine. If you're not familiar with *Dungeon* magazine, let me tell you— that's a major coup.

"It was a great outlet for creativity," he elaborated. "Really energizing."

Heeding the advice of his wife, James realized he should be following that which gave him energy—Dungeons & Dragons—instead of what drained him.

"That's tricky," James said, going on to explain you should be mindful of people you're playing with. "You don't want to get too close to anything that people are not comfortable getting close to."

I know he's sincere but I can't help but laugh at the simplicity of this advice. "I guess that's true in just about every situation."

"If someone has an irrational fear of tigers with backward-facing hands, say, then don't make them constantly run up against rakshasas," James elaborated.

"But isn't that kind of metagaming?" I asked. Technically your character wouldn't know (or care) that the guy across from you left the church in 1978 due to a bitter dispute and has never looked back.

"Yes. It is. But like any aspect of role-playing, you dial it to the level that's appropriate for your group."

It's amazing how much like real life this whole fantasy business is.

of idols. My needs will define my gods and not the other way around. This should be easy.

In the essence of time, I decided to worship five, and to prevent myself from getting overwhelmed by all this religious freedom, I decided I'd stick to one a day. I'd leave the weekend free for reflecting (and because it's Oktoberfest and I haven't found a god that reveres microbrews as much as I intend to on Saturday).

MONDAY'S GOD: AVANDRA

GOD OF: CHANGE

Promotes: freedom, trade, travel, and adventure.

What's in a name? A lot, I hope, because I just love the name Avandra. Maybe I will get another cat.

"What do you think of Avandra?" I asked my D&D-playing boyfriend, Bart, on our way to work.

"The D&D god?" he asked. "I love her. She appeals to my wanderlust."

"I was really just talking about the name. Maybe for a dog or a cat."

But now that he mentions it, I can see why Avandra's commandments would appeal to Bart. He loves traveling so much he got The Fool from the tarot deck tattooed on his shoulder. If his destination requires a series of shots, antibiotics, and adding the American Embassy to his speed dial, then chances are he'll have a great time. Me? I'd be just as happy with a relaxing weekend on the Oregon Coast. And I'm way too noncommittal to get a tattoo. While I do love the excitement of traveling to far-flung regions of the world, I fantasize about what it would be like to spend two weeks *at home*. I could clean out the closets, install pull-out drawers in my pantry, watch Lifetime movies and YouTube videos to teach me things like ventriloquism and caulking my bathtub.

"We should take a vacation," I announced. "A real one. Like to a different country." Whoa! Who said that?

"I've been begging you to!" Bart said, rattling off the countries on his wish list. "Wait, is this a trick? Are you going to book our tickets so there's a four-day layover in Binghamton, New York?"

I didn't tell him about my "deity a day" experiment because I wanted to see if he noticed organically any changes in me. "If we don't take a real vacation I might have to join the army."

Bart could barely contain himself just thinking about the possibilities. "What about India? Or New Zealand? I just heard a story on NPR about Finland. You'd like Finland! They have lots of saunas. And reindeer."

During lunch I logged onto Expedia.com and punched in some random dates in September. How about Seattle to Athens? Oh, I could feel Avandra smiling down at me. Or next to me? Maybe across from me. Where do the D&D gods hang out, anyway? Greece has been on my bucket list for a long time, and I'm thinking with their poor economy, they'd probably love a couple of frivolous, starry-eyed, itchy-footed American tourists.

Or maybe not. Tickets aren't cheap but hotels are pretty reasonable. Especially those on the islands. *The islands!* Santorini! Naxos! Crete! I could visit the home of my beloved minotaur barbarian, Kevin!

"Is there anything important I need to do between September 20 and October 1?" I asked Laura, my boss.

She glanced at the calendar. "I don't think so," she said. "Why?"

"I'm thinking about taking a vacation."

"Ah, going to see Judy. Nice."

"No, not going to see Judy." Jeez. Why do people think I'm so predictable? And great. I can feel the guilt creeping up on me. Maybe she won't notice I'm gone? "No, I'm not seeing Judy this time. But I will be thinking of her."

Click to purchase.

Oh my Avandra, what have I done! I just plunked down enough credit for five sets of end tables and I don't even know if Bart can go during that time.

He can.

"Are you serious?" he asked, nearly sideswiping a minivan in the next lane.

"Pull over and I'll explain."

"I'm good, I'm good!" He's grinning like a maniac. "I just can't believe you went ahead and bought tickets. You realize that's ten fewer days you get to spend with Judy."

"Aw, come on! Why do you have to ruin a good thing? But yes, I know. Maybe she'll come with us."

Again Bart almost hit a minivan.

The next morning during our morning conversation I broke the news to Judy.

"Excuse me?"

"You heard me," I answered. "Bart and I are going to Greece. I already bought the tickets. Avandra made me do it."

"Excuse me, again?"

I explained about my twenty-four-hour experiment. "A new day, a new god. I thought you'd be proud."

"This is how you seek spiritual fulfillment? You buy plane tickets? Say a prayer or light a candle next time."

Just when I was getting cozy with Miss Avandra, it was time to move on. Candles were definitely not part of the plan.

TUESDAY'S GOD: KORD

GOD OF: BATTLE!

Promotes: battlefield prowess, strength, and THUNDER!

Tuesday's child is full of grace and the person who made up that cliché is full of it because I was born on a Tuesday. But this Tuesday it's all about...

"Thunder! Da na na na na na na! Thunder!" I chanted at my desk.

"Stop it," Chris, who shares a low cubicle wall with me, said. "What did I tell you about AC/DC before 9:00 a.m.?"

"Kord pooh-poohs your request! This is my battle cry. *Thunder!*"

"You're in cahoots with Kord?" he asked.

"I am today. I'm filling a void on my friend's kickball team tonight."

"And subsequently a void in your spiritual life," Laura said, sitting down with her tea. "You don't have to pay to play, do you? Because this little experiment of yours is going to break the bank."

I pumped a fist in the air and made devil horns with my other hand. "Nope. No money will be exchanged. But I do get a T-shirt."

And that's about all I knew other than the location for the playing field. It didn't matter because I was *bringing it*.

"It's on like vampire spawn."

"Gross," Laura sneered. "But best of luck to you."

Thunder!

Truth be told, I'm not athletic, and with the exception of my awesome kickball streak in fourth grade, never was. Perhaps it was the growing pains and the amount of baby aspirins I was downing on a regular basis but that year I possessed Hulk-like strength on the kickball field. I was unstoppable. Home run after home run. I could make it from first base to third quicker than that skeeze Jenny Dugan in the seventh grade. My prowess was legendary. I was picked first! *First!* Before the boys. And my popularity on the playground spilled into the lunchroom, the classroom, and living rooms across the west side of Binghamton. I went to every birthday party, had slumber parties lined up for months. Everyone wanted a piece of this future Olympian.

When my gym teacher bought living room carpet from my parent's store, he filled my impressionable dad's head with tales of my athletic inclinations. Dad came home that night with a brand-new pair of sneakers, a baseball glove, and a New York Giants hoodie.

"What's all that for?" Judy asked.

"Our daughter is an athletic powerhouse!" Dad said. "Time to harvest the talent!"

"Ew," Mike said. "You know what harvesting means, right?"

I didn't know but it sounded terrible.

"It's what they do to alien body parts. Dad thinks you're a mutant."

I hadn't quite grown into my head yet, but alien? Really?

But that's how my parents were. A sniff of anything promising in their kids turned into a full-fledged ticker-tape parade. My dad insisted on taking it to the backyard every night after dinner to practice catching pop-ups.

"You got to be well rounded," he explained. "It's one thing to kick a home run but you got to prevent the other team from doing it."

"Okay," I said, kicking up grass with the toe of my new sneakers. I didn't want to catch pop-ups. I wanted to go inside, have a bowl of Rocky Road, and watch *Three's Company*.

"There are no scholarships for kickball, you know," Mike said from his perch in the living room window.

That was probably a good thing because my attempts at catching my dad's pop-ups resembled a pile of bricks being dumped in a straw basket from thirty feet in the air.

"Oops," I said, watching another big, red ball plunge through my encircled arms.

"It's probably getting too dark to see," Dad said. Ever the optimist.

Maybe it was the pressure, or maybe I grew too fast and couldn't get used to my longer limbs. Whatever it was, it ended my kickball career nearly as quickly as it started. Suddenly my signature line drives were going foul. When I kept the ball in bounds I couldn't break the infield. The sneakers my dad bought for my training felt like flippers as I trudged to first base. I pulled off my Giants sweatshirt and stuffed it under my bed. I was retiring.

My dad stopped asking me to practice my pop-ups after dinner. Instead of visors and tube socks he brought home Nancy Drew books.

"You can probably solve those mysteries faster than Nancy can," he said. "You were always good at solving riddles. You could be a detective!"

But now was my chance to make it up to my dad. I would show him that those two and half weeks of backyard practice weren't for nothing. The kickball phenom was still alive and ... well ... kicking.

"Who still plays kickball at our age?" Chris asked.

"It's part of a casual sports league," I said. "They play dodgeball and flag football, too."

My buddy Lars had been playing in the league for years and was constantly on me to try it out.

"It's too painful to go back," I told him. "I'm just not ready."

"It's been, like, twenty-five years," he said. "Besides, we drink beer while we play."

"Okay, I'm ready."

There was no better time to try, what with my newfound alliance to Kord. According to *The Player's Handbook*, "athletes and fighters revere him."

"Eye of the Tiger!" I shouted as I left work.

I met Lars at a park near Lake Union. He and my temporary teammates were drinking Pabst Blue Ribbons out of paper bags. Good thing I wasn't bowing down to Bahamut, the god of justice, today or else I might have had to call the police.

"Shelly's going to be filling in for Jenny," Lars said. "She was the kickball champion of her fourth-grade class."

"Wow. I've got some big shoes to fill," I said, and they all burst out laughing. If the big red ball and nervous stomach didn't already make me feel like a fourth grader, the feeling like everyone's in on the joke but you sure did.

"No, sorry," explained Lars. "I was talking about *your* glory days. No pressure, though, okay? I'm sure the champion still lives within you!"

Great. I hate it when people have expectations. Hopefully my inner champion isn't too busy kicking the crap out of my frustrated artist.

"That was a long time ago," I said in case they didn't notice I wasn't eight years old. Just in case they didn't, I found a paper bag and started chugging.

The team seemed nice enough and I took some comfort in the estimation that people who drink beer out of lunch sacks in the middle of a highly trafficked neighborhood before sunset don't take many things seriously. When the other team showed up, they greeted each other like long-lost friends. In fact, although not "long-lost," most of them were friends.

"We've all been playing together for years," Lars explained. "Sometimes you're on a team together, sometimes you're against one another."

"Ah, such is life," I mused.

Regardless of what side they were on in the park, they were all on the same side of the bar. The first rule of kickball is apparently to get nice and drunk first. I hope this game goes into extra innings because there's no way I can drive home.

I was banished to Jenny's usual spot in the outfield.

"Stay there," some guy named Jack told me.

"Righty-o," I answered, taking about ten giant leaps backward from where he told me to stand. Those playground drunks couldn't walk a straight line. Let's hope they can't kick a ball in one. About four seconds later a giant, arching, growing red dot came crashing toward me.

"You got it, Shelly!"

Kord, damn it! I now know what it would feel like to have Mars spin right off its axis, drop from the sky, and land on your chest.

I opened my arms, closed my eyes, and yelled, "Thunder!"

Whoosh! I felt the breeze as the ball sailed right between my forearms and then, *whack*, bounced back up to smack me in the face.

"Ow."

When I opened my eyes, Sarah, the left fielder, was standing over me. "Oh dear, someone have a towel?"

"Ah wink ah whenaled mah wop whip," I said.

Lars and some other guy (I stopped caring who these irresponsible jackholes were) helped me off the field and gave me a can of PBR from the cooler to hold on my lip.

"That was a good try!" Sarah cooed. "'A' for effort."

Thut up, Thara.

WEDNESDAY'S GOD: IOUN

GOD OF: KNOWLEDGE

Promotes: mental power, prophecy, and skill

I fell asleep with a bag of frozen peas on my face and when I woke the next day, I realized the damage wasn't as bad as I initially thought. My top lip was a bit swollen but the bruising was minimal. At least I could say my S's again.

"You look like Taylor from *The Real Housewives*," Laura said when she saw me.

"Sadly, my nose didn't get broken," I lamented. "I was hoping to get a nip and tuck when the doctors had me under."

"Does this mean your kickball career is over?" Chris asked. "For a second time?"

I wasn't sure what was worse. Being compared to a Botox-addicted bored housewife or having a career-ending injury crush my hopes and dreams for a second time. Didn't matter. Today was a new day, and a new day meant a new god. I sat in my desk chair, closed my eyes, and took a deep inhale, letting my abdominal cavity expand and lengthen. And then I got dizzy and almost passed out.

I'm still learning here, people.

"Om …"

"Oh no. Who are you worshipping today?" Laura asked.

"Today I shall pray to Ioun, the god of knowledge, skill, and prophecy."

"Great!" Laura said. "Then *you* can work on this presentation."

"PowerPoint will not help me bridge my mental and emotional faculties," I answered. "But yoga will. I'm taking a class tonight!"

"What the hell does yoga have to do with Ioun?" Chris asked. "She wants you to seek and distribute knowledge. Educate yourself and others."

"Um, what part of *class* did you not understand?" Look at me distributing knowledge already.

"I'm not sure that's entirely what she means, but go ahead. Knock yourself out," he said, in an unfortunate choice of clichés. "Oh no, wait. Don't do that. Have fun."

"Ha, ha. Very funny."

Sadly, I sort of agreed with him. It would be nice to enroll in a Spanish class or finally learn how to knit or sit in on a lecture at the Seattle Art Museum. But yoga is the only class I could find that was available on such short notice. Just in case Chris was right and I failed to properly educate and enlighten, I'd go to NPR.com and donate $25.

My neighborhood is riddled with yoga studios so I picked one closest to home. Okay, that's not why I picked it. It happens to be across the street from my favorite tap house. Bart is meeting me after class so I can deposit some delicious hoppy calories back into the old reservoir.

I haven't taken a yoga class since … well, ever. I tried to do one of those On Demand videos when I was feeling lazy about not going to the gym for three days but the teacher was so Zen I fell asleep in chair pose and only woke up because of the charley horse in my quad. I was a bit nervous about class until I walked into the studio's lobby, which smelled like my old friend Phoebe. A woman behind the desk greeted me. Her long, lithe limbs were enshrouded in a black body suit. She looked like a vanilla bean.

"Is this the beginner yoga class?" I asked.

"It is!" she said with so much glee I wondered if she thinks I'm from Extreme Yoga Studio Make-Over Edition or something. "Is this your first time?" she asked, handing me a clipboard full of paperwork.

Sure that I will never muster that much glee in my own voice, I just nodded and started initialing things.

My future classmates didn't look very "beginner." Maybe it's because they all had Klean Kanteen water bottles and were wearing those expensive yoga pants and matching tops that I pass over at T.J. Maxx in favor of the cheap cotton sweatpants and T-shirts I find around the office. It's not like I'm going to a bar dressed like this. Bart's bringing me a change of clothes.

Their clothes, on the other hand, you *could* go to happy hour in if you were the kind of person who enjoyed drinking half-price appletinis while showing your midriff.

I did not have my own yoga mat, so Vanilla Bean lent me one. I'm instantly grossed out over the thought that my face is going to get pretty intimate with this rubber cesspool. I exfoliated for this? Why didn't I plunk down the $10 it probably costs to get a mat? Even if I used it only once in an actual yoga class, I'm sure I could have found another use for it. Cushy shower mat? Beach towel? Protecting valuables like those Stuart Weitzman boots I just purchased? Instead I'd probably get a staph infection to go with my fat lip.

I unfurled the borrowed mat next to a woman I perceived to be the least yoga-ish. She was about my age and her sweatpants didn't match her sports bra. I liked her instantly.

She smiled at me as I set up. "Hi, I'm Becky."

"Hey," I said, introducing myself. "It's my first time. I'm terrified. Hold me?" I'm a tad nervous and when nervous, I overshare. "Just kidding. You don't have to hold me. Yet."

"My second," she said. "Wait until you see my killer moves."

Aw, Ioun, I think I love you. I'm already chalking this up as a win. I may not leave with my moon in the seventh house, but I've already met a nice person. Now as long as the instructor is an actual human and not a tape recorder, I think we'll be in business.

She *was* human, and after her welcome, she had us close our eyes and breathe. In and out. Innnnn and ouuuuut. Innnnnnnnnnnnnnn and ouuuuuuuuuuuuuuut.

Snort.

I'm falling asleep again! What the heck is wrong with me? Is there no middle ground between ZEN and REM?

After we had sufficiently expanded our rib cages we moved on to some stretches.

"Is this yoga?" I whispered to Becky. I know there are types of yoga that are vigorous and athletic, but this ain't it. I've done more strenuous moves just turning off my alarm clock.

"It's *this* kind of yoga," she answered, mock yawning. We both stifled giggles.

When the woman in front of us bent over, I got all Sir Mix-A-Lot on her and whispered, "Oh my God, Becky, look at her butt."

Becky did a fantastic job of turning her snort into a cough. I tried to behave.

If I'm not going to justify that beer and barbeque sandwich I might as well get something out of this, I thought. I concentrated on getting in the Zen zone. I opened my mind and my rib cage, ready for enlightenment.

It really was peaceful in there. And the stretching did feel good. Perhaps my spirit guides had come for me after all.

"Now we move into downward dog," the instructor cooed.

Becky, still smiling, slowly bent at the waist and I followed suit. Just as I came mere inches from the mat, I heard something amid the pan flutes and whales calls coming from the CD player.

Pfffffffffffftttttttttttaaaaaaaaaaapppppppppprrrrrrrrrr.

The unmistakable sound came from my right. Oh dear God! Don't laugh, don't laugh, don't laugh! Oh my god, Becky, look at *your* butt! But it was nearly impossible for me to suppress the laughter because when it comes to bathroom humor, I'm an eight-year-old boy. My new friend must have been humiliated. The least I could do is pretend I didn't hear it.

I wouldn't look at her, so instead I focused on the instructor and the more advanced beginner yogis. And oddly enough, they were all focused on me. Wait a minute …

I looked at Becky. "It's okay," she said. "I'm sure you're not the first."

"Oh wait …" I began. "That wasn't …" Becky couldn't possibly believe that was me? Was she that out of touch with herself, she didn't notice an emission like that? Becky needed yoga more than I do.

"Let's move on, class," the instructor urged. "These things happen."

Sure, they happen! I wanted to yell. To *Becky*! I'd barely broken a sweat, let alone wind. The class returned to their downward dog poses, and I spent the rest of the class sneering at Becky. It's not very yogalike, and probably even Ioun would be disappointed, but still … if only I had a fraction of my tiefling wizard Tabitha's magical prowess I'd have cast diarrhea on that fart-framer right then so the class would know exactly whose butt cheeks were heralding the great downward dog fart. But I refrained, and not because I'm not a spell-casting wizard but because I knew I'd never be back.

Namaste, bitches.

THURSDAY'S GOD: MORADIN

GOD OF: CREATION

Promotes: artisans, miners, and smiths

Still reeling from Fartgate, I go into Thursday feeling a little shell-shocked and more jaded than ever. Judy almost busted a lung when I told her about the yoga class. She was laughing so hard she had to hang up to find her inhaler. She called me back a few minutes later.

"Oh, Moo Moo, I'm sorry. I couldn't breathe," she said. She was still laughing. "Which is probably what your classmates were saying, too."

"Oh, ha ha," I said. "*I didn't do it!* I should hang up on you, but Moradin wouldn't think that was exhibiting family loyalty." There. I worshipped.

I was excited to be revering Moradin, as he's one of the more famous D&D gods. His followers have even made some appearances in my D&D games. I feel like Moradin and I share a lot of the same principles. He demands his followers be loyal to their families (duh; got that covered), welcome adversity with strength and fortitude (see "Fartgate"), and strive for making a lasting impression in this world. (If by "world" you mean yoga studio, then *done* and *done*.)

All day I waited for a sign from Moradin, but today appeared to be just another spiritually vacuous day. No dwarves, no miners, not even much love from Judy unless you count laughing so hard at your daughter you bring on an asthma attack. So I decided to visit the place I go when I'm seeking solace and inspiration—a lovely, 187-year-old oak tree in Volunteer Park.

Oh, please. I went to Nordstrom. What? Moradin is also the patron saint of artisans, and no one can deny those Tory Burch riding boots I saw in the catalog are art.

Boots in trunk, I headed back to work, but I wasn't feeling the exhilaration I usually experience post-consumerism. Had my quest for holy happiness bled me dry? If new shoes can't make me happy, I don't know who I am anymore.

After work I headed over to my favorite coffee shop for a tall skinny caramel latte served by one of the finalists in the barista showdown. Yes, that's a real event. This is Seattle, remember? And those little petiole leaves don't just form in the foam themselves, you know.

The coffee is free-range or fair trade or something else I know I'm supposed to care about, but even more important, it's delicious and heavily caffeinated. I come here whenever I'm on a deadline, parking myself at a table near an outlet and away from the toy kitchen set up for the kids who hang out while their mommies complain about motherhood with other mommies. (Once I sat near a group of mommies who did nothing but wax on about the terrors of child rearing. Potty training, preschool enrollments, picky eaters! Their honesty was quite refreshing, really, and I'm sure the kids were much too young to know who their mommies were talking about.)

"For Here" patrons get to drink their coffee out of a large eclectic mug that looks like it was excavated from Jack Tripper's kitchen.

"Hey, Shelly," Barista Extraordinaire said, smiling. "On a deadline?"

"Yes, I need to find Jesus in the next forty-eight hours or I'll have to apologize to my mom."

"Yikes," he said. "Let's make it a grande."

About five minutes into my spiritual revolution, my ADD kicked in. Rather than actually writing, I scanned the room and counted seven men and thirteen women among the patrons. Four of them had ponytails—the majority belonging to men. (Why do guys with ponytails like coffee shops so much?) Out of the fourteen laptops parked on tables, twelve of them were Macs. There was one girl who appeared to be with parents who were not filled with rage by her existence. In fact, they were the opposite, what with the constant patting on the head and conspiratory whispers. Did her dad wipe a tear from his eye?

Every now and again another patron stopped by their table and said something to the little girl that made her smile. When they left Dad would fill up the kid's cup with apple juice and say *cheers!* What were they teaching this kid? Through it all, the family appeared rather fixated on the walls.

Ah, the walls. Right. They were looking at the artwork, which quite honestly wasn't much to write home about. Each piece was mounted on what looked like a piece of sketch paper and pressed into an Ikea frame. The art looked a bit like those ribbon potholders I used to make Judy in second grade, only there was no ribbon—just paint. Caitlin signed each piece with big, loopy, novelty penmanship that said *By Caitlin.* I'm no curator but these looked like a child did them. In fact, that baby boozer up front with her parents could have done these.

"Congratulations, Caitlin!" a departing patron waved to the table. "You are so talented, young lady!"

Wait. We're already offering compliments to kids for their drinking skills? She's not even in high school yet!

Caitlin blushed. Her mom patted her head. Dad filled her cup again. Ohhhhhhhhhhh....

I didn't have a clue what I'd do with the end result but suddenly it became clear what I had to do. Caitlin had produced quite the body of work and had managed to land an art showing right there in my favorite coffee shop. Quite a coup, indeed. I laughed, thinking of what my parents would do if I were Caitlin. She was lucky to get away with some faux scotch and a few cheek pinches.

"Excuse me," I said when I approached the family's table. "Do you happen to know who the artist of these fine pieces might be?"

Again, Caitlin blushed. Her parents looked so deliriously happy I thought the pride swelling their heads would surely cause them to pop right off.

"Caitlin?" her mom whispered. "Do you want to tell her?"

"Me," Caitlin said softly. "I'm the artist."

"Well, your paintings are beautiful," I told her. "I'm no expert but if I had to guess it looks like you practice the ancient art of blue and yellow squiggly brush? Tough medium to master."

Caitlin giggled but her parents acted like they were watching the headliner at the Laugh Factory. And slightly drunk.

"Are they for sale?" I asked.

She nodded her head. The parents were turning an alarming shade of scarlet. Yes, they reminded me a lot of my parents.

Scanning the wall, I found the biggest, most gaudy one and pointed at it. "Is that one still available?"

Caitlin nodded her head.

"Great!" I said, "I'll take it."

"Oh my God, Cate!" Her mom screeched. "Your first sale!"

The dad stood up, smacked me on the back, and immediately apologized for letting the excitement get to him.

"We're just so proud," he said, then whispered, "It's supposed to be $40. But you can pay whatever you want."

"I'll pay $40. Totally worth it."

Cate and company made a big production out of sticking the red dot next to the painting I chose. Caitlin beamed when she told me I could come back in four weeks to pick it up. Lots more congratulations and cheers ensued. Dad was full-on crying.

When I got back to my table, the barista brought over my extra-caffeinated latte. He had crafted one of those Christian fish symbols in the foam.

See? That's why this guy was nearly a champion.

FRIDAY'S GOD: PELOR
GOD OF: SUN AND SUMMER
Delights in: helping those in need and opposing evil

Pelor rocks. This is definitely a god I can get behind. It's all about being nice to people and telling meanies to suck it. Today was to be all about sunshine and laughter, which sort of contradicted the vile and hostile mood I woke up in. Love and light. That's my stupid motto. If I had more time I'd make up little posters with pictures of baby animals on them. Sunshine is the kitty. Laughter is the fuzzy baby chick. They walk side by side through a forest. I gag a little at the thought. Baby steps ...

Oh, sure, I had a lot planned for this day. I fancied myself a bit like Underdog, transforming from a seemingly spiritual inane skeptic into a patron saint of the underprivileged. And when I was done pulling bullies off of scrawny classmates and helping the elderly across streets, I'd throw a massive outdoor block party where the mead and puff pastry pizzas flow like the good intentions that run through my veins.

"No, we cannot have a party," Laura answered when I told her my awesome plan. "Besides, it's horrible outside. No one wants to celebrate *love and light* when there are flash flood warnings."

"Party pooper," I said. "Or rather, Pelor Pooper. Remind me to bring some light to your dark little corner of the world."

She laughed. "When is this experiment over? I sort of miss your cynicism and somewhat questionable ways."

"Passing gas in a sweaty yoga studio is pretty questionable," Chris said, not looking up from his spreadsheet.

"Allegedly!" I shouted. I've told that story to so many people I'm starting to believe Becky's big, fat, flatulent lie.

My first instinct was to throw a stack of Post-it Notes at Chris. And then rid my desk of the rest of its contents in that armsweeping, overdramatized gesture soap opera characters do. Granted, they usually do this when they're about to conduct some hanky-panky on said desk, but still. I bet it would feel good. (The arm sweeping gesture, people. Out of the gutter, please.) I guess Becky and the yoga class still had me all riled up, which is a Major Yoga Fail, if you ask me.

But I took a moment to get centered and managed not to throw anything at Chris other than a sideways glance.

"You're funny," he said. "I know you want to hit me right now."

"Aw, come on," Laura said, "don't get mad and blow a gasket. Emphasis on the *gas*."

Okay, okay, that was pretty funny, but by the power of Pelor, I won't crack my façade with a smile. I just want to be angry and sullen today! Can't a girl get a little down-in-the-dumps time around here? Then I remembered (again) today was supposed to be a day of love and laughter, so technically Pelor would want me to make someone feel good by laughing at their joke. Even if it was at my expense. Oh, Pelor…

So I laughed and then Chris and Laura did and the next thing I know we're caught in that nexus of contagious laughter where you kind of forgot what set you off and are now just laughing at how hard each other is laughing. We laughed so hard my ribs hurt and we all had tears coursing down our cheeks. Our department assistant came over to make sure we were okay. We told her the story and sure enough, she was indoctrinated in our little comedy club.

"I'm going to pee my pants!" she said. "Stop!"

"Well, feel free to blame me for that, too," I said.

I mean, who cares, right? I'll probably never see Becky again, but just in case, I'll be sure to carry a whoopee cushion in my purse at all times.

But maybe I should give her some credit. If not for her flatulent lies I never would have almost gotten mad at Chris, then remembered my pledge to Pelor, and discovered that laughing in the face of adversity is actually more fun than sulking about it. That realization buoyed me all day. I had a spring in my step and dare I say a "sunny" disposition? Nah, too cheesy. But I was definitely in a good mood.

So much so that when someone heated up a disgusting piece of fish in the microwave, causing not just the entire fourth floor to reek like Pike Place Market on a hot August afternoon but my green beans to taste like cheap tuna, I didn't storm back to my desk to compose a company-wide e-mail demanding a ban on cooking smelly office foods. (Not this time, anyway. They probably still have my letters from the first two times.) I barely flinched when another co-worker came over telling me the project I had allocated time for next week was actually due this week. As in *by the end of the day,* which was in approximately twelve minutes.

"I'm really sorry I didn't tell you sooner," she said. "I just found out myself."

Impossible, I thought. She pretty much makes the schedules for these things. Obviously she forgot and now I had to rush to get this taken care of, forsaking a zillion other things on a deadline (not to mention my work-out!). But she really did look sorry and I can't forget the time she baked me homemade banana bread (with Splenda!) for my birthday and helped me lug 3,000 posters to my car and load them into my trunk—*when she was pregnant!*

"It's fine," I told her, much to the surprise of Chris and the delight of HR, who were probably already heading over here. "We've all been a tad overworked lately. Besides, I should know by now around when these things are due."

She half smiled, as if she were afraid showing any more gratitude would turn my passivity into belligerence and I really would blow the gasket Laura had predicted earlier.

"Now shoo so I can get to work," I said.

"Weird," Laura noted. "This whole experiment has made you *weird.*"

I was still in a good mood when I got home and found a typed note under my door insisting that I do everyone a favor and carpet my floors rather than clomp around like a pack of rhinos.

I looked at Zelda, my fat, lazy cat who was in the same spot on the sofa where I left her that morning.

"What do you do here all day?" I asked her, crumbling the note and tossing it in recycling. Yeah, my neighbor can suck it. If he did hear anything, it happened between 8:00 a.m. and 6:00 p.m., which are perfectly acceptable times of day to hear your neighbors. The Shelly of Yester-week would take that note downstairs and shove it down the complainer's piehole. *You're talking about my cat*, asshat, as she's the only one home during the day.

But instead I imagined why he might be home all day with nothing else to do but carp about feline footfalls. Perhaps he recently lost his job and keeps his office skills sharp by typing passive-aggressive notes to his neighbors. Maybe he was home sick with a migraine or worse—brain cancer—and all sounds were amplified. If that's the case I hate to think what kind of note he left our neighbor with the pewter dolphin wind chimes. Or hey! Maybe he's a carpet salesman and is really asking me to do everyone a favor and buy some rugs from him. Regardless, I decided to blow off his clearly instigative little bitch-o-gram (made all the more bitchy because it was typed and unsigned; hmm, complaining about the noises above? I have no idea who this could be from).

It really is easier to make the decision to be happy. I feel more free and lighter than I have in … well … days. I guess there's truth in that old saying "laugh and the world laughs with you"—or least a few co-workers and possibly your cat.

"It's all good," I told Zelda, petting her head. "Sunshine and laughter." She tried to bite me.

"You have a lot to learn about Pelor," I said.

I was in such a good mood I decided to finally tackle her litter box. I was about one clump away from her expressing her displeasure with the housekeeping services on the area rug.

"Sunshine and laughter, love and light," I chanted on the balcony, feeling the goodness of Pelor fill my innards and I dumped Zelda's old litter into a plastic bag. I just might take this experiment into the weekend. Maybe another week. Who knows? Maybe I'll never stop. And then I noticed my downstairs neighbor's car is parked right below. Wouldn't it be awful if I didn't tie this plastic bag tight enough and left it on the balcony overnight? Especially terrible considering the forecast said it was going to get real breezy overnight.

I know, I know, not the most pious move but I'm pretty sure even Pelor would think my neighbor is a prick. And I continued to bask in his sunshine and laughter as I clomped around my living room.

FROM THE SOAPBOX

I always knew religion factored into D&D to some extent, but personally I never explored it, and like the anti-Judy, allowed my ignorance to prevent my characters from subscribing to any one faith. While it's not required that your D&D character subscribes to any particular religion or god, spirituality does exist. Like any aspect of the game, it's what you make of it. It can actually be a fundamental part of D&D, which is ironic considering all the allegations lobbed at D&D players who were thought to have allegiances to the man down under.

Let's talk about those for a minute. I've been playing for more than half a decade (and I think we've established I'm pretty easily swayed by rose quartz, psychics, a strappy pair of wedges, etc.), and so far I haven't felt compelled to so much as squash a spider. Even the spider that decided to summer on my toothbrush. He, and the toothbrush, were gently placed outside on the balcony. (Coincidentally, so was Zelda, my cat. What she may or may not have done to the spider is between her and whatever god she reports to.)

I don't believe a game or a song or a passage in a book can "make" someone commit horrific acts of evil. I understand the need to look for scapegoats when something horrific happens. And of course the media loves a good "the rogue made me do it" tale, but let's be honest: If someone is capable of committing the acts in question, he or she was probably heading down that path long before he or she picked up a twenty-sided die. D&D, like music and books, is an escape. It can provide people with a sense of solace. *Control* in an otherwise out of control existence. But nothing is a guaranteed cure-all. It's just sad when something that likely provided an individual with perhaps the one sense of peace in his or her life gets blamed for making it all fall apart. And yes, I'm totally typing this from a soapbox.

Choosing your alignment isn't easy. Just in case you don't have time to try various gods and goddesses on for size (and fear ending up with weird macaroni art in the process), take a short cut to enlightenment with this simple quiz.

Vacation! You have one week to go anywhere you want. Where to?

A. Time to pack the hammer and tool belt! I'm building a habitat for humanity!

B. Anywhere! I'll decide on the way to the airport!

C. Burning Man, baby!

D. Somewhere quiet and chill. These books aren't going to read themselves.

E. On a seven-day bike tour through the Vosges Mountains! Pedal all day, sample Gewürztraminers all night.

You feel most comfortable in:

A. A cloud of patchouli and Birkenstocks (but only if I have to wear shoes).

B. Something trendy. I pride myself in being fashion forward.

C. Heavy cotton shirts, Dickies, steel-toe boots, and gloves. Protection is paramount.

D. A library.

E. Gym clothes. Never know when the urge to do a few hundred pushups will strike.

When your dice are rolling poorly, you:

A. Close your eyes and pray for some divine intervention. You'll give up cheese and chocolate and basic cable for something with double digits!

B. Laugh. It's the nature of the game! And then pull out one of the thirty-seven d20s you carry around for backup.

C. Destroy them!

D. Go easy on the dice. According to your latest algorithm you should be back on track in about seventeen dice rolls.

E. Jog in place. Maybe do a few jumping jacks. Anything to upset the negative feng shui that's clearly clogging up your play space.

Stop, thief! You're already running late to meet up with friends and see a thug take off with an elderly lady's purse. You:

A. Call the police and then offer the nice lady all the cash you have in your pockets in case the police can't find her bag.

B. Wait for the police to arrive so you can ask if they'll take you on a ride-along sometime.

C. Get really, really pissed. Who the hell picks on an old lady? You walk her home and offer to stand guard outside for the next forty-eight hours just in case the thief checks her license and wants to make a repeat performance.

D. Spend the next fifty-two Saturdays touring senior living centers to offer free self-defense training classes.

E. Take off after the thug figuring you'll have him pinned to the sidewalk in about a block and a half.

A genie offers to grant you one wish. What do you wish for?

A. Nice weather for your barbeque on Saturday.

B. Dealer's choice! Let the genie decide!

C. Rough up the genie. Everyone knows you get three wishes!

D. Money to pay off your student loans.

E. Tickets to the UFC championship. And maybe some new sneakers.

Unfortunately, you're stranded on a desert island that is quickly sinking into the ocean. Fortunately, you have a helicopter! Unfortunately, your helicopter can only fit five people and there are sixteen are on the island. How do you choose who to save?

A. I can't choose. Instead I will fly my helicopter as fast as I can to safety, unload my passengers, and come back for the others! If my mission fails, at least I'll know I tried.

B. Have them flip a coin. Heads they come on board, tails they … well … don't.

C. Women and children first! After that, may only the strongest survive.

D. Decide which five people can offer the most to society. You're basically doing humankind a favor, right?

E. Have them fight it out. Survival of the fittest.

MOSTLY A'S:

Bust out the sunscreen and the Kashi whole-wheat biscuits! You'll need shielding and sustenance as you bow down to the temple of sunny and selfless Pelor. And no, there's no tax write-off for taking inane quizzes with absolutely no scientific merit behind them. Now go let the sunshine in, you do-gooding hippy.

MOSTLY B'S:

Have you ever actually seen a Cheshire cat smile? No, because that would be creepy. However it's not creepy to have a little Lady Luck smiling down on you like the god of your choosing, Avandra. I know, I know, you probably changed your answers a million times, and believe me, Avandra approves. Now really test your luck and buy a lottery ticket and try to get front row parking at Trader Joe's.

MOSTLY C'S:

You're a maniac, maniac, on the floor.... Oh, sorry. Every time I think of your god, Moradin, I think of that montage scene from *Flashdance* where Jennifer Beals dances her leg warmers off in an old converted warehouse. Why, you ask? Because she worked as a welder by day. Moradin would totally approve. In addition to being a maniac, you're also probably darn pleased with the results of this quiz. And if for some reason you aren't, who would know? You'll bite your lip, put on a brave face, and craft a set of bunk beds out a few hundred discarded hubcaps until you feel better.

MOSTLY D'S:

Hey, there. Sorry to interrupt while you're out there curing diseases, launching rockets into space, and rereading War and Peace while waiting for the clerk to finish bagging your groceries. I just wanted to give you the results of that quiz you took. Boy, you must love quizzes, huh? So does your deity, Ioun. Anything that engages your brain and provides a little insight into the inner workings of that giant brain of yours just makes you warm and tingly. That's all. Carry on with your little hobbies now.

MOSTLY E'S:

Two, four, six, eight, who do you contemplate? Kord, Kord, Kord! That is when you're not painting your face in your team's colors or training for your next Iron-whatever competition. So wave that foam finger up in the air and eschew those weaklings you leave in your wake! And I really hope you're happy with these results because I don't want you to take your aggro frustration out on me. (Even though Kord might want you to.)

CHAPTER 3

CRITICAL HIT-ONS

ME: Ugh. I think I'm turning into my mother.

JUDY: YOU SHOULD BE SO LUCKY.

ME: Well, it's not lucky for my friends, as they're the ones who are going to suffer for this.

JUDY: OH DEAR. WHAT ARE YOU ABOUT TO DO NOW? IS IT AS BAD AS THE TIME IN HIGH SCHOOL WHEN YOU WROTE A PLAY ABOUT YOUR FRIENDS' EATING DISORDERS AND SEXUAL PROMISCUITY AND DIDN'T BOTHER TO CHANGE THEIR NAMES WHEN YOUR ENGLISH CLASS PERFORMED IT?

ME: That eventually saved Megan's life.

JUDY: AND NEARLY ENDED YOURS. OH, THEY WERE SO MAD AT YOU. EXCEPT THE PROMISCUOUS ONE. IF I REMEMBER CORRECTLY HER POPULARITY ROSE EXPONENTIALLY FROM YOUR ENDORSEMENT.

me: I'm not planning on outing anyone's lewd behavior, but I do plan on giving out ringing endorsements. At least for Jodi.

judy: Jodi is single? Oh, good! I have a great book for her!

me: No! Leave her alone. She's *my* project!

judy: Why is she single, anyway? She's so sweet and nice, I can't believe she'd even need your help in that department.

me: Well, she didn't exactly *ask* for it. I'm just kind of doing it. My match-making services are like those obnoxious, out-of-the blue offers from Dish Network. Anyone with a TV is eligible.

judy: Just be careful. Some people might not take well to you butting in and taking over.

me: Oh, that's rich! Are you the pot or the kettle?

judy: Very funny. What's Jodi's e-mail address? Really. If she *Acts Like a Lady But Thinks Like a Man . . .*

me: I said no! I have it under control. Besides, Jodi is too nice to tell you where you can stick your advice books.

judy: No offense, but you're not exactly an expert on relationships. How long did it take for you and Bart to finally realize you were more than best friends?

me: Six years. And I think even your pal Oprah would agree that some of the best relationships start with that foundation.

judy: *Humpf.* My grandkids could be going to kindergarten now if you were a bit more perceptive.

me: Or you and I could be bitter enemies because your incessant pro-creation badgering put me over the edge. Finally.

judy: I doubt it. I've been badgering you for years. You won't budge. Tell Jodi to try online dating. I just saw the commercial that says one out of five couples meet online. And I know just the book to help her write a profile. They were just talking about it on TV. Oh, what show was that—

me: I'm not putting her online.

judy: There are apparently key words that men subconsciously gravitate to and ones that instantly repel them.

me: If only there were words that would instantly repel mothers. But don't worry. It's covered.

judy: Why? Are you giving her that bottle of human sex pheromones I ordered for you from the Philippines?

me: No.

judy: The glitter love dust from New Orleans?

me: No.

judy: The rose quartz from the psychic I met in the Bahamas?

me: No.

judy: What could possibly be more powerful than a psychically charged piece of rose quartz; the pheromones from the most attractive, fertile Filipino women; and good old-fashioned voodoo?

me: A set of pink dice; a bodacious, bad-ass barbaric alter ego; and some good old-fashioned role-playing.

judy: No! You're a terrible friend! Jodi doesn't even play D&D.

me: Minor hurdle. She's just going to look the part. The rest will fall into place.

Judy: I still think the book I heard about would be better. The author is a renowned couple's therapist. She knows what works! Come on, what show was that—

me: What's the difference between *your* books and my D&D books?

judy: My books are written by experts. The authors are world authorities on relationships and psychology. They have proven track records! They've been in *USA Today*!

me: My books are written by experts. Dungeon Masters are experts on relationship psychology. D&D's been around for more than three decades, so that's a pretty decent track record. D&D has been in *USA Today*.

judy: Really?

me: Really.

judy: Well, I still think you should give me her address. You know, for backup.

me: No way. Talk about being a terrible friend.

Let's pick on single people, shall we? What? Everyone picks on them. At least it seems like that from the pile of self-help available to this lot in life. I feel like I can offer my own advice here (but not make fun of them) because I have spent 99% of my own life in this camp and 98% of my life fending off the advice of Judy and other well-meaning friends.

Saying things like, "How can you be single?" and "What's wrong with these guys?" doesn't help. First, I hadn't really thought about why I was single or what was wrong with all my possible suitors. Are you implying that I had all the tools at my disposal and have somehow messed up, therefore guaranteeing me a lifetime of spinsterhood? Or that my potential suitors are all broken, flawed, idiotic, or too wrapped up in their action figure collections to give me the time of day? And *that's* the pool I get to choose from? Thanks. (And for the record, there are worst things than action figures for a guy to be into: raising and slaughtering goats, meth-making, and the *Twilight* saga, to name a few.)

Second, people always assume that single people don't want to be single, which may or may not be true. Hey, you don't know what kind of baggage I'm toting around that prevents me from coupling. Maybe the onus isn't on the guys. Maybe there *is* something wrong with me. Maybe my shrink staunchly advised against dating, fearing for the safety of others. Maybe I'm sorely in need of a shrink! (And also, for the record, there's nothing wrong with having a shrink. Especially if your insurance plan covers it.)

Third, *single* does not mean *alone*. Do you know single people have the freedom to date as many people as they like? At the same time? Just because someone isn't in a *committed* relationship doesn't mean they're not having relations.

While I may have tried to give people that impression because I was sick of answering their *why what how* questions, it was definitely rooted in frustration rather than reality. The only "relations" I was having were with the sandwich artists at the Subway down the street and Fred, the guy who delivered my pad thai every Thursday night.

By contrast, we have my friends who are always in a relationship. One's been dating since nursery school and has never gone more than three months without being "the other half." And we're talking good, healthy relationships, too. She was the first one of my group to get hitched and she probably already has a cabin booked to celebrate their golden anniversary on a Carnival Cruise to Cozumel.

Me? I was a late bloomer. Don't get me wrong. I went on dates. I had tons of crushes that were more fun to not act on and a few long-term relationships. Most important, I got very good at ignoring Judy's musings on what it would be like to have a son-in-law and my cousin Lulu's inquiries into my sexuality. Hey, Lulu, if you thought I was gay because I was single, then wouldn't that just make me a single lesbian? I'm not getting how one excludes the other. Whatever.

Having a boyfriend never defined who I was. Either I was single or I wasn't. And when I was I always had seemingly endless fodder to write about, like why people are so obsessed with single people.

I admit that I, too, am obsessed with single people, regardless of my own relationship status. Or more to the point, obsessed with setting people up. I'm quite good at it, too. Just pick someone from column A, match them with someone from column B, and presto! A couple!

Matchmaking is the kind of butting in I can get behind. While I was always the friend everyone claimed they couldn't believe was single, no one ever tried to fix me up, claiming they didn't have any friends they thought were "good enough." Seriously? Then why are you friends with these people? Truthfully, I think no one had any idea what kind of guy I would be attracted to. He'd have to be part Simon Le Bon, part Simon Doonan, and part golden retriever. Hmm … now I can see why I never went on blind dates.

But seriously, why can't we leave the single people alone? Shouldn't we put all this "find a cure" energy into something meaningful like cancer or adult acne? And by "we" I mean "mothers." And by "mothers" I mean "Judy."

Judy treated my singlehood the way an experimental doctor might treat a rare, recursive virus.

"Try online dating! I'll pay for your first three months!"

"Try going out more! I'll buy you a new outfit!"

"Try reading this book! It and thirty others just like it are on their way!"

The books! There are more books promising to find the lid for your pot than there are Italian cookbooks for beginners. It's true. I counted. I knew what Judy's motivation was—a bad case of Grandma Envy. Finding me a mate wasn't so much about making sure I always had someone to pick me up at the airport as it was about ensuring there would be a small person with her delicate ankles and a button nose sitting at the kids' table on Thanksgiving.

"That's not true," Judy insisted when I told her my theory. "I just wanted you to be happy. That's all any parent wants for their kids."

"But again, you're equating happiness with couplehood. I know plenty of couples who are anything but happy."

Even Judy had to agree with that. But "happy" to her means *someone to take care of you.* "What if you needed to go to the hospital or had the flu or slipped in the bathtub?"

I reminded her of the time I stabbed myself while de-pitting an avocado, *in front of Bart,* and had to calm him down before removing the paring knife from my palm. Neither of us is good with crisis, I'm afraid. But it was nice having someone to open the wine bottles while my hand was bandaged.

I have another speculation as to why single people get picked on. It's because they're an easy target. Everyone thinks they know how to manage someone else's sad, lonely life better than they do. I mean, obviously, right? These people are sad and lonely. Look up "single" in the dictionary and that's exactly what it says. I'm kidding, of course,

AND MY SOUP'S COLD, JERKWAD

Dave Barry said, "A person who is nice to you but not nice to the waiter is not a nice person." I believe it and think of that every time I'm out to eat with someone. I also believe there's truth in the saying, "A person who is nice to you but not nice to the Dungeon Master is not a nice person." The DM is essentially your host. You wouldn't be playing D&D without him or her. That reason alone warrants at least a thank you, not to mention a six-pack and a pizza.

The same goes for how the Dungeon Master treats his or her players. You don't want to play a game with someone who uses it as an outlet for their control issues.

"Ahh, the dragon rolled 119 damage! You all die horrible, flaming deaths! Good-bye and get out of my house!"

Ladies? Don't date that guy. And guys? Don't ask that girl if it's that time of the month. In fact, don't ever ask that stupid question. Even if it isn't she'll lie and say it is so when she smacks you upside the head she'll have a good defense.

I don't know what's happening in your home or work life but none of that that should ever make its way to the playmat. I'm not the one who deleted the series finale of Lost from your DVR (although I would have if I could have; why did everyone love that show?). Don't punish my poor little adventurer by throwing her down a trap door with nothing to cushion her fall but a throng of bugbears. She's just trying to make a living here!

but that is the way it seems if you spend any time perusing the self-help books Judy sent me. (And don't look at me like that! Of course I at least peeked at them.)

Sadly, there is no end to the amount of books geared toward fixing the lovelorn. And what's up with all the titles—they always have YOU in big letters. *How to Find the Love YOU Lost. How to Stop YOURSELF from Falling for Another Loser. Why She Chose Him and Not YOU.* It's like YOU have gone out there and made a big, fat, lonely mess of YOUR life and now these little paperback martyrs have to go out there and clean up after YOU. Can't YOU just hear their passive-aggressive little paper sighs? "Oh, fine, I was relaxing here on this shelf checking out that molten chocolate cake on the cover of *1,000 Chocolate Delicacies*, but okay, I'll take care of you. Again. Good job, mate. Nicely done. Need a paperback to fight all your battles?"

Had I only known the key to unlocking my inner half of a happy couple was to buy some dice and roll up a character, I could have saved Judy thousands of dollars. Dollars she could have sunk into slot machines or Omaha Steaks or providing nutritious food for a child in Honduras. If there's one stereotype about D&D that *is* true it's the one that implies only guys play it. Well, sort of true, anyway. *A lot* of guys play it. Oh sure, women play, too, but your odds of being the only girl in the room are great (and not in a creepy, bad-judgment sort of way that Lifetime movies are made of).

Oh sure, I give my Dungeon Master(s) a hard time during the game, but I know they can handle it. It's all in good fun. It's kind of like yelling at the ref during a hockey game when he makes a bad call. Actually, I take that back. I've seen how some people treat refs during a hockey game and I'm not *that* bad. For instance, I've never thrown meat at my Dungeon Master. It's more like how I treat my trainer when he tells me to do pushups.

"Quit telling me what to do!" I say this knowing full well that telling me what to do is exactly what I pay him for.

When my group gets out of hand with the "you're cheating!" and "Nope, thirty-four doesn't hit my level five armor class," our Dungeon Master lets us know. No matter what happens in the game I always make sure to thank him, tell him that it was fun, and offer to carry his minis back to his desk. He usually lets me, too. Sucking up is just one of the many ways to make your DM feel appreciated.

There are tons of stories out there about couples meeting each other around the D&D table. "He was a shifty rogue," "She healed me," "He was my Dungeon Master" (the latter of which I'm assuming is a reference to D&D; maybe not). This hypothesis is just itching to be tested. That's where Jodi comes in.

She's the perfect accomplice to test my theory. She just embarked on a new career in aesthetics, which she loves (and is really, really good at; if you need someone to tend to your skin care needs, let me know). She's smart, funny, outgoing, and beautiful. Most important she's now the official friend none of us can believe is single. At the risk of sounding like Judy, what *is* wrong with the guys around here?

Over a delicious dinner of vegetarian Sloppy Joes and a bottle of Riesling, I told Jodi how I thought D&D was great for couples and potential couples.

"If more people knew about D&D and its matchmaking wonders, Dr. Phil would be out of a day job," I said.

"That's some good motivation to get the word out," she offered. "I'll join that cause."

While much subtler, Jodi's mom has been known to quote Dr. Phil-isms. Single women hate Dr. Phil. (Remind me to talk to R&D about creating a Dr. Phil-inspired monster.)

"You and Bart could be the poster children for how D&D brings people together," Jodi added.

It's true, D&D brought Bart and me together, or more specifically our jobs working on D&D brought us together. I thought he was a perfectly nice guy and liked him right away in that co-workers-I-wouldn't-hate-having-lunch-with sort of way. According to him he liked me, *liked me* the first time we met.

"You were nice, even if you were a little too chatty," he said.

"Well, you were nice, too," I said. "Even if your glasses were from 1987."

It didn't matter how we felt about each other then because I had a boyfriend. But I still classified Bart as someone with definite potential, so I dropped him into slot A and set out to fix him up right away. My friend Des had a friend named Bethany whom I had never met but Des gave a glowing review.

"She likes reading and camping and is superfunny and cute."

"Hmm, camping?" Bart asked, when I told him about my prospect. "The reason I have a job is so I *don't* have to sleep outside."

But he overlooked Bethany's affinity for sleeping on dirt and agreed to meet her for a blind date. While they had drinks at a bar in Queen

Anne, Des and I texted back and forth, trying to pinpoint the exact moment they fell blissfully in love. I went to Bart's desk before my own the next morning.

"Well?" I asked. "Are you heading to REI to buy a sleeping bag, Wilderness Jack?"

"I hate you. And you owe me two hours and $29."

What? How could this be? Des had nothing but positive adjectives reserved for her friend. And all of my fix-ups have always resulted in at least a third date. Judy was right! There was something wrong with the guys around here!

"There's a reason that girl is single," he continued. "I had more fun counting the salt specks on my French fries."

"But Des said she was funny and smart . . . "

"Would it have killed her to use some inflection while telling me about her days as an intern with an actuary?"

"And cute . . . "

Bart informed me that when a woman describes her friend as "cute" it's usually a sign she's . . . well, not. (I don't believe this. I have plenty of friends who are across-the-board cute. But just in case he's for real, please note I have described Jodi as beautiful.)

Bethany was actually surprised that Bart didn't call for a second date. Surprised and disappointed. I had to make up some story to Des about Bart not being over his ex-girlfriend and therefore not ready to date after all rather than explain her friend is about as interesting as a rice cake. We still talk about Bethany when we're stuck doing less than scintillating tasks like caulking the bathtub or facing cans of tomato soup when we volunteer at a food bank.

"Would you rather be stuck in a submarine, listening to Bethany lecture about the proper way to lick a stamp, or in a small, dank supply closet organizing cans of soup based on their sodium content?"

Much to Bart's delight, I didn't try to fix him up again.

For years our timing was never quite right for dating. By the time I broke up with the guy I was seeing, Bart was dating someone else. But over the course of five years we became the kind of great friends men and women can be if you're sure they'll never see you in your birthday suit. Bart was my workout buddy, drinking pal, and confidant. I made him study the huge zits erupting on my chin, I could belch him under the table, I told him about my penchant for Saturday afternoon Hallmark Channel movies. You know, the stuff you tell your best guy friend when you have no intention of actually dating him.

But then Bart's relationship ended, and he moved to my neighborhood.

We were working out, drinking, confiding, *and* carpooling together. And for the first time we were single at the same time.

One day in May I invited him to join our friend Sarah and me for a hike at Mount Si. Sarah was training to climb Mount Rainier. Now, here's some unsolicited advice for you: do not, under any circumstances, climb giant mountains with friends training to climb even bigger mountains. While Sarah pretty much ran up the 4,100 feet (with a thirty-pound pack strapped on her back), Bart had to push me (and the Luna bar strapped on my back) up at least 2,100 feet.

"I'll give you half of my Mediterranean wrap when we get to the top," he promised. "And homemade butterscotch cookies. You just have to get there."

"Go without me. Save yourself! Your cookies can't help me now!"

Four million switchbacks later we made it. Sarah was nearly done with her sandwich by the time I face-planted on a boulder.

"You did it, Buddy," Bart said. "Not bad for your first hike."

"Please insert cookies into the slot on my face," I said. "My limbs have forsaken me."

We were exhausted by the time we returned home but managed to rally for Chinese food, several pints of beer, *Sex and the City* trivia, and a bottle of Trader Joe's Tempranillo on Bart's front porch. I was hoping he could help decipher the mixed signals I was getting from an Argentinian rugby player.

"I can't figure the guy out," I said. "He asks me to do stuff all the time. Just us. Date-like things. But then when we're out, he treats me like a kid sister. I *think* there's chemistry. What's his deal?"

"The deal is the guy is an idiot," Bart said. And then he kissed me.

I'd like to say "and the rest was history," but it wasn't.

"Don't forget the couple of months I spent wooing you," Bart likes to add when we tell the story. "You put me through the wringer."

It's true. But only because I thought the idea of us as a couple was worse than the dreaded reverse-bob hairstyle. Why?

"Because it will ruin our friendship," I insisted. Yep. What would Dr. Phil say about that? I'll tell you, as channeled through Judy.

"You love spending time together, have a ton in common, share your deepest, darkest secrets. You're right, Shelly, run for the hills!"

Oh, whatever, Dr. Judy. I came to my senses, okay? And while we're at it, here's some more unsolicited advice for anyone single: Look at your best friends. I mean *really* look at them.

For Jodi, I have some different advice. Or rather, a proposition.

"How would you like to take part in an experiment?" I asked her,

BEST SUPPORING CHARACTERS

Hey guys! Want to know what it's like having Judy for a mother? Let me give you some unsolicited advice!

Have some kooky, harebrained, peculiar notion floating around in that brain of yours? Try it out on your D&D character first. If the party lets you get away with it, you might have a shot in real life. If the party threatens to loot you and feed what remains to a pack of displacer beasts, perhaps you best nurse that idea of yours a little longer.

Bart's a great guy but I would never date his D&D character. Holden Cawfield, a kenku assassin, is an instigator, a troublemaker, a what's-behind-door-number-3'er. He's also a creepy little bird man. Knowing Bart, Holden represents a slice of his personality— the instigating, troublemaking, questioning-door-number-3 part. Although Bart would love to venture off into the great Forgotten Realms with nothing more than a backpack and some trail rations, in real life he's much more pragmatic, rational, and easygoing. D&D is a great outlet to express unrealistic ideals. I mean, I'd much rather Bart topple a bookshelf and use the fallen books as a ladder to get to the upper tier of a ziggurat in D&D than, say, at Judy's house to try to escape out a window when she starts questioning him about our future together.

as I filled her wine glass with more Riesling. "We could erase Dr. Phil from the minds of mothers everywhere!"

"Okay!" she answered. Jodi is always agreeable, but under the influence of wine she's downright impetuous. "Wait, what kind of experiment? I'm not cutting my hair or getting pierced. Learned that the hard way."

"Oh no, nothing like that," I said, opening another bottle. "Not this time, anyway. You know how you're always saying it's hard to meet people? Well, I have a great conversation starter for you."

"Keep talking," she said, sipping her fresh glass of Riesling.

"I'm going to outfit you in some new gear and send you out on the town. Movies, beer gardens, a jog around Green Lake. Of course, I'll pay for everything."

Jodi is a sucker for new clothes. Even if said clothing involves barbarians and skeletal monsters.

"Wait, you're going to buy me new clothes?" she asked, narrowing her eyes.

"Well ... not so much *buy*," I explained. "More like borrow some things from the office. Some D&D things."

"No chain-mail bikinis!" Her voice may have said no but her glassy eyes were saying yes. Or maybe that was the Riesling.

"Guys dig girls in D&D gear!" I said, having no evidence of this but I'm afraid I'll lose her when she sees the duds I'm talking about.

Jodi took the wadded up black T-shirt I handed her. "Rock me, Asmodeus? Is this supposed to be funny?"

"Yes. To those in the know, anyway."

She studied the shirt for a minute before concluding Asmodeus looked just like her boss from her days working at the skating rink. "I thought he was hot. But then again, I was fifteen."

"Asmodeus is believed to be the prince of lust," I told her. "Wear him with care."

A few days later I found Bart tearing around his bedroom. His dog, Sadie, was following anxiously behind him like a novice cop who just spotted her first perpetrator and kind of wished she hadn't.

"Did you by chance borrow one of my T-shirts?" he asked.

"You're confusing Sadie. She thinks some guy in a 'Daddy' costume is breaking into her daddy's house."

"I just saw it...."

"I'm sure you have another shirt you can wear," I said. "Like the one you have on, for instance."

He sniffs it and dismisses it. "I want to wear my Asmodeus shirt. Ernie will love it."

"I'm sure Ernie will love your Chicago Bears shirt just as much. Or what about this perfectly good one from Banana Republic?"

He's undeterred and because I made the assumption he would never, ever miss that shirt and gave it to Jodi, we're going to be late. We're having dinner with his friend Samantha from the Peace Corps and her husband, Ernie, tonight. I'm not sure where we're going—Bart made the plans—but I hope Jodi and an 11th-level paladin aren't there, too.

I haven't met Samantha or Ernie yet, but they're already convinced Bart and I are soul mates.

"She plays D&D?" Samantha wrote in an e-mail. "You're a perfect match!"

Sweet sentiment and maybe it's true, but that's not the only reason we're wellmatched. We both love books, and *The Office*, and cupcakes. We get cranky if we miss a workout and make up voices for our pets and . . . well, you get the idea. But I can see why Bart's friend would call out our mutual interest in Dungeons & Dragons. Bart is exceptionally passionate about D&D. He's been playing for years. It makes sense that couples that play D&D together should stay together because it's not just about having one thing in common—it's something people are incredibly invested in. Of course you'd want to share that with your significant other. (I'm still working on Bart's appreciation for *Tabatha's Salon Takeover*. Baby steps.)

"I love that you play D&D." Bart said with the sincerity and sentimentality of someone saying, "I love that you are nice to animals" or "I love that you gave me a kidney."

I suppose if you're going to spend an entire Saturday afternoon (possibly the evening, too) playing a game, it helps to have your partner sitting next to you. And playing D&D is a great insight into someone's character. I think instead of speed dating, people should do "swift encounters." How that guy handles two armed guards with their backs to the party is very telling.

At the wedding of Bart's best friend from childhood this past year, I met the rest of his original adventuring party. For the wedding, Bart was asked to write a story that captured the essence of their friendship, which is a lot of pressure for one story. (The wedding was also on a ranch in the wilds of Idaho, which was a lot of pressure on a city slicker who lacks sensible shoes or anything made of fleece. But that's another story.) These guys go back nearly twenty-five years, so there's a lot of history there, but Bart's story focused on the hours spent playing D&D. After the wedding they waxed nostalgic about their favorite characters, the crawl space in Bart's hallway where they would hide out—with candles—so they could read the adventure and see the map. Bart's mom yelled upstairs every thirty minutes to make sure they were okay. Obviously she didn't know about the candles in the crawl space, and according to him she had no idea what they were doing other than playing some game that required "make-believe." It was better than the trouble they could get into outdoors.

Samantha's comment about us got me thinking about D&D and couples. Well, that and the e-mail I got from Judy.

TO: Shelly
FROM: Judy

BECAUSE YOU WON'T GIVE ME JODI'S ADDRESS, I'M SENDING THIS TO YOU.
PLEASE PASS IT ON. ARRIVING TUESDAY.

This madness needs to stop.

"Absolutely," one co-worker answered when I asked if playing D&D with his significant other strengthened their relationship. "D&D, and gaming in general, is a huge part of my life. It's not just the game itself that I love. It's the culture, the relationships, shopping for dice. The fact that we can share that together is hugely positive."

That seemed to be the general consensus around the office, but then again, most of the people I asked aren't just working at Wizards because they need to pay the rent. They're here because it's their dream job. Anyone who would move across the country just to be near the same zip code as the company who publishes the game they love is probably surrounded by people who share that passion. But just to be fair I kept asking people until I found a rebuttal.

"It's actually better that she doesn't share my interest in gaming," my friend Ben said. "Couples need to have their space. D&D is how I get away. It's my time with my friends."

I get that. I love Bart and all but I don't want to look up from the carnage of a pillaged clearance end cap at Target to see his smiling face. No man should have to see the woman who might bear his children in that state.

Hmm, would Bart and I be a different couple, better or worse, if we didn't play D&D together?

I'm pondering just that when Jason from shipping drops by my desk with a box.

"Another care package from Mom," he noted. It's the third package from Amazon this month.

"I'm becoming a better person," I told him. "Notice anything different yet?"

"Tell her to send brownies so we can all experience a little enlightenment."

It's true, Judy's brownies are so delectable, you'll have clean karma for lifetimes to come.

I read the back cover. Apparently this book had: "Found USA Dan a wife in just two weeks!" "Turned TJ's sour dating life around!" "Made Stormy Weather get in touch with his inner, romantic demons and realize he'd have to slay them. Eventually."

Hmm ... one might think someone who chooses the handle "Stormy Weather" might be beyond a few simple solutions to find Mr./Mrs. Right in Cyberspace. Jodi will never see this book. Instead it goes in the ever-growing to-be-read-if-I'm-ever-housebound-for-two-years-without-cable-television-or-shampoo-bottles-or-VCR-instruction-manuals-or-anything-good-left-to-read pile.

A few days later, I got a call from Jodi that opened with, "I'm going to kill you."

"That doesn't sound promising," I said. Good thing we're on the phone and not standing at the top of a steep staircase.

"I wore that stupid lust-man shirt for my walk around Green Lake. Honestly, I didn't know it was the D&D one. I thought it was my bon jovi slippery when wet tour 1987 one."

"Which is much cooler," I interjected.

"But, oh well," she continued. "A clean shirt is a clean shirt. Or so I thought."

"Wait," I stopped her. "Is this conversation going to end with 'pick me up from the ER' or 'stop at an ATM for bail money'? Because you can skip the details and just tell me where you are."

"No!" she answered all huffy. As if *that's* never happened before. "I'm home and thankfully alone. You'll be happy to know that T-shirt attracted all sorts of attention."

"Wait! Let me get a pen!"

"You can just use the same language from the lawsuit I filed against you."

"Please continue," I said. "I can't wait for the papers."

"So at first I thought people were looking at me funny, but that could be for a number of things. I let the new stylist at the spa color my roots and they're ... well, colorful to say the least, but then I actually saw people do double takes. Weird looks I can handle. Double takes that zero in on my boobs is completely another."

"That must be how Vince Vaughn felt post-*Old School*. Moobs are a career killer."

She continued. "Then I realized these two guys were following me and whispering. I picked up the pace and they picked up the pace and I felt exactly how Tracey Gold feels in pretty much any movie she's in. Then I remembered it was broad daylight and I was in a crowded, public park. So I stopped and turned around and asked them what the hell they thought they were doing."

"Again, if you're in jail or the ER, will you please just save the details and tell me?"

"So they apologized and said they couldn't help notice my T-shirt and wanted to know if I played D&D."

"What's bad about that?" I asked. People are always saying Seattleites are aloof and too passive to make friends with strangers. This could be really good for T-shirt sales.

"I'm like, 'Hello, I'm working out here!' but they were so excited. They started telling me about their game on Wednesdays and their characters and asking me all sorts of questions about my levels and paths and who I was campaigning for, which I thought was a strange diversion."

"I think they were asking what campaign you play in," I explained. As if it mattered. Jodi was even more loquacious than her usual self. She wasn't asking for the *Player's Handbook* crib notes.

"I told them I hadn't played in a while, which is true. I haven't played since that time you plied us with Pinot and forced us to."

"Forced, encouraged, drugged, whatever."

"And said they'd be happy to roll down a character for me."

"Roll up," I said. "Keep talking."

"So now I'm back to walking, really fast, trying to shake them while still managing to strike a balance between polite and disinterested, but they kept up! So then I lied and said I had a strict training schedule to maintain and took off running. Running!"

I laughed. Jodi has been known to say she'd only run if someone were chasing her. And then only if he had a long-range weapon.

"Sounds like you met two potential friends and managed to get in an even better workout than expected. I think you should thank me."

"I can't feel my legs," she said.

I made her an appointment with a massage therapist the next day. A few days later I got an e-mail from her:

TO: Shelly (home)
FROM: Jodi (sent via Blackberry)
SUBJECT: You are a bitch.

Have to avoid Green Lake so I don't run into my "friends" again so I went to Seward Park. Had to wear your stupid dragon shirt again because the kitten peed all over my clean gym clothes. Grrr . . . that's a different story. Anyway, about ten minutes in, this guy walks up to me and asked where I got my shirt from. I told him from my bitch friend who bullied me into wearing it for some weird social experiment in exchange for wine and Sloppy Joes. He then asked me what we were experimenting with and I told him about your book (sorry! I hope it wasn't a secret!). Turns out he used to play D&D up until college but his group fell apart and he's yet to pick it up again. Although he does stay in touch online. OMG he knew your name! Points for him. But he doesn't read your column. Negative points for him.

So get this—we're halfway up that dreaded hill before I even realize we've been walking and talking for at least a mile. And then two miles and then—oops! Passed my car! I know my legs are going to kill me tomorrow but he was so much fun to talk to. Finally we both had to admit we walked about three miles more than we needed to, so we decided to rebuild that calorie deficiency with banana bread and cappuccinos at Starbucks. Another hour of great conversation went by until he finally asked if maybe I'd like to meet him at the lake again for a walk sometime. I'm thinking, *weird. No ring, nice guy, cute, fit, fun to talk to, has a job. What's going on here?* And then it hits me. The reason I'm not a bumbling idiot around this guy and actually enjoying myself is because—he's gay! He confirms my suspicions about two minutes later when he asks if his partner and their adorable pugs, Zsa Zsa and Garland, could join us. Oh well. Maybe I'll make two new friends. And I do love pugs. And yes, damn it, he did mention his friend Mark who loves D&D just moved here from Phoenix, is single and apparently ready to mingle. I'll give you half a point.

Hey, can you get me a couple more T-shirts? I bet these guys would love them. Oh, and I just got a package from your mom! She's so sweet!

XO,

Jo Jo

D&D BY THE NUMBERS

Think playing D&D and dating are mutually exclusive? Can playing D&D negatively affect your dating life? Not according to the informal market research study I conducted around the office. Surprise! I work with a few guys who play D&D and have significant others. And by a few I mean about 210.

Here's what my super-sleuthy investigative skills turned up.

10: Number of guys who play D&D who are in relationships that I could round up on short notice

3: Number of their significant others who play D&D

1: Number of significant others who *played* D&D until they felt like their boyfriends were using a fantasy setting to hash out real-life relationship problems

1: Number of boyfriends who were using a fantasy setting to hash out real-life relationship problems

8: Number of guys who tried to get their significant others into D&D

7: Number of guys who initially hid the fact they played D&D from their significant others

8: Number of guys who would love to have a regular D&D game with their significant others.

2: Number of guys who are happy to have D&D all to themselves

4: Number of guys who bought their significant others *Confessions of a Part-Time Sorceress* in an attempt to get them to play D&D

3: Number of significant others who enjoyed *Confessions of a Part-Time Sorceress*

1: Number of significant others who thought *Confessions of a Part-Time Sorceress* was vapid, silly, and too girly

1: Number of significant others I hope gets a nasty bladder infection the day of our company holiday party and, sadly, won't be able to attend

Shelly Mazzanoble

CHAPTER 4

BABBLING'S IN THE EAR OF THE BEHOLDER

ME: And then Roxy said—

JUDY: Did you see the **HOUSEWIVES** yet?

ME: Mom? I'm talking. I was telling you a story.

JUDY: Oh, I know. But it's taking too long. And I want to talk about the **HOUSEWIVES** before my nail appointment.

ME: But you can't just interrupt someone when they're talking. I'm not done with my story.

JUDY: Of course not. Because you have to fill in every detail. What the temperature was, what you were wearing, what you wished you were having for dinner. Is that really important?

me: Yes, because that's part of the story! The temperature was unseasonably warm so I didn't need a jacket. Instead I wore the pashmina wrap Roxy brought me back from Paris when she went there on their honeymoon.

judy: But that doesn't have anything to do with your homeowners association meeting! Isn't that what the story is about?

me: It does if you just let me finish!

judy: Your stories are wonderful but sometimes the details are … how can I say this … excessive.

me: Some might say flowery or *narratively gifted.*

judy: No, I'd still say excessive. Sometimes I want to shake you and scream, "Get to the point! I don't care what color the tablecloths were or how much salt was in your gnocchi!"

me: Well maybe that *is* the point! Maybe it's part of my story!

judy: You were always like this. When you were little you'd start off telling me about your lunch and how much you hated Beth and how you'd absolutely die if you didn't get a new Papa Smurf and how mad you were that Mrs. Munroe's class gets a pet rabbit and all you have is a sunflower and, oh yeah, you love Rocky Road ice cream so much. Turns out you were trying to ask for help with your math homework.

me: I wanted to share things with you. I can't believe you're making this into a bad thing. Would you rather I had been one of those teenagers who hate their moms and never come out of their rooms?

judy: When you were a little kid? Maybe. It was much worse back then because on top of your effusiveness, you also had a stutter.

me: I stuttered?

judy: A-a-a-all the t-t-t-time. You don't remember?

me: Wow. I probably blocked out this painful memory because my primary caregiver mocked me.

judy: Or the shock therapy we put you through eliminated most of your long-term memories. Yeah, that's more likely it.

me: Can I please tell you what happened at the homeowners meeting? It was pretty terrible. Like leave-carpenter-nails-under-my-car-tires terrible.

judy: Good thing I renewed your AAA membership this year.

me: I bet my neighbors would toilet-paper my home if only they could figure out how to do it on my share of the building only.

judy: I'd love to hear, but I don't have time. I have a doctor's appointment. *Tomorrow.*

me: You are a horrible person.

judy: Oh, stop. It's not that I don't like talking to you or enjoy your stories. Sometimes I wish you had an edit button. Remember how frustrated you'd get when Mike would finish your sentences?

me: That was—.

judy: Annoying. We told him to do that. You know, to help you along.

me: I don't believe this. Half the things he interjected were lies. Like, "I want to eat Chinese food!"

judy: You loved Chinese food.

me: No, I didn't! I hated it! *He* liked it! He used me to get sweet and sour chicken!

judy: That's so weird. I can't believe you don't like Chinese food. Do you remember how mad you'd get if you thought people weren't paying attention to you anymore? You'd start crying and stomping your little feet and yelling, "Mommy, make them listen to me!"

me: These are horrible memories.

judy: I know! I can't believe they're all flooding back to me. You should go off on tangents more often. Oh, wait . . . what am I saying?

me: Very funny. Now I know why I spent so much time alone, with just the voices in my head to keep me company.

judy: That makes sense. Maybe it's not your inability to finish one thought. Maybe all of your personalities are extroverts.

me: Or maybe I was starved for attention and the only thing I could do was tell inane stories.

judy: Don't blame me for your issues! I tried to help! At least with your storytelling. Did you ever read *How to Win Friends and Influence People* by Dale—?

me: *No!*

judy: Well, maybe you should. Before your next homeowners association meeting.

I will never speak to you again if you tell my mother I said this:

She's right.

A little.

I can be a bit wordy. Oh, stop! I know what you're thinking. How many trees had to die because *someone* doesn't know when to say when to a paragraph? And this after some vigorous editing.

It's out of my control. There are perfectly good words out there and no one is using them. Punctuation marks unemployed! I see a tangent and I have to jump on it like Denzel Washington on a runaway train. It's just that my story about that one time I tried stand-up paddle boarding might remind me of my thirtieth birthday in Hawaii, which triggers a memory of the unbridled crush I had on Rick, Magnum P.I.'s sidekick, which brings me to . . . well, you get the picture.

The road to "the point" is a long, meandering, sometimes detoured route for me. I'm a rambler. A subscriber to the "tell, don't show" philosophy. And when I sense I'm losing you, I talk faster. Sometimes I act like Tootsie, the separation-anxiety-plagued black lab I fostered, and will follow you from room to room if you try to get away.

I love telling a story. I love details. I love a rapt audience. But I never realized until my mom told me to *shut the hell up* that perhaps others didn't appreciate my wordiness.

"Brevity is the soul of wit," Bart informed me when I told him Judy nearly hung up on me today.

"You know, I have to disagree with the old Bard on that one. Everyone knows a good joke is one you invest your audience in. There's got to be that buildup. Even a knock-knock joke has some suspense."

"Ah, but in Shakespeare's day 'brevity' referred to 'intelligence.'"

I should note that Bart was an English major.

"So you're calling me stupid? Because I like to tell long stories? Here's a story for you. There once was a boy who called his girlfriend stupid. She hit him with a frying pan. The end."

He laughed. And moved a few inches away from me. And took the frying pan I was drying out of my hands and put it away.

"I am doing no such thing," he said. "But even you admit that you have trouble articulating your point, especially under pressure, in an argument."

It's true. If you think just everyday story retelling is bad, you should hear me debate. Forget it. If it's something I'm passionate about, I never get the words out quick enough. It's like they get clogged up in transport from my brain to my mouth and just sit there all frothy and foamy until someone acknowledges I'm yelling and lets me win the argument. Or I burst out crying before it gets to that point. Either way, I win the argument by default.

And when the argument ends I can't stop thinking about it and all the clever, cool, pithy things I should have said. I remember facts and anecdotes to back up my claim. Sometimes I even go so far as to craft an e-mail (it could take days) that explains all that I was trying to say when I was gurgling and choking and throwing rigatoni at you. (Yep. Did that.) Usually I send the e-mail, much to my opponent's surprise. In D&D, I believe this is called *delaying your action*.

Case in point: the recent homeowners association meeting. Now these things aren't ever riotous good times. Usually we have barely enough for a quorum, a tin of Danish butter cookies, and lots of bitching about the property management company that includes empty threats like *this will be the year we fire their asses*. As far I can tell from the meeting minutes, they've been saying that for at least twenty-three years

This meeting, however, was different. After the board met with a team of structural engineers, it was discovered that *parts* of our thirty-one-year-old stucco abode were showing signs of water intrusion. I know what you're thinking—stucco in the Northwest? Right. It's like wearing stilettos to a hoe-down-themed wedding. (Been there, worn that.) It doesn't make sense, but in 1979 I'm sure it looked darn good. (Just like my stilettos, thank you.)

Water damage is the cancer of architecture. It can lead to all sorts of fun things like mold, rot, collapsed foundations, and above all else, panic. For the first time in the thirteen years I lived there, we had 100% turnout at a meeting, mostly due to the two words on the meeting agenda: Potential Assessment.

Skip, the homeowners association president (and keeper of *the worst* volunteer job in America), made sure we all had a copy of the engineer's report before the meeting. Not being an engineer myself, I took one look at the photos of *giant wet spots* between the stucco and interior walls and surmised *ohmygodwehavetofixthisnow!* If we were to replace the entire exterior of the building then we'd be looking at upward of $700,000. That's roughly an average assessment of $40,000 *per unit*. Holy hell, right? But what choice did we—rational adults who want to protect not just our homes but also our years of equity—have?

"Well, obviously the problem isn't going to correct itself," I said, believing I was stating the obvious. I had visions of my cat, my wardrobe, my DVR stuffed with unwatched *House Hunters* episodes, lying beneath a heap of soggy, mold-laden drywall. "We'll need to fix it. All in favor?" I was in a hurry, I admit. The aforementioned DVR had a ton of trashy television I was dying to rot my brain with. Way more fun than an engineering report.

Apparently my friends and neighbors were of a different mind. "Fix it?" Cheryl from downstairs asked. "Fix it how?"

"With hair dryers and ShamWows," I said. I see *someone* didn't read the report! "Or, you know, with, you know, professional engineers. Like how they discuss on page forty-three of the report Skip gave—"

"You a crazy one?" Aella—the superloud, bossy, overbearing, gossipy Croatian woman who grows the most fantastic tomatoes every summer—shouted.

"Who are you talking to?" I asked. It's really hard to tell with her because she's constantly rolling her eyes.

"I think to you," bitchy banker girl whom I never officially met so I have no idea what her name is said. Andrea? Adrian? Airhead? Whatever. "It's crazy to think we've all got scads of cash under our mattresses just looking for something to do. But then again, you and your pashmina probably do."

"Are you freakin' kidding me?" I asked. "First of all, hello. I'm Shelly. Nice to meet you. Second, this was a gift." I hold out my beautiful orange pashmina. It is fabulous but hardly a sure sign my ficus plant is really a money tree.

"It's a scam," Aella continued on her tirade.

"Yes, Aella, it's true. You can get knockoffs on any corner in Manhattan, but I assure you this one is real. My friend brought it back from Paris. She was on her honeymoon and still thought of her friends, which is supernice—"

"Not-a the scarf-a!" Aella shouted. "The report! It's a ploy-a between the engineer-a and the property-a management-a company! They want-a buy-a building!"

"That is wholly ridiculous," I said. "Why would they want to buy a waterlogged, thirty-something-year-old building in Seattle's twelfth most-popular neighborhood? You people need to come back to reality. Go toward the light, Aella!"

"Hold on," Joseph, the quiet guy from upstairs who gets a ton of packages from TimeLife, said. Finally, a voice of reason. "How do we know this report is accurate? I mean, if your doctor said you only had two months to live, you'd probably get a second opinion, right? Why should we trust these guys?"

"Because we paid them $8,000 to tell us so!" I shouted. How was it these people had no recollection of the thirty-seven bids we had to get from engineers all over the Pacific Northwest to just be able to *look* at our building! It took three months to settle on this company—a company we all met and liked. A company that provided twenty-three references who had nothing but glowing things to report. A company who even Google couldn't dig up dirt on!

"It's water damage," I said, trying to remain calm but I could feel the frustration taking form as a lump in my throat. I would start foaming at the mouth any second. And then I would cry. "It's not completely unreasonable where we live. We're about to head into winter—an extremely rainy winter! Do you really want to pretend this report never happened?"

"*Yes!*" they shouted together like they had been practicing.

"But that's insane!" I tried to reason. "Aella, wasn't it you who complained about condensation along your window sills?"

"*No-a.* You make crazy talk again."

"Joseph, your bathroom ceiling caved in two years ago when we had all that snow! You got hit in the forehead with a hunk of plaster! I gave you bandages from my Doggy First Aid kit. Remember? We laughed that you had to go to work with a bandage that read *Licks Make It Better.*"

"Oh, I think that was because I forgot to turn my bathroom fan on," he said. "I'm sure the roof is fine."

"And Cheryl, weren't you just saying how great it would be to sell your condo and move to Phoenix to be with your daughter and grandkids?"

"Umm, no, I don't think I'd like Phoenix."

"Too hot," the airhead said.

"So brown-a," Aella agreed.

This was unreal. Not only were they out-of-their-tree crazy, delusional, and ill-advised, but they were liars. I have meeting notes that prove every single one of the things I mentioned above. But did I say that? Not really. Did I calmly go over the list of reasons why now, of all times, was when we needed to be vigilant about protecting our investments? Not quite. Did I try to offer compassion and solidarity given the serious financial stress this would be putting on all of us? Not so much.

I took a different route in my attempts to win friends and influence my neighbors. I stood up, pounded a butter cookie with my fist, and proclaimed the room was "chock full of assholes!" and stormed out.

"You're just like your father," Judy said when she finally let me finish my story. "Whoever makes the most noise wins."

"Or smashes the most cookies."

As much as I'd like to believe her, that would be an insult to my dad. While he may be a yeller, he's also very eloquent. He wins fights with astute comebacks and staunch reasoning. And he's quite scary when he raises his voice.

"But Dad would never have beaten a cookie, run out of a room, and called his neighbors assholes."

"Oh, God no," she said. "He would have started with that, made them believe they were assholes, and convinced them that he was their only hope for salvation. They'd be writing him checks for $40,000 with one hand and carrying him and his folding chair above their heads with the other."

See? Not like my dad at all.

Not long after the homeowners meeting, I met up with my friend Karen for drinks and to discuss my options. Her condo went through a similar situation with their siding and she's on her board. If anyone can give me tips on how to convince a bunch of lunatics on the brink of retirement to fork over their 401(k)s, I'm hoping it's her. But condo talk took a backseat to her love life. Honestly, I was glad. I needed a break from the HOA.

Karen is single and was having trouble meeting a decent guy. She tried online dating, speed dating, and blind dating. Nada. I know how hard it is to meet people, so whenever I come across a quality single guy, I offer him up like a bowl of oatmeal and maple syrup to the tree gods. Surprisingly, the guys don't mind.

I thought one co-worker in particular was a great catch, so I threw him into the sacrificial ring and rattled off just a smattering of some of his best qualities.

"He's really smart and funny and a great cook," I said. "In fact, he gave me this wonderful vegan cookbook for my birthday last year. *Veginomicon*, I think it's called. Have you tried vegan food? Don't be scared of it. It's really delicious. I made these delicious tempeh nori rolls. I should give you the recipe. Speaking of which, did I lend you my copy of *The Glass Castle*? I'm starving, we should order!"

"So..." she started. "About your friend?"

"You should order, too. I'm *really* hungry. No sharing."

She did that "banging your head on the Formica table" thing people do when they're frustrated. Weird. I wondered why she was frustrated.

"Your vegan friend."

"Vegan? Who? Oh! The guy I want to fix you up with. He's not vegan. He just gave me a vegan cookbook because he thought I would like it. But he is nice to animals. Has two dogs."

"Sounds great. I'd like to meet him."

"He is. And he likes his mom but not *too much* and oh, yeah, he's a great Dungeon Master."

"Dungeon Master?" she shrieked. "Are you joking with me? You think that's a *selling point*?"

"Well, maybe I wouldn't have ten years ago but I kind of do now."

"I thought vegan was bad...."

"He's not vegan!" Now I was pretending to bang my head on the table. "And do you even know what a Dungeon Master is? It might not be what you think it is."

"I know what it is! It's the leader of the nerd cult you're indoctrinated into!"

You say "nerd cult." I say, "just another day at work." Whatever.

"Where would we go on a date?" she continued. "An arcade? Maybe a skating rink? Or, I know, his mom's basement so we could read comic books and eat Cheetos?"

"Hey, 1982 called. It wants its preconceived notions and antiquated stereotypes back."

She laughed. Scoffed, is more like it. "Ha, ha. I'm sure he's nice enough. Just not what I'm looking for."

"Do you know how much work goes into Dungeon Mastering?" I asked her. "You've got to be clever, creative, charismatic! The amount of prep time and paperwork is second only to what an escrow agent does on a daily basis. They're incredibly dedicated people."

"You're nuts," she said. "I want a guy who spends time with me. Not someone who pores over his monster books trying to devise intricate ways to kill his friends."

"It's not just about monsters and killing your friends," I explained, but it was no use. My friend wasn't just backing away from the sacrificial ring—she never even approached the coliseum. It's no easy feat to be a good Dungeon Master, and anyone who doesn't know that isn't worth my friend's time.

I left the coffee shop thinking about Dungeon Masters. They're special people. Where would players be without them? Lots of people DM, or have at least tried their hand at it, but there's plenty more that won't touch it with a ten-foot pole. Dungeon Mastering obviously appeals to a certain type of person: someone who is calm in crisis, can think on his or her feet, is spontaneous and creative, and enjoys a captive audience. Dungeon Masters are articulate, gifted storytellers and expert time managers. They are professionals of plot, geniuses of gab, authorities of anecdotes. Players depend on DMs to lead them through stories; very detailed, meandering, sometimes tangential stories. But stories with a purpose.

And that's when I got an idea. I, too, could be an expert leader like Dungeon Masters. All I have to do is become one of them.

Like I said, I dabbled in Dungeon Mastering but I can count how many times on one hand (and a thumb). Let's see, there was that time when I was writing *Confessions of a Part-Time Sorceress* and if you read it you know how that went. If you didn't, fine, I'll tell you: I was nervous and drank too much and had barely enough knowledge of how to be a *player* let alone a Dungeon Master so I ended up way over my head. I'd done it a few more times since then and each time it got a little bit better. My favorite time was for a group of women who had never played before, but unlike the first time, these women actually wanted to play. I used an existing, prewritten dungeon delve appropriate for their level but tweaked the monsters a bit.

I didn't think they'd be so motivated to fight a band of kobolds as they would various reality television stars, like the Kardashians and Hugh Hefner's bimbo girlfriends. When I told R&D about my brilliant use of improvisation they commended me—for my knowledge of *Star Trek: The Next Generation.*

"I'm impressed," Mike Mearls said. "I had you pegged as a *Bridezillas* kind of girl."

"I am a *Bridezillas* kind of girl!" I said, getting defensive. I suppose he thinks I have no regard for pedicures and aromatherapy, either.

Turns out there's a species of extraterrestrials in the *Star Trek* universe called the Cardassians. Incidentally, the *Star Trek* Cardassians and the E! Kardashians have much in common: Both are humanoids with reptilian features who travel in predatory packs in search of the dominant position in social gatherings. I'm not making this stuff up!

While I would identify as a player, I'm not ruling out Dungeon Mastering. Especially not now.

What is it about this role that attracts some and repels others like Drakkar Noir and custom rims? (Sorry guys. I hope I didn't just burst your bubble.) I must find out and bring my hard-earned research back to the people in a clever, concise, coherent manner.

"I have a great idea for a chapter," I told my editor. "I should travel the world interviewing Dungeon Masters and find the one common denominator that draws people to this very important role."

"Uh-huh," Nina said, nibbling on her cheesy fiesta potatoes. "I'll have to check but I don't think we have the budget for world travel."

"Well, it worked for Julia Roberts," I said. "And look how popular *Eat Pray Love* was."

"Elizabeth Gilbert was the author. Julia played her in the movie."

"Whatever. Who do you think would play me in the movie about my quest to discover what drives Dungeon Masters? Wait. I could. I was a theater major, after all."

She offered me a potato, which is her nice way of saying no.

"You could come, too," I told her. "In fact, you have to. It's mandatory."

"Sure," Nina said. "Ask your boss. It's her budget."

"Hmm," said Laura, offering me some of her volcano burrito. Clearly those two had lunch together. Probably to discuss my book tour. "So that's two around-the-world all-expense-paid trips you're asking for?"

"Not *all* expenses paid. I wouldn't expect Wizards to pay for things like souvenirs and anything over two glasses of wine per meal. Or the new wardrobe I'll have to buy to ensure I'm dressed appropriately for the 194 countries I'll be visiting."

"That's very generous of you," she said. "And who would do your job while you're out there gallivanting?"

"Not *gallivanting*," I said. "This is important work. So important that it *would* be my job and therefore I'd be doing it so no need to replace me. There. Problem solved."

"Months?"

"Maybe weeks? Several?"

"Maybe you could rein it in a bit," she suggested. "Like go hang out downtown. I'll cover your parking."

Disappointed I'll miss out on a trip to Palau, I start my knowledge quest a little closer to home. Like from my desk. This office is teeming with Dungeon Masters. Probably more than the entire population of Palau. I think of the most renowned DMs in the building and write their names in my new secret research notebook. (Weirdly, they are all named "Chris.") Next week I will study these Dungeon Masters. I will watch them with rapt attention. I will analyze their every move, exchange, and gesture and discover what it is that makes them masterful. And then ... I will become like them. Nope. That doesn't sound creepy at all.

THE PASSION OF THE CHRIS

Monday morning, I approach work with a renewed sense of vigor. I'm excited to get Project Dungeon Master off the ground and start winning some arguments! About midday, Laura realizes we're doublebooked for meetings that afternoon and would have to tagteam.

"Do you have a preference for which meeting you go to?" she asked.

Technically, one is for a project I'm deeply involved in, but the other one is helmed by Chris Tulach. This is a great opportunity to study the ways and means of this guy. Plus in a meeting no one will think it's weird if I'm taking notes. Even if my notebook is covered with hand-drawn cupcakes.

"I'll go to the meeting about Game Days," I told her.

She crinkled her forehead. "Are you sure? You're probably needed more in the conventions meeting."

"Oh, you can just fill me in," I said. "Besides, it's important for me to be well-rounded, right? What if you got hit by a bus tomorrow and had to be in traction for a year?"

"Umm ... right. Good point, I guess. Way to be a team player."

In Chris Tulach's meeting I noticed his presentation style. He stands up. He writes on the white board. He moves with a frenetic energy common to kittens and toddlers. But I notice everyone in this meeting is iPhone free and rapt with attention. Why? He's passionate. And he knows his subject.

THE FANTASTIC FOUR

So who are the elite masters I chose to study? Ladies and gentlemen, may I present to you the Master Class of Dungeoneering.

CHRIS PERKINS, DUNGEON MASTER TO THE STARS:

In addition to being our superstar Dungeon Master, Mr. Perkins is an exceptionally nice guy, with freakishly good handwriting. I think it's what the Century Gothic font is modeled after. He has DMed for such luminaries as Wil Wheaton, the guys from Penny Arcade, Dan Milano and the Robot Chicken crew, R. A. Salvatore, Ed Greenwood, and the writer of the IT Crowd, Graham Linehan. Just to name a few. When people line up to watch these games live, they're not just there to see Wil Wheaton's character bite it. They want to see the authority behind the screen. There's a reason they call them Masters.

Chris is never shy with giving advice. He doles out his secrets with the same sincerity and earnestness Mrs. Gable used to dole out apples on Halloween. (Except no one chucks Chris's advice into his chrysanthemum bush. Ingrates.) Surely he will teach me to take over the world. Or at least the board of my homeowners association.

He's clearly put a lot of thought into the topic, and besides it being just rude to *not* pay attention, he's got me thinking how much I *want* to pay attention. I mean, if whatever he's talking about has got him this jazzed, it's got to be good, right?

I'm reminded of the stint I worked at a men's clothing store. Tina, the tweaky manager (who once stole a $400 sale from me and I'm still pissed about it) gave me a tip: *Just sound like you know what you're talking about and they'll buy it.* Not to be stereotypical but let's just say *some* guys didn't know much about fashion. And they didn't care about it until they had a function—a wedding, a date, a parole hearing—to attend. It wasn't exactly difficult to outfit them in a grandpa cardigan and pair of relaxed-fit dark indigo jeans and send them on their way. But those bigger ticket items were harder to sell. That's when we'd have to pull out the big guns—a few choice adjectives like *band collar* or *bouclé* or *British-style versus Mandarin-style* suits. Band-collar shirts are ugly but I sold hundreds of them because my clients were so impressed they had a "name" and they trusted me because I knew it. Fancy name = instant expert.

Is Chris doing something similar here to sell us on his new Game Day program? Why shouldn't we funnel thousands of dollars into this? He sure sounds like he's the authority. And if an enthusiastic D&D player like himself is behind it, then surely other D&D players will follow. Yes! Fantastic idea! I'm about to reallocate my entire marketing budget when I'm reminded that:

A. I don't have authority to do things like that (for good reason, I guess).

B. There's a long process that needs to take place before we even start talking marketing dollars. No matter. I came away from that meeting with all the information I had hoped to glean from it.

Key Takeaway #1: Kill 'em with enthusiasm, eagerness, and expertise.

THE DEVIL IN THE DETAIL (LIKELY A TROLL, TOO)

Tuesday rolls around. (Get it? A little D&D humor?) And that means it's time for my D&D group, the Wyld Stallyns, to meet and kick some kobold. Half of the group and Chris Youngs, our DM, are there when I arrive. He's got his tackle boxes full of minis, magnetic nameplates, wet-dry markers, tokens, and laminated playmat. If only there were tackle boxes to compartmentalize my scattered thoughts, I'd be in business.

"You're early," he said, looking at his watch.

"It's ten after," I said.

"Uh, yeah. Early."

Whatever.

Key Takeaway #2: Guilt your audience into submission.

Chris starts with his "Previously on Dungeons & Dragons" spiel. It's always a welcome recap because a lot has happened to me in the last 168 hours so I can't possibly be expected to remember what happened to Tabitha. Unfortunately, I keep making the mistake of believing the same is true for Mr. Youngs. But noooooooooooooo! The guy has a memory like an iron vault. Or in this case, the stone sarcophagus the party is trying to open. Again.

We succeed, but of course doing so unleashes the ire of about 900 stirge-like creatures.

"Tabitha uses her shield!" I shouted in response to my little wizard getting attacked.

"No, she doesn't," Chris Youngs said. "She used it four rounds ago."

Now, I know what you're thinking. *Four rounds?* A gnat has a more robust short-term memory than I do. But understand "four rounds ago" was maybe six weeks ago. We don't get to play as often as we'd like, thanks to these little things we like to call day jobs.

"No, I don't think so," I said. "You must have Tabitha confused with another tiefling wizard who is about to take enough damage to bloody her. Not me. Nope. This shield is brand spankin' new. Not a clink on it."

"Nice try," he commended. "Take nineteen damage. And put your shield away before you trip on it."

Now, did Tabitha really use her shield already? I don't know, but I didn't argue (much) because I trust that Mr. Youngs has a better head for such inane details than I do, so I go with it.

And that's where we get:

Key Takeaway #3: Dazzle your audience with your keen ability to remember more than they do. Then use it against them.

COMMAND PERFORMANCE. AND ATTENTION. RESPECT, TOO.

On Wednesday, Chris Lindsay operates like a well-tuned cuckoo clock. Around 10:00 a.m. I see him hunched over his desk, pencil poised over index cards, elbow deep in miniatures. Then he turns his chair 180 degrees and stares out the window for a good seven to ten minutes.

"Working hard?" I asked. I can tell a lot about our lunchtime D&D Encounters game by how Mr. Lindsay responds to this question.

"Oooooh yeah," he said, rubbing his pencil furiously between his palms. "Very hard...." And then he smiled.

It's the smile that says it all. The you're-going-to-squirm-and-I'm-going-to-love-it smile.

Maybe it's because the six-inch wall between us offers me a vantage point to see how much work he actually puts into our games, maybe it's because I'm always starving at noon, or maybe it's because I'm really afraid of him, but I'm never late for our lunchtime game. Regardless, we only have an hour to play, so we speed through the encounter to make the most of every minute.

First thing I notice, now that I'm paying attention, is that Chris sits on the long side of the table. He does this every game. This strikes me as odd for two reasons.

CHRIS YOUNGS, TUESDAY AFTERNOON DUNGEON MASTER TO THE WYLD STALLYNS:

Mr. Youngs has been playing D&D since he was five. He got into it sort of how I got into hockey—his brother and friends needed a fourth to round out the party. Little did they know the student would soon surpass the teachers and Chris would be writing his own campaigns and running the group through them. He's a social, creative guy, which lends itself to being a good DM, but there's got to be more than that. I mean, I'm social. I'm sometimes creative. I mean, check out those little cupcakes I drew all over my super secret research notebook. That counts, right?

Oh, and did I mention Mr. Youngs smells divine? Like rosemary and mint? Yes, in fact, I have. Many times.

CHRIS LINDSAY, WEDNESDAY D&D ENCOUNTERS DUNGEON MASTER:

Mr. Lindsay joined the D&D Brand team after spending years in Wizards' Game Support division. Obviously he knows what he's talking about if he can handle all those calls and e-mails that come in asking some of the most obtuse rules questions in D&D history. He sits next to me with nothing but a six-inch cube wall between us. Not only is he a PowerPoint guru, but also he's our litmus test when it comes to "is this too nerdy?" It seldom is, if you're wondering. Again, knowing the rules and the boundaries of nerdiness is one thing. How to keep your players coming back for more in a D&D is another.

CHRIS TULACH, TOURNAMENT ORGANIZER EXTRAORDINAIRE:

I swear, Mr. Tulach was put on this Earth to work for Dungeons & Dragons. Sometimes in meetings when I hear him talking about a play program he's working on or an in-store event he planned, or the lemon cookies he baked for his home game campaign, I try to imagine what in my life is equal to D&D in his life. Chubby Hubby ice cream? Beer? The Real Housewives? No, I'd get sick of all of them eventually. I have yet to find it but I'll let you know when I do. I could learn a lot from him, no doubt, if I could only get him to sit still long enough to study him. Hmm ... I think ... studying the notes in my secret research notebook.

Exceptional Dungeon Master trait #1: Must be named Chris.

It's like kids named Troy and Brock are destined to be professional football players and girls named Bambi have to ... well, just don't name your kid Bambi. Perhaps the Chrises of the world have been predestined to become great Dungeon Masters. Answer the call, young Chrises! Young scholars like myself are looking to you for guidance. Let my crash course in Chris-like behavior begin.

1. Those "leading the meeting" usually sit at the head.
2. With his screen, minis, index cards, adventure book, and lunch, he is taking up an inordinate amount of space. So much so that none of us can sit on that side of the table. Rather, the five of us are sort of forced to sit across from him, crammed next to each other, like we're eager campers waiting for our counselor to tell us a scary story. I'm constantly elbowing Liz every time I shove a Brussels sprout in my mouth and can feel the vibration in *my* chair whenever Bertrand's cell phone alerts him to a new e-mail. The last two players to arrive have to sit so far from the playmat you have to ask your buddy to move your character six squares.

"There. No, there. Back one. To the left. Right. No, not right—
correct. Now one to the left. Good! Wait, what do you mean I
can't hit them both with my burst from right there?"

I used to think this was nothing more than poor meeting etiquette, but
now I'm not so sure. The whole camp counselor formation might have
some value. I don't ever plead blackout and ask what happened during the
last session. I seldom try to use my daily powers twice in one encounter (I
mean, I do try but I'm well aware that I've already used them). The game
moves at a steady clip because everyone greets their turn with swift tactical action and moves on. There is very little table talk in Mr. Lindsay's
game. While we may joke around outside of the game and tease each
other like a brother and sister, our relationship is very student/sensei in
the game. Weird!

Key Takeaway #4: Force your subject's focus and respect by manipulating
your surroundings.

As I pondered this, I heard my name. Or rather my character's name.
"What's Stormin' Norman doing?"
"What? Oh, um, you know. Just chillin'. Looking at . . . stuff."
"Well, while he's chillin' and looking at stuff he feels something skitter
across his boot."
"Oh, no. Ew. Um, guys, something just skittered across my boot!"
And just like that I'm back in the game without even knowing I was out.
Mr. Lindsay winked at me and I realized whatever it was that skittered
could have crossed anyone's threshold. Employing the age-old school
teacher tactic of calling on someone who appears not to be paying attention, I am bound and determined to be mindful of every facet of the
forty-eight minutes we have left in our game.

Key Takeaway #5: Demand attention by calling on those drifting off.

THE IMAGINARIUM OF DOCTOR PERKINS

I always found Chris Perkins's voice to be soothing and calm. In fact, it's
so much so that I had to quit listening to the Penny Arcade podcasts he
DMed for in my car because not only did I nearly fall asleep at red lights,
I gave up chewing gum, impulse buying at the grocery store, and developed a sudden urge to quack like a duck whenever I smell jasmine and
honeysuckle. Still not sure why.

Once I saw him walking to a meeting carrying a laptop. Only I didn't
see the laptop, just the cord that trailed behind him, and I thought, *It's*

true. He is *a computer.* Although I haven't had the pleasure of sitting in on one of his games, there's enough footage out there showing him in action.

So what if he knows more about D&D than probably any resource, human or otherwise, out there? Who cares if he's a prolific writer who pens his adventures from scratch? Pay no attention to the fact that he has elaborate three-dimensional set pieces built to his specs. There's got to be something in here an average Josephine like me can use.

The first thing is obvious: commitment. Mr. Perkins is nothing if not dedicated to providing his players with the utmost in entertainment. And maybe it's walking into an arena filled with 1,200 fans eager to watch your character tromp through the landscape Master Dungeon Master has provided for you, or maybe it's because these podcasts usually involve people who work in highly creative fields, but I can't help wonder if just being in Mr. Perkins's aura puts your imagination into overdrive.

Key Takeaway #6: Instill Inspiration with Your Indisputable Infatuation

When I worked as a receptionist for an insurance company in high school, Betty, the office manager, told me that I should always answer the phone with a smile on my face. Betty was clearly nuts as this was way before the days of Skype. Perhaps those little kerchiefs she wore around her neck were cutting off some much-needed oxygen.

"Why would I do that, Betty?" I asked. I was in high school after all and therefore a pro at patronizing my idiotic elders.

"So they can hear the happy in your voice," she said, through the stiffest, most practiced smile I ever saw. Oddly, she didn't sound happy when she said this.

It does work. (Sorry, Betty) and I swear Mr. Perkins must practice this sort of thing when he DMs. Only his smile is genuine, because even with his lips sewn together you could still hear how much he enjoys his place behind the screen. And because of that his players and (in his case) the audience enjoy it, too. There is truth to the old adage "kill 'em with kindness." Especially when you're a Dungeon Master.

Mr. Perkins also does something clever, and that's interweaving a story arc that's unique to each character. Way to keep them interested. It's like wiggling a big fat magical sword in their faces.

Key Takeaway #7: Appeal to their selfish sides and let them know they have something at stake, too.

So you know how sometimes you're talking and there's silence, which may be the sound of *people actually paying attention,* but you mistake it for disinterest, discontent, or worse, sleeping, so you fill the void with more chatter? Sure you do. Well, perhaps there is something to that old "brevity is the soul of wit" cliché. Mr. Perkins gives the players just enough information to make sure you know there's a whole lot more where that came from. His silences are usually met with dumbfounded faces or pensive head-in-hands moments. He manages to come across as droll and succinct, which of course makes him my hero. I wonder if he's available for HOA meetings?

The Monday of the following week arrived and I affectionately refer to this as Eviction Day. It's bright and sunny and again on the unseasonably warm side.

"Good," I told Judy. "I can sleep with the sunroof open when my car, a.k.a. my new studio apartment, is parked under the viaduct tonight."

"Oh, it won't be that bad. I'm sure they've had enough time to calm down."

"Well, even if they haven't, I feel confident I can win them over to my side."

"Uh-oh," Judy said and sighed. "Who'd you catch peeing in the elevator this time?"

I scoffed at the notion. "Gross! I never caught anyone doing that." Unless she meant my old dog Charlie, but that was only because she was on prednisone and arthritic and I couldn't get her downstairs in time.

"Well, then, how do you think you'll win them—oh my God! You read the book! Dale Carnegie showed you the way!"

"No, Dale Carnegie showed me nothing but the inside of a recycling bin. I've been studying the real masters of manipulation: Dungeon Masters."

Judy's turn to scoff. "How dare you equate a globally accredited, most influential business leader of the twentieth century with your little dragon storyteller friends?"

"Easy. What do you know about Dungeon Masters?"

"Umm, you have to be nice to them or they will kill you."

I think she may have had Dungeon Masters mixed up with mafia bosses, but I got the spirit of her comment. "If that were true, I'd say that's pretty influential. But there's more to it than that."

Just as Betty could hear the happy in my smile, I could hear the absurd in Judy's eyes rolling. "I'm sure it's a tough, undervalued, disrespected job. Just like being your mother."

Just in case she couldn't hear my eyes rolling, I sighed loudly.

She ignored me and continues with her diatribe. "I always thought I'd make a wonderful Dungeon Master."

"Always?"

"Well, since you started talking about this stuff," she said. "I used to make up stories all the time for you and Mike. And I'm good at voices."

"That's not all there is to Dungeon Mastering. They're experts at winning friends and influencing people, too."

"That so?"

I went on to explain that once Dungeon Masters get behind that screen, they're in control. They're powerful, all-knowing controllers of the universe. It's really just a matter of bringing it to the front of the screen, so to speak.

But Judy was not totally buying it. "Maybe they're all knowing and masterful because they feel safe *behind* the screen and being in front of it would just turn them into wobbly, panic-stricken blobs. Ever think of that?"

"No, I haven't, and there's no time for that. I have a homeowners association to win and neighbors to influence."

I left the pashmina upstairs and opted to wear an old Mariner's sweatshirt and my Chuck Taylors. I'm a woman of the people. I support the home team. I can run like hell if I need to.

When I arrived there are five other homeowners in attendance—Skip, Cheryl, Joseph, Aella, and her husband, Alexander. Obviously this is big business because Aella only trots him out for special occasions. If Aella is all fists and fury, she's practically a baby bunny compared to him. He doesn't speak English very well but he speaks angry fluently. Even when he was explaining the correct ratios between nitrogen and potassium in packaged fertilizer, it was like he was Mel Gibson telling me why I could give up the dream of alimony. You do *not* want to be on the business end of Alexander. Good thing I was geared up.

Fortunately, Skip and Joseph sat at the heads of the table and the rest of the group was spread out along the same side. I sat on the opposite long side and proceeded to spread out my paperwork two seats to the left and right of me. I almost came to blows with three guys in their twenties for doing roughly this same thing at a bar last weekend. Kids these days.

"I think we're expecting more people," Cheryl said, looking at my plethora of paperwork.

"That's fine," I said, creating neat little piles. "I have enough copies for everyone."

Within a few minutes, we had enough homeowners for a quorum. Skip started the meeting off by asking if it was okay to *start the meeting*. A few unsure "ayes" are mumbled around the table, which totally sets Aella off.

ROLE CALL

Four out of five D&D players identify themselves as Dungeon Masters. How do I know this? I conducted an informational Facebook poll. Seven minutes after my post, I got sixty-three responses. And here's an interesting tidbit about Dungeon Masters and Player Characters: Once you go behind the screen it's difficult to come out.

"I've been DMing for more than twenty years," Ben said. "In that time I've probably helmed over a hundred games and maybe played a character in three."

Megan, a control freak, believes she wouldn't be nearly as enchanted with D&D in any other role. "I don't like watching stories or characters get derailed. I need to have more control of the environment and the people who live in it."

"I play both roles," Brian said, "but I like DMing because I like telling stories."

"What the hell are you talking about?" my brother posted on my wall. "And Mom wants you to call her."

"Call-a this meeting-a to order!" she shouted. "All in favor?"

"Fine, whatever," Skip said. "All in favor?"

A stronger chorus of "ayes" echoed around the table. I could feel Aella's fury from across the table. She had her house keys in her hands and was crouched at the tip of her folding chair. Her body language was screaming, *Tell me what I want to hear or I'm leaving and you won't have your quorum!* Alexander looked on like a restrained Doberman who just caught a couple of intruders. Can someone give me a diplomacy check?

Skip pulled out a legal pad and rumpled notes from the last meeting. It made me wonder if Aella would crumple them up and throw it at poor Skip's head after I left.

"Last time we met, we had a discussion about the potential water damage on the south and west sides of the building."

"Not so much a discussion," Aella said, sneering at me.

"And not so much *potential*," I answered as I sneered back.

She didn't bat an eye.

"It was more of an ill-educated suggestion to move forward with repairs, which was shot down. Why are we here again? I thought this was settled."

Ill-educated? Great. How could I speak to them in a language they'll understand when they couldn't even properly string together an insult? But I was not deterred. I was a calm, cool, collected master of manipulation.

"I have the notes right here," I said, passing out copies for everyone. "I also took the liberty of printing out copies of Star Engineering's references and rating report from Angie's List, Yelp, and the Better Business Bureau."

Some of my neighbors nodded their heads as they sifted through the piles of paper. Others tossed it aside and growled. "We don't need no stupid-a references. We need to tell these-a scam artists where they can-a stick their report-a. Nothing wrong with the building!"

Ooh, we're rolling for initiative.

"I understand your concern, Aella," I began. "And I appreciate your dedication to ensuring everyone in this building is protected. I share your concern, so I took the liberty of looking into some case studies about stucco buildings built around the same time as ours. Turns out nearly one in three buildings thirty years and older experiences similar cases of water intrusion like what Star Engineering found on our building. If you turn to the graph on page six you'll see what I mean."

Does a 19 beat your armor class, Aella? Why, yes, I believe it does.

Nothing says "I know more than you and therefore you need to trust me" like a graph. If they looked closely they might notice some of my math was off, but they don't. This graph was purely for visual impact, and impact it had.

"Very impressive," Skip said. I can tell he was thankful not to have to run one of these cat-herding contests.

"Oh, sure," Aella said as she snorted. "But can your graphs generate a million dollars, huh? This just paper! You need-a money to fix-a the problem. We no have-a money!"

Aella casts *Bless,* granting all targets a +1 power bonus to attacks.

While graphs are aesthetically appealing, you can't beat the emotional influence of the money card. The same heads that nodded at my graph and references nodded at her. Stupid lemmings!

I cleared my throat. "Look, I know some of you have lived here even longer than I have. *Cheryl*, you were one of the very first homeowners!

There are plenty of places you could have lived, but you chose to live here. *For decades.* And let me tell you—wise investment! But that investment is in jeopardy if we don't do something about the water damage. At the rate we're going we face substantial structural damage that will add additional hundreds of thousands of dollars in costs. I assure you, *Joseph*, we will have to make these repairs eventually and if we wait much longer it will cost double, even triple this initial bid. You could lose *all* of your equity."

I said that last bit looking at Patty, who I know has grandiose ideas about hanging up her nursing scrubs and moving her and her overweight tabby to a cabin in Ocean Shores. I felt bad when she averted her gaze and frowned at my presentation packet. But it was no time to go soft!

And Patty is dazed. Save ends.

"If you don't believe me, look at page eleven and see what happened to the Garden Heights over in Bellingham," I said. Patty would not like it.

I gave them time to read the overview. It didn't take long, seeing as I bulleted, bolded, and highlighted the important stuff.

"Maybe we could look at just replacing the south wall," a weakened Amanda/Adrian said to my surprise and delight. Never underestimate the power of a sweatshirt and a bar graph.

Amanda/Adrian's next-door neighbor, Joy, bobbed her head in agreement. "And then we could replace the stucco with a nice, more modern material."

"I love it!" Amanda/Adrian said. Mind you, these are the same people who wanted to paint underwater murals on our front doors.

"It will look like a cool art piece," Patty said. "Like an accent wall. Maybe corrugated metal."

Even Joseph got inspired. "Maybe we could paint the stucco a brighter color while we're at it. Like a nice burnt sienna?"

Okay, not to be an ingrate and all but that wasn't what I had in mind at all. I mean, I was excited that they were getting on board but to slap a piece of corrugated metal onto a 1979 stucco building in Seattle's twelfth-most-popular neighborhood?

Fortunately, Aella didn't agree with this strategy, either. "That still be $400,000 dollars! Plus more for your *arty* materials!"

Alexander was getting upset. His face burned scarlet and there were veins emerging from parts I didn't know had veins. "Ohhhhhh puurrfff-phhhh ickles guppppppkle … "

"You are correct, Aella!" I said, smiling at her. "And I think Alexander might need a glass of water. In the meantime, please turn to page nineteen for a detailed cost breakdown. You'll notice that by repairing the entire building envelope all at once, we save just over 20% in the long run."

MASTERING THE MYTHS

Is Dungeon Mastering really that hard? Do you really have to have a Mensa membership before you're allowed to purchase your first Monster Vault? Do you really need to invest in a storage unit just to house all your equipment?

There are tons of reasons people shy away from taking a turn at DMing, but lots of them are just misconceptions:

WORK WORK WORK: Really? These are your friends! They love you! They love playing in your game. No one does the voice of the wererat like you do! What if your friends said, "Oh, I'd love to celebrate your birthday but that involves getting you a card and thinking of something sweet to write in it and driving six miles to your favorite restaurant so I can chip in for your $14 dinner and it's a work night and 30 Rock is on and I really just want to go to bed and get up early but thanks, anyway! Here's to next year!"

In case you don't have much time dedicated to prepping your adventures, fear not! There are tons of resources out there that make DMing easy. Dungeon Delves, prewritten adventures, D&D Encounters. You get out of it what you put into it. And really, this is a small price to pay for the praise and adoration of your friends.

RULES RULES RULES: Oh, sure, there are rules, but you don't have to know them all. You just need to start the story, guide the players, and attack them with a few monsters now and again. If you can think, you can be a Dungeon Master.

"Yukbaukukuk!"

"I'm sorry?"

"He say you-a going to-a have to buy us out!" Aella said on behalf of Alexander. "We no pay for repairs. You buy us out and we move to new apartment."

As much as I loved the idea of an Aella-and-Alexander-the-Grump-free zone, their latest idea just proved how out of touch with reality these people are. Buy them out? Who are we, Wal-Mart?

Thankfully I didn't have to explain the preposterous nature of this because Skip was all over it.

"That's not an option, Aella. The Association does not purchase units just because an owner is disgruntled."

Oh, snap! Skip hits with an acid arrow.

MONEY MONEY MONEY: Well, sure you could buy every book and set of dice out there. Even invest in a few really nice mechanical pencils and fancy DM screens, but I'm going to tell you a secret: You don't have to. If you want to try your hand at DMing you can make your own playmat with graph paper and pencil and use pennies, bottle caps, and cat toys as monsters. Just like the kids of the 1970s and 1980s did. The rest of the story comes out of your head, so unless you're charging yourself a consulting fee you're probably not spending too much there.

I would, however, be remiss if I didn't at least suggest you enhance your game by investing in a few accessories. Trust me—there's nothing like watching your players' faces when you pull out a giant blue dragon from behind your screen. A pewter napkin ring just doesn't have the same appeal.

"Then we sell," she said. "Wash our hands of you." She mimed washing her hands for extra emphasis.

"Well, good luck with that, Aella," I said. "Really. Just from the few days of research I did, it looks like selling when the building is in such a state of uncertainty is all but impossible. I can't imagine there's a mortgage lender in town who would finance a building with a potential assessment upward of half a million dollars."

"You-a can't keep us here!" she shouted.

"Oh, I'm not keeping you. Your denial about the building's structural damage is what's keeping you. When we fix it, you leave." I washed my hands for extra emphasis.

"We should start talking to our respective banks," Joseph said. "We're probably better off getting individual loans rather than an association loan."

I smiled at my prodigy. "I couldn't agree more."

Just like our Tuesday game and lunchtime Encounters game, and Mr. Tulach's speech about in-store play programs and anything our Dungeon Master to the Stars touches, I left them wanting more. I packed up my remaining papers, grabbed my keys, and bid adieu.

"If anyone has questions, just let me know. I kind of went overboard with the research. I just want to be sure we know our rights and are as educated as we can be. I realize it's a big expense for all of us. Not pashmina big, but up there."

They thanked me for my hard work. Told me how much they appreciated the effort I put into this.

"Your opinion matters," Patty told me, clutching my wrist.

"Imagine taking a bath and not living in fear of getting a concussion!" Joseph said wistfully.

"Yes, imagine that," I said, vowing to not imagine *that* at all. I hope someone was taking notes.

"Arizona, here I come!" said Cheryl.

"Sorry to cut this short but I have an appointment I can't miss."

For all they knew I was off to meet with an engineering firm and a property management company to stage another coup on an unsuspecting condo association in a subpar neighborhood. But I just went back to my condo and created a new graph. This one showed how many out-to-dinners, eyebrow waxings, and On Demand movies I'd have to forgo in order to pay my share of the upcoming assessment. Tell me again whose dumb idea this was?

CHAPTER 5

WHO MOVED MY CHA?

ME: Bart wants to move in.

JUDY: It's about time. You're too old to be living alone with a cat.

ME: You're my mother. How can you condone living in sin?

JUDY: The sin is overshadowed by the fact that no one will call you an old maid anymore.

ME: Seriously? That's why you support Bart and me taking the next step in our relationship? And what do you mean *anymore*? Who is calling me an old maid?

JUDY: Well ... me. But I'm sure people are **THINKING** it.

me: I'm sure they're not, but let's get back to the situation at hand. I live in a one-bedroom, one-bathroom condo. Zelda is more territorial than I am, and Sadie may or may not have killed a cat when she was a puppy. It's never going to work.

judy: Zelda is a bitch. She needs someone to put her in her place.

me: That's your grandchild! And her place is sleeping on the couch. Not torn in little pieces around the baseboards.

judy: You're projecting your issues on Sadie and Zelda. They're not the problems here. You and your inability to break out of your comfort zone are.

me: I break out of my comfort zone all the time! Just yesterday I went to QFC instead of Safeway. I didn't know my way around. It took me at least fifteen minutes to find peanut butter. But I did get a great deal on frozen spinach.

judy: Who moved your cheese, honey?

me: I don't know. I wasn't shopping for cheese.

judy: You're just like Hem and Haw when you should be like Sniff and Scurry.

me: Seriously, what are you talking about?

judy: You didn't read it?

me: I have no idea what you're talking about, and now I'm scared. Are you having a stroke? What year is it? *Who is our president*?

judy: I'm talking about the book, *Who Moved My Cheese?* It's an international best seller, revolutionary, totally changed the way people like you live. For the better, I might add. I sent it to you a long time ago.

me: Oh. Weird. I must have *moved* it into the trash.

judy: Well, you need to read it before Bart moves in.

me: No one said he was moving in! We're just talking about it.

judy: Oh, please. You'll save a ton of money. Money you could put toward therapy.

me: No amount of therapy could undo the damage you've caused.

judy: Just make sure the living situation is a short-term one. He's not going to buy a cow if the milk is so cheap.

me: Oh, it will be short-term. The first time he leaves his wet towel on my $400 duvet cover, he's out.

judy: See? Loosen up. It's a wet towel, not a dead body.

me: And toothpaste all over the bathroom sink. I've seen how he lives and it ain't pretty.

judy: It's not supposed to be pretty, he's a bachelor! He'll step it up when he's got an old battle-axe for a roommate.

Shelly Mazzanoble

me: He shaves in the bathroom sink instead of the shower. There will never be enough time in the morning for me to properly exfoliate and moisturize if I need to share the mirror! And what if he uses my conditioner and I run out?

judy: You're just like your father. You're both so paranoid about being unprepared. Where have you ever been that you couldn't just buy a contact case or tube of Neosporin if—heaven forbid—you forgot to pack some?

me: What's wrong with being prepared?

judy: Once on our way to Florida I mentioned wanting a sandwich and your father pulled over, yanked out a cutting board, set of knives, fresh ciabatta bread, cold cuts, and a dozen condiment packets he'd pilfered from fast-food restaurants. All from the trunk of his car!

me: Once on our way home from a Christmas party, my friends and I got stuck in a freak snowstorm. We couldn't get up the hill to Nina's house so we had to walk. Good thing I had an extra pair of boots, scarf, hat, and reflective vest in my trunk!

judy: Maybe you should try living like the rest of us and then judge.

me: Oh, look! It's 8:22. I have to take my vitamin and clean out the crisper drawer in the refrigerator I keep in my bedroom for emergencies.

judy: Look for your cheese while you're in there!

"What's wrong with enjoying a good ritual now and again?" I asked my friend Jodi as we walked the path around Green Lake. (*Counterclockwise*, because everyone with any sense knows that's the *right* way to walk around Green Lake.) And I'm not talking "ritual" in the same sense Tabitha, my wizard, might enjoy one.

"A ritual?" she asked. "Or a routine?"

"What's the difference?"

"A ritual is more of a ceremony," she explained. "A routine is a habit. One might even say a rut."

"Well, one might be wrong," I said. "I'm not in a rut or stuck in a routine. I just like things a certain way."

Jodi scoffed. "To say the least."

"Hey, we went on vacation together. Do you think I'm hard to live with?"

"Ooh," she said as she squirmed. "I'm not sure it's the same thing. We had room service and housekeepers, not to mention separate beds. But

Bart is pretty laid back. I'm sure he knows what he'd be getting himself into if he moves in."

If. There's that word again. Why can't I pull the trigger on this? There's no one I'd rather spend time with than Bart. Plus, if he moved in, I could maybe start using some of the gazillion recipes I've collected over the years instead of opening a can of beans and a jar of salsa and calling it a night.

"I'm trying to be as honest as I can be. I've lived there for twelve years. Every nook and cranny in that place is filled with stuff. *My* stuff."

"Good reason to get rid of the clutter," Jodi said. "We could have a garage sale!"

I glared at her.

"Not that your stuff is clutter," she backpedaled. "It's perfectly useful and necessary stuff. All of it."

Ah, who am I fooling? Even though I make at least one trip a month to Goodwill it doesn't mean I couldn't do with a lot less. "You know what? I just found a winter coat from eleven years ago. I kept it as my 'dog walking' coat. I haven't had a dog in six years. Maybe I am in a rut."

"Why? Just because every Sunday we come to Green Lake," Jodi said. "Not one of the other nineteen thousand parks in Seattle. And we have to walk counterclockwise because you said that's the 'right' way to walk around. Oh, and I think you always wear the same pants."

What? Now Jodi is on Team Judy? When did she start recruiting my friends?

"Okay, there is a *right* way to walk around the lake. Everyone knows that. I walked *the wrong way* once and nearly pulled my hamstring. Coincidence? And yes, I probably do wear these pants on Sundays because Saturday is laundry day and my good workout pants are air drying."

Jodi laughed. "Well, I like Green Lake. And I love traveling with you because I know if I forgot something, you'd be able to replace it. Your carry-on bag is like the offspring of a Seven-Eleven and a Nordstrom."

It's true and not just for carry-on bags. My glove compartment is like hotel gift shop. But if there's one thing I know how to do, it's pack a suitcase. Have you any regard for how hard it is to pack everything that matters in one 22" x 14" x 9" bag? Sure, Judy is right. I don't live in a third-world country, and I seldom have to travel to one, so chances are good that if I ran out of conditioner I could always buy more. But it might not be *my* conditioner! My hair and therefore my well-being will suffer the consequences.

This is a bit of a problem in my relationship. Bart is a man of little baggage (and I'm not just talking about the emotional kind). He once got on a cross-country flight to visit my family and me with only his car keys, iPhone, and wallet. That's it. Not even a book, because as he explains, "It was a red-eye and I wanted to sleep." Who does that? I mean, the airlines, as stingy as they are, allow you to have up to two carry-on bags! You need to take them up on that.

Of course Bart's connection was canceled, he was rerouted to an airport an hour and fifteen minutes away from my parent's house in upstate New York, and my dad and I had to drive to Ithaca to retrieve him. I brought him a bag of toiletries (from my own TSA-approved personal collection) and a change of clothes (from my brother's closet) and took him to a bathroom at a state park to freshen up. For two days I made him repeatedly explain why he decided to get a on a plane with no carry-on bags.

"I didn't need anything," he explained. Again.

"Of course you needed something!" What was wrong with this guy? "A toothbrush, three days worth of clothes, a digital camera, trail mix, *US Weekly*, a bathing suit, two pairs of shoes (at least), a first aid kit, a can opener, contacts cleaner, ear plugs, slippers. A couple of paperbacks. The list goes on!"

(And the list exists as an Excel spreadsheet. I'll e-mail it to you if you want.)

Sure, there might be a happy medium between my hypercompulsion and Bart's laissez-faire attitude. I'm just not comfortable enough to find it.

As for routines, yep, I've got them. I watch *Good Morning America* every morning preshower and then yesterday's recording of *All My Children* postshower. If I'm good about fast-forwarding through all the commercials, it runs for exactly as long as it takes for me to get ready.

When I come home from work, I prepare dinner. (Either a can of black beans, salsa, sour cream, and half an avocado *or* four soy nuggets from Trader Joe's. Both options include a massive salad with romaine lettuce, dried cranberries, fat-free feta cheese, mushrooms, and cherry tomatoes.) I watch *E! News* while I prepare dinner and something from my DVR while I eat. Maybe two half-hour episodes of *House Hunters* or a full hour of something like Kathy Griffin's *My Life on the D-List*. There are shows to watch while eating dinner, as opposed to the shows to watch while balancing your checkbook (*Top Chef*); shows to watch while in a complete vegetative state (*Say Yes to the Dress, Bridezillas*); and shows to watch as a reward for being productive (*Mad Men, Project Runway*).

Sex and the City called these things "secret single behavior"—the secret habits you would never let your significant other catch you doing. I call it "truth in advertising." I believe it's important to let all the bad stuff out right away. It's the same reason I don't wear foundation or cover up pimples or wear ... er ... form-falsifying under-thingies. I couldn't bear the look of disappointment when the curtain was lifted. It's not like I'm concealing a smaller zit under the gigantic one on my chin. What you see is exactly what you get.

Although I might not subject Bart to it, I don't hide any of these things from him, either. It's not like I went on about my love of the History Channel and then acted all confused about how a *What Not to Wear* marathon invaded 98% of my DVR space. In fact, I've seen *House Hunters* on his own DVR (because he won't delete anything!). And he's watched enough snippets of *All My Children* to be able to inject commentary like, "Ryan had another aneurism?" or "Scott and Marissa slept together? What hypocrites!"

Now, let's talk about lunch. What I eat has proven to be a major source of contention for Bart and a huge source of entertainment for my co-workers. Why? I don't know.

"Because you eat the same exact thing every single day!" Bart explains (unsolicited).

"So?" I counter.

"Stupid, cold veggie burger with the same amount of ketchup and honey mustard," he goes on. "Same amount of carrots. Same little, tiny chocolate bar for dessert."

Hmm. Maybe there are some behaviors you shouldn't let your significant other be privy to.

He's right, though. I do eat the same thing. Veggie burger wrapped in a tortilla shell, eight ounces of steamed carrots, and one tiny piece of chocolate to clean the palate. In my defense, I change the seasoning on my carrots. Sometimes it's Jamaican jerk, sometimes it's lemon and pepper. So there. I'm a regular renegade when it comes to spices. I will only go out to lunch if it's a co-worker's birthday or if something major happened at work and we all want to talk about it. I will loosen up on weekends.

Bart used to send me studies and statistics he'd find on the Internet about how soy is bad for you and eating the same thing every day wreaks havoc on your metabolism and 89% of veggie burgers actually contain beef. Again, unsolicited. I thought women were supposed to choose men who were like their fathers.

"What?" I asked regarding the last alleged survey he unearthed. "Says who?"

"Uhh … me?" he admitted. "I just wanted to see if you'd eat a baked potato or Subway sandwich if I told you the leading soy bean producer donated money to a mink-raising farm."

People are fascinated by my lunch. Seriously. Just as I am fascinated with their cans of soup or leftover pizzas or frozen Lean Cuisines. Sometimes a different one every day!

And seeing as we're on the topic, I'll confess another one. I'm a rules abider. Like, annoyingly so. No parking? Okay, fine. I'll keep moving. Please take one? Sure! One is all I need. I've seen Bart angry two times in the six years that I've known him, and both times it was due to my unwillingness to allow him to break a rule.

The worst time happened just recently, when we were flying home from Idaho. He put his backpack in the overhead space (above someone else's seat but let's not go *there*) and then tried putting his laptop in the overhead space above his chair. Sound the alarm! Everyone knows one personal item goes under the seat in front of you. You have no idea the amount of dread I experience before boarding a plane. And no, it's got nothing to do with terrorists or lazy mechanics. That whole pack-my-life-in-a-carry-on thing? Well, fat lot of good it's gonna do if they make me gate-check my bag. And because my bladder is even more high maintenance than I am, I have to sit on the aisle, which means I'm going to be one of the last zones to board. If even half of the passengers who board before me have the barefaced disregard for airplane etiquette that Bart exhibits, there's not going to be room for my appropriately sized and laboriously packed suitcase. And that, my friends, fills every cell in my hyperparanoid body with apprehension.

I had no choice but to call Bart out. Surely there were others in zone four like me. And surely my good karma for ratting out my boyfriend would one day ensure that my carry-on bag miraculously finds solace in an oversold airline situation.

His response was rather snarky, and that surprised me. "It's not like there's a rule about it."

"Um, yes there is!" I shouted (maybe loud enough so that the people sitting within five rows in either direction could hear). "And you're going to get some bad travel karma if you disobey it."

"Is that so?" he snickered, still not making a move to retrieve either of his bags from overhead. "That's the actual cause and effect of this little situation? You put two bags overhead—when there's plenty of space to do so—and on your next flight you have to sit by a baby with an ear infection?"

"And digestive issues."

I know that gives him pause. The only thing worse than dog poop is baby poop. What are they eating, anyway? But it didn't give him *enough* pause because he just kicks back in his seat and makes a big production out of stretching his legs all the way under the seat in front of him.

"Ahhh . . ."

"You will pay," I told him.

"Nobody cares," he whispered. "Just chill out."

THE CHEESE MOVES, BUT IT DOESN'T STAND ALONE

I deal with some changes better than others. I like changing my hair color. I like changing my shoes. I like changing the channel when the Kardashians come on. But some changes I'm just not a fan of. I am not alone. How do I know this? Because I play D&D.

I'm just going to say it. D&D players? Not huge fans of change. It's cool! I can relate! And just so my inbox doesn't get (even more) clogged up with hate mail, I'll acquiesce and say "some" D&D players. In its thirty-six years D&D has only had four editions. That's crazy! Just think of how many hair styles you've probably had or will have in that time. But when D&D changes it's a tad more noticeable than a bang trim. An "edition" is essentially an update to the rules system. To some that's a much needed and well-received overhaul. To others it's the equivalent of bandits pillaging your home and then torching it. While you're home. You know those horrid news stories about people who lost their houses to wild fires? And they're sobbing into the camera and yearning for the photo album that contained pictures from baby's first Christmas and their first teddy bear and their (gasp!) second edition D&D books and you can see the pain and longing and pure hatred for the stupid flames that are skipping and prancing like little hippies at a Phish concert up the other side of the mountain. Well, to some, Wizards of the Coast represents the flames.

Contrary to popular belief there is no law that prevents one from playing an earlier edition. If you loved third edition, play it! There are no Edition Police who will come to your house, confiscate your second edition books and replace them with fourth. We tried hiring for that position, by the way, but HR put the kibosh on it.

Oooh! *Just chill out.* I hate it when people tell me that!

No sooner did the flight attendant come on the intercom and explain that this was a full flight and, yes, they did in fact care where your carry-on baggage went.

"Please use the overhead space above for your larger carry-ons and the space under the seat in front of you for smaller personal items, like laptops and pocketbooks."

"Oh, really?" I said as I smiled. "That's so weird. There *is* a rule where your bags should go."

"I'll tell you where your bags can go," Bart said as he laughed, pulling his laptop down from above and shoving it under the seat in front. And then he made a spectacle out of trying to stretch his feet and them getting all caught up in the canvas muck under the seat.

"My shins!" he bellowed. "Oh, God, they feel like they're stuck in a meat grinder!"

"Really, Bart? A meat grinder? That's what it feels like?"

The guy next to him, and that would be the middle seat if you're minding the details, was about six foot nine and sound asleep. I pointed him out to Bart.

"He's not asleep," Bart said. "He's unconscious from the pain. It's unbearable!"

The woman to my right laughed with us. "You're *so* getting married," she said.

"You're *so* channeling my mother right now."

Please make no mistake—I don't want to be like this. I know people are stashing more than one personal item in the overhead bins just as sure as they're bringing more than two personal items on board. (A rollerboard suitcase, purse, and Starbucks shopping bag are—count 'em—*three* bags. *Three!* And no, I'm not buying that's your baby's backpack just like I don't think having a baby in the backseat should count as a carpool.) But still, I don't want to tattle on these people—I want to be them!

In kindergarten my teacher was staunchly against tattling. So much so that if we dared rat out a fellow classmate, we were forced to wear The Tattle Tail. Yes, Mrs. Fox would pin a ratted, old, beaded belt to the elastic bands of our pants and send us out, branded as a nark, into the wilds of crafts and nap times. (I still think letting the world know that Benjamin Grovers was sticking his boogers in my crayon box was worth the humiliation.)

Creative use of a homophone there, Mrs. Fox, but perhaps I would have benefited more from a little afterschool adventuring with Dungeons & Dragons. What deters so many from getting involved with D&D is what appeals to me—the many layers of seemingly complex rules. No, I don't know every one of them. Not even close. But I guess I find some comfort in knowing that even in my fantasyland, there are certain things that *just can't happen*. Or so I thought.

It was this concept that prevented me from trying my hand at Dungeon Mastering even though I was secretly dying to. I can make up stories! I can make up characters! I can be the center of attention! But I didn't know all the rules and therefore I would surely lead a trusting band of adventurers right into a gargoyle-filled chasm or worse—a terrible time. It was unfathomable!

It wasn't until the very same people who make the rules gave me permission to break the rules that I learned to loosen up a bit.

"What do you mean I have the freedom to make things up?" I argued with Mike Mearls, Group Manager for Dungeons & Dragons Research and Development. "It's your job to *put rules in writing*! Why go through all that trouble if you don't care what people do with the rules?"

"Because we want people to have fun," he explained simply.

It sunk in, albeit slowly. Like when I DMed a game for my parents who up until that moment kept telling people D&D was like the game of Life except with a dungeon. Oh, and a few dragons. My dad kept asking where the board was.

"No spinner? No egg timer? I don't get it."

Obviously I wanted them to have fun, and part of the fun was beating up monsters and reaping the reward. My mom played a dwarf, who to someone who's barely five feet tall wasn't so much fantasy, but she quickly fell in love with her alter ego, Jubunsky.

"She's very talented in the ways of dwarves," Judy claimed.

"What ways would those be?" I asked.

"You know, picking things up. Moving heavy objects. Cooking. Cleaning."

"Sneezing?" my dad asked. He insisted on playing a pirate who was more Captain and Tennille than Captain Kidd.

"Oh, Tom," Judy sighed. "I'm not *that* kind of dwarf. I'm a big, burly, hairy, testosterone-charged lady dwarf. Like your Aunt Edna."

Obviously letting my dad play a pirate instead of a paladin was "breaking" the rules. And so were those "math errors" I made allowing Judy's low rolls to hit the javelin-throwing goblins. She was so excited to use her *spinning sweep* power. What choice did I have?

I DMed a few more times for new players, and because I wanted them to have a good time, too, I gave in to the luxury of making up and breaking the rules a fifth of my co-workers labor over. All that pressure to know every little thing? Nonexistent once I remembered this was a *game*. No one noticed Marcy moved seven squares when her speed was only six. No one cared that if there was a chasm big enough for a gargoyle to fly out of it, the party probably would have seen it when they walked in the room. It wasn't just fun for the players, it was fun for me, too. And because I was having fun, their first impression of D&D was a good one. Man, there's a lot of pressure on Dungeon Masters.

The only thing that has more rules than D&D is, well, me. But if I could loosen the coils on the D&D machine, perhaps I could in real life, too.

D&D adventurers don't have the luxury of waking up every day after the automatic coffeemaker has just finished its final perk. In fact, Tabitha doesn't always get a chance to wake up because chances are she was too busy fighting her way out of a dungeon to sleep. She doesn't travel with Tumi T-Tech rolling suitcases and thirty-seven mini bottles of conditioning agents. She doesn't even get to make her own choices because her fate lies in someone else's hands—mine. Or really the dice. How does she manage?

Judy may be right about one thing. Bart and I taking the next step is a good thing. But if I'm ever going to be okay with sharing my crisper drawer with someone else I should probably figure out how to live like a true adventurer and untether myself from my routine.

"What if I did an experiment where I took my routine totally off the rails and lived like ..."

"A normal person?" Jodi asked. "I'm sorry. I didn't mean normal. I meant ... no, sorry, again. I did mean normal."

I nodded. I knew what she meant and she was right, hence my desire to inflict change and hopefully emerge a better person.

"I'll spend a whole week off from my secret behaviors and daily routines," I said as I planned. "But weekends are mine! If I hate this, I'll need a good forty-eight hours alone with a can of beans and a *Say Yes to the Dress* marathon to feel like myself again."

"But isn't the point to *not* feel like yourself?" Jodi asked.

"Well, to feel like myself but a self who can do things like wear white after Labor Day without spontaneously combusting." Egads! I'm sweating just thinking about it. Good thing I always have a stick of deodorant at arm's length. Or had. Before I can properly live like a D&D adventurer I need to do away with all remnants of my civilized life.

"Good lord, this is going to be a long week," said Jodi.

"What am I supposed to do with these?" my neighbor asked when I brought him a sack full of frozen veggie burgers.

"Whatever you want. Eat them, store them for the zombie apocalypse, write your cryptic, anonymous notes on them. But please make sure to tell them I love them and this was not their fault."

"But I hate veggie burgers," he whined. "These will take up valuable freezer real estate that should be used on important things like corn dogs and Tombstone pizza."

"Oh, fine," I said, wrenching the sack of soy from his paws. So much for a peace offering. "I wouldn't want you to fall into a nutritional void because of my selfish experimentation."

I brought the burgers to a second neighbor, this time on my floor. It was a little close to comfort with her being right across the hall. I could practically smell them in her frying pan.

"Veggie burgers," she cooed. "Right on." She took the sack and slowly shut the door.

Seriously? No questions? People just show up with random bags of groceries often?

I stuck my foot in the door, preventing her from shutting it. "Don't you even want to know why I'm giving them to you?"

"I know why," she said, opening the door wide enough to stare at me with one eye while she spoke. "I'm starving, you know, but I can't get up to walk to the store because I have these plantar warts. It's like I manifested these veggie burgers. The universe brought them over."

Whoa. Has this chick been intercepting my mail? Come to think of it, when *is* the last time I got a package from Judy?

"Um, it's me," I said, speaking slowly. "The universe did not give you those. I did."

See? Rules. I want the credit here. Sorry, universe.

"The universe worked through you," she countered. "You're the messenger."

Holy cow. This stuff sounds even more like bunk when actual human beings spout it off. "Thanks!" she said, closing the door.

I thought about banging her door knocker (which sounds like a euphemism for this girl's mental state) and demanding my burgers back, but decided to let it go. In a way the universe did give her those veggie burgers. Who am I to argue? Besides, I had more important things to debate, like what I was going to eat for my next ten meals.

That night I supped on veggie dogs and kidney beans. (I usually have black beans, okay? That was a departure for me.) And I geared up for phase two of my what-would-Tabitha-do quest: Lose the baggage.

Oh, har, har, *baggage*. Get it? In this case I mean it in the literal and figurative sense. All that stuff in my glove compartment? It exists in my purse, too. Although it is important for adventurers to be well-equipped before going out into the wilds to fight orcs and bugbears, Tabitha probably doesn't need a worn-down eyeliner nub in a color I haven't worn since 1998, a Library of Congress card (not here in Seattle, or in the Forgotten Realms for that matter), a recipe for cucumber mango salsa (should a cucumber and a mango ever wind up in my purse together with nothing to do), thirteen rubber bands, four headbands, and twenty-seven bobby pins (because my hair grows really fast and I never know what stage it will be in when I go to the gym), a coupon to Bed Bath & Beyond that expired in 2007 (I know they'll still honor it), and The FURminator (I was letting my friend borrow it for her Shih Tzu, okay?).

It all comes out. Everything but the wallet, hand cream, ChapStick, cell phone, pen, and datebook. On second thought I take the datebook out. Would Tabitha care if she had a 3:30 appointment at the consignment shop or Sarah's baby shower on Saturday? Of course not! I'm amazed at how light my purse feels. In an odd, metaphoric way, so do I.

Using that momentum I tackle my "bonus bag," for lack of a better word. If I had a dollar for every time someone commented on how many bags I was lugging I'd be rich enough to not need a day job and could instead stay indoors all day preparing my earthquake survival kit. (Note to self: Don't forget to put rubber bands and blister plaster in there.)

The bonus bag is what I carry to work every day in addition to my purse. This bag is the vessel for pens (in case I can't find the ones in my purse); a coffee-stained, worn-down informational brochure about Honda's roadside assistance program (I drive a Volvo); my lunch (on the way to work); dirty Tupperware (on the way home from work); and most important: gym clothes. About a week's worth of gym clothes *every day*. You never know what the weather will be like, and I'm sorry, but not having socks is no excuse to skip your workout. Oh, and I should explain that we have a gym *at* work. (I know! How awesome is that?) And even more awesome is that because of me, my less prepared co-workers also don't have the excuse of not having socks to miss *their* workouts. That's why they call me Lady Footlocker. At least I hope that's why they call me Lady Footlocker.

Next stop on the Change Express is taking it to the streets, or rather the parking lot where my car is parked. This is a tough one as I like to treat my car like a mobile Walgreens. Out go the deodorants, lotions, sunscreen, ChapStick, and emergency ponchos. Good-bye Fiber One bars, tissues, more extra gym clothes, TomTom, atlas (holy cow, an atlas? Better save that for the Smithsonian), aspirin, ice scraper, flip-flops (in case of emergency pedicure), and pens. The only things staying are the owner's manual, insurance card, hand sanitizer, cell phone charger, and the reusable grocery bags in the trunk. No need to pit Mother Nature against Mother Nurture. And okay, maybe the flip-flops. Ruining a perfectly good polish job won't teach me anything.

After I tackled my car, there was only one thing left to do: prepare for adventure. There's no shortage of resources out there advising on how to maximize your D&D character. I've got several books touting just that on my bookshelf, in fact. It's like R&D is made up of a gaggle of Judys, which is weird considering I don't think any of them are mothers. I select a handful of books from my shelf and start researching. Let the spontaneity begin! Wait, it's 7:00. I'll get started right after *E! News*. I promise.

MONDAY

EXPECT THE UNEXPECTED. THEN EAT IT.

Obviously, if I wanted to live like a Tabitha, I had to break the hardest habit of all. Tabitha doesn't know where her next meal is coming from, let alone exactly what it is. At least for the next five days. I spent half of Sunday looking for my Crock-Pot and the rest finding various recipes for vegetarian chili. Is everyone an expert on how to turn a few cans of beans and diced tomatoes into thirteen weeks of lunches? Man, one Google search turned up about 4,829 results. I guess millions of 1970s crock-pot cooking households were right after all. (Unless you count key parties and high-waisted bell-bottoms. Those were definitely wrong. I'm talking to you, Jessica Simpson.)

I didn't mean to make so much food, but that darn Crock-Pot took one kidney bean and churned out about four pounds of chili. Those things are amazing! (Look for me on an infomercial near you.)

I love chili, and this batch is pretty darn good, if I do say so myself (thankfully, considering how much I made). The ban on veggie burgers shouldn't be a problem at all.

When lunchtime rolled around on Monday, I forced myself to finish a project I was working on before I allowed myself to go to the kitchen. I'm all about prolonging the agony *and* the payoff. Usually I'm in there between 12:05 and 12:17 every day, and so are lots of other people, as I always see the same bunch waiting for the microwave. My body is apparently used to being fed between 12:05 and 12:17 and it was starting to express its displeasure at the delay.

"Oh my God, was that an earthquake?" Laura asked.

"No, I think a train just went by," I answered, and much to my delight no one questioned this, even though there aren't any train tracks nearby.

It was my stomach, but I wasn't about to admit that. My sugar levels were dropping faster than *Project Runway*'s ratings after moving to the Lifetime channel. If I prolong the agony any longer I'll be at risk of getting a write up from HR for:

A. Yelling at a co-worker
B. Throwing scissors at a co-worker
C. Taking a bite out of a co-worker

I'm in the kitchen at 12:19. Success! I lived outside of my comfort zone.

If it's one thing I can rely on more than my food scale, it's my lack of a short-term memory. I couldn't find my lunch! I mean, there was my lunch bag (it's gold lamé so it's pretty easy to spot) but that wasn't my lunch inside. Instead of the usual tin foil square and small Tupperware container filled with carrots, it was a large Tupperware bowl and a small Ziploc bag filled with blue corn tortilla chips.

"Aw, man!" I groaned when the realization hit me. "It's chili!"

A different batch of co-workers were in the kitchen heating up their lunches as this was not my regular kitchen time.

"Do you have someone else make your lunch?" one asked.

I scoffed at the preposterous notion. Who did this person think I was? Oprah?

"No," I said. "I make my lunch!"

She raised an eyebrow. "Weird. Did you make that like fourteen years ago or something?"

"No."

"Then how did you not know what you were having for lunch?"

Okay, these 12:19 people sure are nosy. The 12:05ers would be much too busy debating the new chip choices the vending machine had to offer to even hear my complaints.

"I just forgot, okay?" I made a big to-do out of tearing the lid off the Tupperware and throwing it at the microwave. I should have just emptied the whole thing in the trash and gone to Kidd Valley for a veggie burger, but I feared my hunger would negatively impact my driving abilities. Besides, that chili had a tendency to multiply. If I tossed it in the garbage it was liable to regenerate as a swarm of bees and mow down my co-workers on its way to punish me. That for sure would be an HR violation.

Aw, suck it up, Tabitha said. *Try eating journeybread for thirty-three days straight.*

"I would love that, Tabitha. Sounds right up my alley."

"Who is Tabitha?" Nosy co-worker number 2 asked.

Oh, I so don't like this 12:19 p.m. kitchen crowd.

"Oh, never mind," I mumbled to her stupid face. (Author's note: She doesn't have a stupid face. That was the chili talking.)

Back at my desk, I tried to regain some of the enthusiasm I had yesterday for the chili. Wasn't I Googling chili cook-offs so I could enter my sure-to-be famous chili? If the contestants on *Big Brother* can eat slop week after week, certainly I could eat this for lunch. But whose dumb idea was it to include apple slices for dessert? I made a note to stop at the co-worker's desk that I normally avoid because she always has a bowl of chocolates ready for the taking. I'll do that on my way to HR to turn myself in.

When Laura got back to her desk she asked, "What smells so good?"

Seriously? What was wrong with these people?

As I was about to write up my own incident report, I noticed something written on my napkin. It's inscribed just like Judy used to do, but it's my handwriting.

"Change Happens," it reads.

Sometimes I hate me.

TUESDAY

USE PROTECTION (AND WE'RE NOT TALKING ARMOR)

I thought I'd be soy-deep in veggie burger withdrawal by today but I'm still associating them with my wackadoodle neighbor's plantar warts, so for now I can resist. Today I bring a Field Roast sandwich loaded up with sprouts, avocado, and pickles. Yum! But it didn't fill me up like my usual fare did. Maybe it contained less fiber. Maybe it's subconscious. Or maybe I was just looking for an excuse to get a bag of Sun Chips and Fudge Stripes cookies out of the vending machine. Fudge Stripes cookies are food of the gods!

My friend Audra and I decide to meet at Panera Bread for dinner. A Mediterranean sandwich and Greek salad will more than make up for my less-than-stellar lunch. (Excluding the amazing Fudge Stripes cookies. I'd almost give up carrots altogether for another taste of them.) I was at a red light near the mall when I noticed a strange aroma emanating from nearby. Nearby, as in *from my body*.

"What the heck?" I muttered. I took two showers today, one in the morning and one after that hellaciously hard workout in our company gym—the only space in the building that appears to be free from air conditioning. If there's one area I should be a little flexible with it's my workout times. If working out at my usual 3:00 p.m. time means passing out from heatstroke and sporting a magenta, sweaty face for the rest of the afternoon, then by all means, I should go in the morning.

But that smell. That's not a stench that emanates from *me*. That's an odor reserved for high school gyms and New York City subways. In fact, I take lots of steps to ensure this is a smell that I'm never responsible for. Was it possible I forgot to put deodorant on after that second shower? I got some new lotion and I was excited to use it. (It won an *Allure* beauty award. Tell me that's not exciting!) Perhaps my excitement caused me to forgo a very important step?

Experiment aside, my personal hygiene should not be sacrificed, nor should Audra's pleasant dining experience. I mean, would Tabitha set forth without a sunrod and some tindersticks? Or maybe a sprig of lavender tucked in her rucksack in case she found herself in a glandular emergency? The bloom can come off even the most expensively scented rose.

Fortunately, it's also not a problem for me because I've got some backup deo—oh, no! The Great Car Clean Out! How could I be so stupid as to leave the owner's manual in and take the deodorant out? Maybe I had time to stop at a drugstore on my way but that would mean driving eight blocks in the wrong direction and Audra was already in a time crunch. I may be uptight, overprepared, and rigid, but I'm not tardy. There had to be something in the car to mask the smell. Some antifreeze, maybe? Or perhaps I could pull into a Shell station and dab a little gasoline behind my ears. I checked the glove box, under the seat, and the pockets on the back of the seats. My car wasn't this clean when I bought it! Was that red light taking longer than usual?

I was really sweating, which was bringing this situation up to an orange alert. And seriously, what was up with this red light?

By some stroke of divine intervention (or maybe cantrips by Tabitha), a trial-sized bottle of hand sanitizer materialized under the passenger's seat. I dabbed a few drops under my arms, even though I suspected it would be like trying to mask a decomposing corpse with an unscented candle. And yes, I did just compare my underarms to a decomposing corpse.

I really wanted to go home, take a shower, and eat some instant oatmeal for dinner, but this was the new world order. Would Tabitha forgo a meal because she was a little ripe from crawling around a dungeon all day? Probably not. And I'm really craving Panera's black bean soup.

"Why do you keep scratching your pits?" Audra asked when we sat down, right on time. "You look like Koko the gorilla."

Looking like a gorilla I could handle. Smelling like one was a different story. The hand sanitizer stunk enough to temporarily mask the smell, but it was sticky. The drier it got, the pastier it became under my arms. Perhaps it was the extra onions I ordered for my salad but Audra seemed none the wiser about my less-than-fresh feeling. Or maybe she was being polite.

"Seriously, Shazzer, you need to stop with the arm flapping," she said, laughing. "You're making me nervous."

Nah, definitely not being polite.

WEDNESDAY

DON'T MAKE MOUNTAINS OUT OF MINOTAURS

Ugh. My stomach hurts. And why does my mouth taste like a gym shoe? Oh, that's right. I ate my body weight in onions last night. I bypass the usual cup of coffee and Facebook morning routine in favor of taking an extra-long shower. I need to double the dose on my ginger body wash just to cut through the stench. I have onions coming out of my eyeballs. Maybe I should make an emergency appointment with my aesthetician.

Last night's dinner coupled with today's ginger moisturizer is probably making me smell like a big bowl of spicy Thai noodles, but I'll take it. In fact, I'd take it for lunch over what I find in my lunch sack—a frozen black bean and mango Kashi meal. The people in the commercials look so happy and carefree as they lift a hearty, seven-grain forkful to their healthy mouths, but I'm already dreading it. At least I have my workout to look forward to. Wednesdays Nina and I go for a run, and it's less like exercise and more like happy hour with your long-lost bestie. I know what you're probably thinking. If we can chat it up for the entire run, we're probably not working as hard as we could be. We think you're wrong. Obviously, it's being in incredible shape that allows us such pleasures.

I reach into my gym drawer to pull out clean clothes when I'm overwhelmed by a cold terror. My clothes! I forgot my stash was cleared out, and worse—I am not in the habit of bringing my daily duds. Oh, no! I called Nina right away.

"Emergency!" I screamed into the phone. "I need gym clothes!"

"Um, hold on. I have to call you and borrow some."

I gently reminded her of my weeklong experiment, and then we were both depressed.

"But I was going to borrow some socks," she said.

"Haven't you learned anything from me?" I asked. "Why don't you have backup?"

"Because I have you!"

Whatever. What I should be asking is what would Tabitha do if she was faced with a mighty quest and lacking the proper robes? Well, being a wizard and all she could probably conjure some up with an enchantment.

I guessed I could rush over to Macy's and conjure some up with my credit card, but a quick glance at my work calendar showed that couldn't happen unless I could suddenly pull off a six-minute mile in jeans and heels.

My Tabitha miniature stared down from my monitor.

"Wimp," she said. "You'd find a way to make it work if you were hard-core like me."

"Look, you mouthy mage," I responded. "You live in a fantasy world. If dragons are things you see on your daily commute you can't tell me how to live in the real world."

"What kind of adventurer are you?" she asked. "You're going to let a little thing like Spandex keep you from accomplishing your goal?"

"Spandex? What decade did you teleport to?"

"Are you on the phone?" a co-worker who snuck up behind me asked. I hate not having a door.

"No. I mean, yes," I pick up the phone to continue my conversation with Tabitha.

"No one wears Spandex unless they're competitive bike riders or super-heroes," I whispered. "And whatever. I can work out tonight at home. I'll do one of those On Demand programs."

"Liar," Tabby said. "Big Brother is on tonight. You'll be sprawled out on the couch with your fat cat wallowing in the self-superiority complex you stupid humans get whenever you watch people melt down on national television."

"Wow," I said. "Those are some pretty big words coming from someone who isn't even two inches tall."

"I'm just saying," she continued. "I wouldn't back down. Neither would the Wyld Stallyns. We've faced bigger challenges and always rise to the occasion. Time for you to rise up, too. If door number 1 is locked, try door number 2."

"And if door number 2 is locked?" I asked Little Miss Know It All.

"That's what the rogue is for."

Right. Okay, I see what she meant. And she's right. I've seen firsthand how the Wyld Stallyns have found themselves in some tight places, grossly outnumbered, and ill-prepared. And yet, they emerge victorious. I can't imagine the Wyld Stallyns chillin' at a tavern while an innocent patron gets hassled by a couple of trolls and not doing a darn thing because some-one forgot to pack flint and steel. Well, actually I can because sitting in a tavern knocking back a few pints of mead sounds pretty darn good right now, but in the spirit of this experiment, I feign otherwise.

"Oh, fine," I sighed. This conversation had already cost me seven of the sixty minutes allocated for working out. I'd have to re-imagine today's routine. If only I had flip-flops in my car. Okay, fine, I do. I didn't take them out. Busted. Pedicures happen. On my way outside, I stopped at Nina's desk.

"Get your sneakers. We're going for a walk," I told her. "It's a beautiful day. We should at least get some vitamin D."

Our walk was peaceful and refreshing and because we had to get back in time for a meeting we walked at a brisk pace. Maybe it was the flip-flops or maybe it was the speed walking, but dare I say I could feel the beginnings of some deep muscle soreness. Nice! Good thing my plans for the night included sprawling on my couch and feeling superior.

THURSDAY
TAKE A REST

Crazy day! I was on my way to work when I saw a school bus topple into a ditch and flip over! Even crazier was that the bus was filled with meerkats and sea otters on their way to the Seattle Aquarium! What choice did I have but to pull over and save them all! I'm a hero! Hooray! Got to go! The mayor is taking me out to dinner.

Okay, I lied. It's just that nothing really good happened today. Maybe I'm getting used to this whole living-life-by-the-seat-of-my-pants thing?

Oh, and I had popcorn and a pack of butterscotch Life Savers for lunch. On second thought, let's hope I'm not getting used to it.

FRIDAY
AND THEN AN EXTENDED REST

When the phone rings before 7:00 a.m. or after 11:00 p.m. it's never good. That's why I choose to let it ring. And ring. And ring again twenty minutes later. Why wake up just to hear bad news? This, my friends, is reason number 529 why you should not put me down as your emergency contact.

When I roll into work, my boss spins around in her chair so fast she knocks a stack of Game Day kits off our shared table.

"Easy, Tiger!" I said cheerfully. It's amazing what thirteen hours of sleep can do for you.

"Where the hell have you been?" she asked. "I've been calling you!"

"That was you?" I asked, secretly glad I didn't answer it. I don't like answering work questions when I'm here, let alone when I'm knee-deep in slumber land. "Sorry. I thought it was an emergency."

"Umm, it was," she said. "You missed two meetings. One of which you were presenting at."

"Oh. Did I?"

"There you are!" my friend Bre said. "I was so worried!"

"Worried about what?" Jeez. I thought it was just a meeting about marketing tactics. "I'll e-mail you the presentation."

Bre grabbed me by the shoulders. "Because Judy hacked into your brother's Facebook page and posted an APB on his wall. You didn't call her on your way to work and you didn't answer your cell when she called. Apparently she's been calling you all morning."

"Really?" I asked, digging around in my desk drawers for some oatmeal. Part of busting out of my routines means calling Judy at random times during the day. "I didn't check my phone."

"What the hell?" Laura asked. She's really not into this whole missed meeting thing. "Were you at the doctor? Did you get a flat tire? Were you held hostage by a band of Labrador puppies? Where were you?"

"I was tired," I told her calmly. "And needed an extended rest. This whole week of living like an adventurer has taken its toll on me. But the good news is I feel invigorated! It's like I got all my daily powers back!"

Laura and Bre stared at me. Probably marveling at my glowing complexion and the bright whites of my rejuvenated eyes.

"I'm going to call Judy," Bre said, walking away.

"It's 11:45," Laura said. "You missed two meetings, one presentation, and forced your mother to post an AMBER Alert on Facebook. You're three hours late and when you finally do roll into work you claim your tardiness is due to needing an extended rest?"

"Did you know that your cells produce more protein when you're sleeping? And can bolster your memory?"

"Good," she said, but I wasn't getting a sense she was entirely impressed. "Now you can remember to set an alarm."

I called Judy.

"You are a BLEEEEEEEEEEEEEEEEEEEEEEPING BLEEEEEEEEEEEEEEEEP," she screamed, after hanging up with Bre on the other line.

"Jeez, Judy," I said. "Loosen up."

"What the BLEEEEEEEEEEEEEEEEEEEEP is wrong with you? I thought you were dead!"

"Nope. Just sleeping."

"I'm going to BLEEEEEEEEEEEEEEEEEPING kill you! What were you thinking?"

"What was I thinking? That our morning routine is like a big hunk of Gouda," I said calmly. "And I took your advice and moved it."

Yay! The experiment is officially over. It's a beautiful day, Windex-blue sky and warm breeze and I plan on spending it at Safeway stocking up on veggie burgers and carrots. I can barely contain my excitement!

Before I got to the frozen food aisle, I saw a picnic end cap. Wine, baguette, wheel of brie. Roasted red peppers, macaroons, grapes the size of ping-pong balls. What a great idea! I buy everything on the end cap and drive to Bart's house.

"Get in the car!" I told him. "I'm taking you on an adventure."

"Okay!" he said. So agreeable it's almost like he's expecting me.

I raided his cupboard for the items Safeway didn't think to include on its display—paper plates, napkins, and those cheap wine glasses we got when we went to Woodinville for wine tastings. If it was a week ago, I'd have these things in my car.

We rolled down the windows, opened the sunroof, and cranked up the air conditioner. I didn't have an idea of where to go, just a picture of what we'd see when we got there. I kept driving until we couldn't go any farther because Puget Sound spread out before us.

"We're taking a ferry?" he asked.

"I guess so," I answered, getting into the lane the attendant is pointing to. "I wonder where this one goes to."

Forty-five minutes later we arrived in Bainbridge Island. It's the stuff postcards are made of. Seriously. I have the postcards. We spend the whole trip on the outside deck, asking tourists to take our picture in front of the diminishing Seattle skyline.

"Make sure you get the Space Needle in there," I told a woman wearing a Green Bay Packers sweatshirt.

"Where are you from?" she asked as she handed back my camera.

"About seven minutes north of the Space Needle," we answered.

Bainbridge is a lovely destination, with the town center clustered nicely within walking distance of the ferry terminal. We drove past tasting rooms and shops and cafes and coffee houses until we found Battle Point Park.

"Nice place for a picnic," Bart mused.

"Funny you should say that," I answered, opening the trunk. Even Tabitha wouldn't be that prepared.

After our picnic we found a trail and went on a long, leisurely hike that left us hungry again. We headed back into town and grazed on asparagus salad and vegetable cassoulet at Cafe Nola.

"I don't want to leave," Bart said. "I feel like I'm on vacation."

I, too, felt that way. I'd been rocking that carefree, everything's-just-as-it-should-be feeling all day. The mortgage was paid, the iron was turned off, and I wished my friend a happy birthday. Yep, everything was as it should be.

"So let's stay," I said, then looked around to see who said that.

"What about Sadie?" Bart asked, referring to his aging sweet pit bull. "And that four-legged demon who takes up residence at your house?"

Ah yes, Zelda. Maybe absence will make her heart grow fonder.

Not to be deterred I came up with a solution.

"Jodi has your spare key so she can take care of Sadie, and Zelda has more than enough food to last a night."

Seriously. Who's talking?

"But you don't have your provisions," Bart noted. "We don't even have toothbrushes. Let alone a place to stay."

He said this but I can tell he's already sold. If Jeff Probst came into the restaurant right then and offered to whisk Bart away to a deserted island with nothing but a bandana, he'd do it. An overnight in a resort town is a cakewalk.

I was about thirty-nine steps from saline solution. I'd be okay.

"I guess we could stop at a drugstore," I said. "It's Bainbridge, not Burma."

And I was okay. What made our spontaneous trip to Bainbridge Island so much fun was just that—it was spontaneous. We hopped on a boat with nothing more than picnic supplies and debit cards. What more could an adventurer need?

"You know," Bart said as we cracked open our second bottle of wine, "You couldn't have planned it better."

I agreed. So much so that I insisted we make one final stop on our way home.

"To the hardware store," I instructed. "We're getting you a copy of my house key."

ADVENTURING GEAR—FOR REAL

While I respect R&D's attempts to outfit adventurers just starting out with basic gear, the standard adventurer's kit is missing quite a few essentials. Yes, I know, not everyone has a bag of holding, so space is limited. If you really want your character to be able to survive any situation, and more important to enjoy themselves, swap out R&D's essentials for my essentials. You're welcome.

R&D'S WAY	SHELLY'S WAY
Backpack	TSA regulation-size roller bag. Hey, if Southwest says you can have 24", you take 24".
Bedroll	This sounds suspiciously like a sleeping bag. Why on Earth would I need a sleeping bag when I'm staying at the Westin? (Hello! Heavenly Beds, anyone?) I don't care how portable these things are, they take up way too much space and will never be as comfy-cozy as a cashmere eye mask, travel throw, and pillow case.
Flint & Steel	Ridiculous. You'll never get that past TSA. Ditch it and use the space for a couple of paperbacks.
Trail rations	Yes, definitely. Here R&D and I see eye to eye. Never leave home without several varieties of PowerBars, bottled water, gum (Orbit Sweetmint; lasts all the way to your first connection), trail mix (the kind with M&Ms in it, not the "healthy" kind), soy jerky (oh, fine, have beef if you must), Nutter Butters cookies (they're hardy and won't crack under the pressure of two tons of toiletries, not to mention they're delicious), Popchips (several varieties), pretzels (braided; keep it real), and cocoa roast almonds, for example. See why a stupid fanny pack wouldn't work?

R&D'S WAY	SHELLY'S WAY
Belt Pouch	OMG—a fanny pack?! Call it what you want, but if it walks like a duck and makes you look like one from behind, it's a fanny pack! This is not okay in any realm, R&D! No. Just … no.
Rope	This is not a terrible idea, actually, although I much prefer bungee cords.
Sunrods	My dad, also a master of preparedness, goes to the dollar store every year before Christmas and stocks us up on essentials like rain ponchos, amber vision sunglasses, and these little key chain flashlights. They may be smaller than a tube of lip balm and cost less than a dollar, but man, those things are mightier than those annoying HID headlights that always seem to follow me home from work. I have night blindness, people! Anyway, my dad's dollar flashlights are way more practical. Can you hang your keys on a sunrod? I think not.
Waterskin	Besides sounding like something Hannibal Lecter would wear to bed, a waterskin is just plain ugly. Get yourself a nice, stainless steel BPA-free water bottle instead. Happy packing! But remember, no fanny packing!

CHAPTER 6

NEVER SPLIT THE PARTY

ME: Thank you for your recent order: *Marriage Fitness: 4 Steps to Building & Maintaining Phenomenal Love.* Unfortunately, the intended recipient is no longer at this address. Please stop sending her mail.

JUDY: Oh dear. Please tell the intended recipient that now that she and her partner have decided to cohabitate, she might appreciate a little romantic advice.

ME: It's not appropriate for mothers to send daughters books that promise to teach *Phenomenal Lovemaking*. It fact, it's gross.

JUDY: It does not say **LOVEMAKING**. Does it?

ME: Whatever. The premise is there. Besides, Bart and I are not married! I should hope you would have laid off the Sambuca long enough to remember the ceremony.

JUDY: I'd probably die from the anticipation before I get to take my first shot.

me: Well, things will be just fine with Bart. I don't think we need any help from your paperback preachers, thanks anyway.

judy: Knock on wood. I just thought you'd like this book because it's about fitness and you two seem to like that stuff.

me: It references fitness in the title, but I'm pretty sure this isn't about how to flatten your abs in six easy steps. Now, those books I *would* read.

judy: Maybe it *is* about flattening your abs. You'll have to read it and find out.

me: I won't. I'm much too busy henpecking, belittling, and emasculating Bart to read a book.

judy: Do you think Bart will still like you after living with you in your natural habitat?

me: What do you mean *still like me*? Ever think he's the one who should be worried?

judy: No.

me: Well, maybe he should be. Once at his house he left out a whole carton of milk for two days! I went there to walk Sadie while he was playing D&D and I thought she had died. Like died on the heater or something. It smelled that bad. Poor dog couldn't get out of the house fast enough. So I tossed the milk, right? And then he got all pissy the next day because he was out of milk and couldn't make a smoothie. Who does that?

judy: I don't know. I would think yogurt would be much better in a smoothie.

me: No. Who leaves dairy products out for two whole days?

judy: Men do that. There's something in their genetic code that prevents them from reopening cupboard and refrigerator doors once they close.

me: What a waste. It's almost as bad as the trail of baby powder he leaves from the bathroom to the bedroom. Once Sadie must have stepped in it and walked all over the house. I came over to what looked like the set of *Paranormal Activity 3*! It was terrifying!

judy: You need to soften your start-up.

me: Excuse me?

judy: Solve the solvable problems by softening the start-up. Didn't you read that book by John Gottmann?

me: John who?

judy: Oh my God. He's a brilliant marital psychologist. And he's local! He teaches at the University of Washington.

me: Oh, well then, I'll just go visit him during office hours and ask how I can teach my thirty-something-year old boyfriend that moving piles of discarded newspapers and junk mail from the kitchen table to the coffee table doesn't constitute cleaning.

judy: Wow. You're really uptight. I have no idea where you get that from.

me: Oh, please. Weren't you the one who had us living in fear of little pieces of paper? God forbid I tore something out of my notebook and left a little bit of fringe on the carpet.

judy: That's because you and your brother used to tear up months worth of newspaper to use for New Year's Eve confetti. I was still finding those scraps when you left for college.

me: You mean the cleaning lady was finding them. Speaking of which, I need to find one.

judy: Or you could create a *shared meaning experience*.

me: Here we go.

judy: In Gottmann's *The Seven Principles of Making Marriage Work*—

me: Again, not married.

judy: Fine. For making *cohabitation* work. You need to create rituals and traditions around housekeeping. Maybe after he sweeps the living room floor he gets a cupcake.

me: Ew, Mom! That sounds like I'm moving in with a six-year-old! I will not bribe Bart with baked goods! He should see the mud he tracks in from walks with Sadie and sweep it up. With or without the promise of a cupcake.

judy: By establishing traditions around basic household tasks you'll in turn be celebrating each other's roles.

me: I fail to see how getting cupcake crumbs on a newly swept floor will celebrate my role.

judy: If your role is a controlling naghead then it might.

me: Naghead?

judy: You might want to at least learn how to make *repair attempts*. You know, acknowledge the things he does correctly before you jump all over him to wipe down the bathroom mirror.

me: It's true. There are times when I'm afraid living together will make us parodies of ourselves. Like all of a sudden we'll become a stereo-typical sitcom couple. When did I care about fixing the bed and not using the guest towels? When did I get guest towels? I don't want to become that woman!

judy: Yeah, I don't blame you. She sounds like a real pain in the ass. But rest assured. You don't have to resolve your major issues in order for your marriage to thrive.

me: *We are not married!* And I hardly think leaving chin hair in the sink after you shave is a major issue. It's more of a courtesy issue.

judy: Would it kill you to have some Clorox cloths under the sink? Just make wiping the sink basin part of your routine.

me: It's not my chin hair, Mom! And why do you know so much about this book. Did you read it?

judy: Honey, I've been married for more than forty years. You think it's all love notes on the coffee machine and romantic nights watching *Law and Order SVU*?

me: I can't even fathom how romance fits into that, but then again, I don't want to know. It's you and dad we're talking about.

judy: You could learn a lot from us. But probably even more from John Gottmann. I'm downloading something to your Kindle right ... now. Isn't technology great?

Here's the story of a lovely pair of brown suede wedge heels; a girl who was obsessed with them; a pit bull who was also obsessed with them; and a boy who was about to feel very, very bad.

One night, I met Bart and his friend Sean out for drinks and Mexican food. It was a beautiful night, clear and warm, and the forecast showed zero chance for precipitation. This is what I like to call a "fancy shoe night." The weather cooperates, I don't have far to walk, and my pedicure is still looking good. Yes, the stars had aligned.

Fancy shoes are *special* shoes. *Special* because I paid an arm and a leg for them. (Actually, that's an idiom that doesn't work here. Why would I give a leg for a pair of expensive shoes? Kind of a rip-off, don't you think? Maybe an arm and an ear?) Anyway, I got them at Bloomingdale's in New York and they are truly fabulous. Buttery brown suede ankle boots with a wedge heel. They're definitely "top shelf" shoes, meaning I keep them in their shoebox on the top shelf of my closet. Can you see where this is going?

So I wore my special boots and felt special all night because of it. Bart marveled at how tall I was and Sean said my "ginormous heels" make me look like a centaur and I, for some reason, took that as a compliment. I felt *that* special. We filled up on guacamole and Mexican beers and then took it across the street to a bar known for their delicious, creative cocktails and truffle popcorn.

After we parted ways with Sean, Bart and I headed home, tired and happy. And really buzzing. I don't do cocktails very often, and when I do,

I usually lean toward the kinds that taste like bubble gum or bananas or butterscotch Life Savers. You know—the kinds you drink *a lot* of without realizing how many you drank? Perhaps that's why that night I left the boots on the bedroom floor and not wrapped in their shoe bags and stowed neatly in their box on the top shelf. The next morning through my sleepy haze, I woke up to the smell of pancakes and vegetarian bacon. (Don't judge: It's delicious.) Even with the dull ache in my head and my lower extremities knotted up with the charley horses I got from my chubby cat taking up three quarters of the bed and forcing me to sleep on the diagonal, I was feeling pretty happy. Ahh, life was good!

As I was enjoying my breakfast, I heard Bart mumbling from the bedroom. I figured correctly that he was talking to Sadie.

"Umm, Buddy?" he called. "You might want to come in here."

"Okay," I said.

"But stay calm."

My first thought was that Sadie had finally snapped and killed Zelda while we were sleeping. But Zelda jumped out from behind the love seat and landed an ambush attack that resulted in a four-inch scratch down the back of my calf.

My second thought was that Zelda had killed Sadie. What an awful mess that would be. That thought was almost confirmed when I saw Bart standing over a limp and cowering Sadie.

"Oh my god, is she okay?" I sobbed. "Did Zelda take her eyes? I'm so sorry, little puppy head! Auntie is so sorry!"

Bart held what very well could have been an electrocuted animal in his hand. "Um, she's okay, but, err, these aren't."

He held the deformed object out to me.

"Ew!" I shouted. "A dead thing! No! Wait, is that . . . oh my god, oh no!"

"I'm really sorry, Buddy."

Yes. Yes, it was. To be fair, it wasn't a "these" it was a "this" and I found that to be much worse. It was my left boot and it was torn to shreds. Part of the heel was chewed through. The suede was sopping wet with dog spit. The sole had been gnawed from heel to toe. And it happened in front of the right boot. How would it ever recover from seeing that?

"Please tell me Sadie pulled that thing from the jaws of a displacer beast," I said fighting to remain calm. "And I will herald her a hero. Otherwise, look for her profile on Petfinder in about eight minutes."

"Um . . ."

"No, no, no!"

"I'm so sorry," Bart said, backing away from me. "I don't know what happened. Sadie never chews shoes."

"Well, clearly she does!" I yelled.

Sadie sighed deeply and put her head down, covering her eyes with her paw.

"Don't pull that remorseful crap with me, dog! You're a bad, bad dog! How dare you? Those were my favorite!"

If you think you've seen this scenario play out in a very similar way, you're right. It happened to Carrie on *Sex and the City* with Aidan's dog, Pete. They broke up, I reminded Bart later.

"Because the dog ate her shoe or because Aidan was a wuss?"

Well . . . maybe a combination of both.

But back to the shoe at hand. Seriously, I was *mad*. Like way more peeved than I ever thought I could get at an animal. In fact, I *couldn't* get that mad at an animal, so I directed it all toward Bart. Sure, it was Sadie who ate the shoe, but she's his dog! He adopted her. Never mind that it was me who found her at the shelter, guilted him into fostering her, and later tricked him into adopting her by making him think the paper he was signing was just a rabies vaccination. (He was going to do it anyway, no biggie.)

The brutal assault happened while he was awake! Probably while he was watching *Superman 2* or Googling where to find shaved noodles in King County or preparing me breakfast in bed or any number of idle things instead of watching what his dog deemed appropriate for chewing.

"I gave her a bone," Bart said. "I thought she chewing that."

"Does Manolo Blahnik make bones?"

"I have no idea what that means, but I'm guessing no?"

And that is how we celebrated the eve of our cohabitation.

"I can't believe you're living with that dog," my brother said over e-mail a few days later. "Mom said she ate your expensive shoes and when she was younger she ate a cat. You are either crazy or really desperate to have a boyfriend."

"Allegedly," I wrote back. "On the whole eating-a-cat thing. Sadie says it was self-defense. The shoe incident is true. And I will not comment on your 'desperate to have a boyfriend' accusation."

Needless to say it was a rough few days adjusting to our new living state. The Great Shoe Massacre was just the beginning.

The day after, two giant men from Boston boxed, wrapped, and taped all of Bart's worldly possessions in just under two hours and thirty-three minutes and carted them off to a storage facility in Seattle's Georgetown neighborhood for an indeterminate amount of time.

"Wow, Georgetown," I said, regarding the neighborhood filled with big old brick warehouses and a growing community of artists. "Your stuff is so hip and trendy now."

"You know what they say," he said. "D&D minis and comic books move in, the hipsters and restaurants will follow."

It wasn't just Bart's comic books and minis in those boxes. It was his board games and photo albums from the Peace Corps, the tiki bar decorations we got at Big Lots, the Walter Payton-signed Wheaties box, and the backyard horseshoes game. Almost everything near and dear to him. We spent weeks packing up his stuff and I was feeling terrible he'd have to give up so much, even temporarily, even for a good cause, even if it meant we'd save his rent plus utilities every month and put that toward a house. That is, until we got to the cobalt dishes.

Bart's had the cobalt dishes since he was in college. They've been boxed and moved to sixteen different apartments. *Sixteen!* And no, they're not family heirlooms. Unless Bart's related to JCPenney.

"You're taking great care in wrapping stuff that's just going to Goodwill," I said when I found him using the entire Arts & Leisure section to coddle a soup bowl.

"Oh," he said, staring at his papered bowl like it was a gift of myrrh and frankincense. "I thought I'd take this with me."

"With you to Goodwill?"

"No, with me to your house."

"Oh."

All right, I thought to myself, sensing a red-flag situation. *Tread lightly. This is a touchy situation all around. He's the one being displaced here. I've lived in my condo for more than a decade! That's longer than he's lived in Seattle! If the guy wants to bring a soup bowl, he should bring a soup bowl! It's his house, too!*

"If that's the bowl you like to eat soup out of, it should come," I announced, feeling proud like a fourth grader who just spelled *poultry* correct.

Judy was wrong. I can live in peace and harmony with another living being. A human being, even.

He cocked his head to the side and looked at me like I suddenly was a fourth grader. "Not just the bowl. The whole set. It's good stuff. I've had it for years!"

That's the difference between the two of us, I guess. To me, *had it for years* implies it's *time to go*. To him that just means *sturdy and irreplaceable*.

"But I have perfectly good plates and bowls," I said. "And matching coffee mugs!"

Chill … it's just some soup bowls! Besides, you'll probably get all new stuff in a year or two. Who cares what you eat off?

"It's just," I continued, "we don't have a lot of room. So maybe we stick with just one set of dishes for now."

Bart looked at the soup bowl he cradled in his arms and then to its cobalt blue brothers and sisters. "But why can't this be the one set we stick with?"

Choose your battles! Is this really worth it?

I thought of dinner parties and the placemats I bought that complement the colors of my dishes and how I have ten of everything because if there are more than ten people at once I invoke my right to use paper plates. (Not like plain old white paper plates—but nice, decorative ones you get at party supply stores.) I couldn't figure out what the heck was so appealing about his set of plates. He didn't even have a full set.

SUPER-MODEL ME

You know why people like creating D&D characters so much? Because you can filter out the bad parts of your own personality. And yes, you have bad parts. Maybe they're not all documented in a book, but still. They're there. When we create a new character we design their backstories, pick their personalities, quirks, family histories, and mannerisms. If you don't like something you can erase it. My characters are flawed to an extent—they'd be horribly boring otherwise—but they don't have real imperfections. They probably never sweat the small stuff. They hardly ever have meltdowns. They're not OCD and anal about things like how to properly stack the colanders in the cupboards or how to fold dishtowels. They probably don't even get morning breath or digestive issues. Basically, they're Victoria's Secret models, which means they're also incredibly depressed and envious of those like me who consider a one-pound bag of M&Ms a perfectly reasonable dinner. Suckers!

"You don't have enough," I said. And it was true. He only had four dinner plates and three salad plates. And we may never find that one soup bowl under all that newspaper.

Thankfully he saw my reasoning but wasn't totally convinced he wanted to give them up completely.

"I'll put them in storage," he decided.

"But why?" I whined.

Oh, I know. Just let the stupid dishes go to storage. But I couldn't help it. Ideally the next time we saw any of this stuff was when we move into a brand-new (to us) home. Even I'll want to replace my beloved dishes when we get there.

"Maybe our kids will need them when they go to college," he said.

I smiled, waiting for him to laugh, but he just stared at me. Oh, wow. He's serious. And how am I supposed to argue with that? At once it's poignant and charming and reeks of the sentiment that we'll be together at least long enough to populate the earth with a child that's able to get into college. And at the same time we're talking *at minimum* eighteen years from that very moment assuming I am currently *with child* (and I'm not, thank you; I'm a stress eater and moving is very stressful).

"What makes you think our child would want dishes that are twenty-eight years old? I mean, it's a sweet gesture and all but maybe we could celebrate them getting into college by buying new stuff."

"Or maybe they'll like the idea that these are the same dishes Mommy and Daddy used to eat off of. Besides, it's economical."

I sighed. "Fine. The dishes go to storage," I said, wondering how much it would cost to get those giant men from Boston to lose the box marked "dishes."

After that, Bart and the remaining 5% of his stuff sat in my living room. The living room I had lived in for thirteen years.

Alone.

I told you. When I plant roots, they stick.

"You know what's going to happen," Bart said flipping through the saved shows on my DVR. "We're going to argue so much about those dishes that they'll become this huge iconic figurehead in our relationship. We'll dredge them up every year and argue about what we should do with them and because we'll never agree we have to keep them."

"And really the dishes are just a symbol for something that is dreadfully off in our relationship," I added. "Like when I say 'why did you keep those stupid dishes' I'll really be saying 'why didn't you roll over our 401(k) so we could retire, damn it?'"

"We'll force our kids to eat off of them and therefore resign them to a life of repeating our mistakes."

"They'll live in the same fear of those blue dishes that I had of my mom's wooden spoons. Ouch. My butt still stings when I walk past the housewares department at T.J. Maxx."

"They will taste our resentment with every bite."

"We'll definitely need a reality show," I said.

"Especially around the time they go through puberty," Bart agreed. "I would have loved to have had those awkward years projected into America's living rooms."

"It's not too late."

With that we raised our cans of Fresca and toasted to all the ways we could screw up the next generation.

Later that night the wind picked up and the snow fell in cold, icy sheets. If you're not familiar with how the people of Seattle deal with snow, allow me to fill you in. *They don't.* That is unless you count ditching your cars in the middle of I-5 and running for your life down the highway shoulders as "dealing." Schools announce closures at the mere threat of snow. The TV news was already showing scenes from the apocalypse and the snow wasn't even sticking yet.

"We're not going to work tomorrow," Bart predicted. "It actually might be cold enough to stick."

"In that case, let's open a bottle of wine."

When I went to get the wine opener, I tripped over a rollerblade.

"You rollerblade?" I asked Bart.

"Sure!" he answered.

Weird, I thought. Not in the last year and a half at least. And certainly not in November.

I looked around my once organized and artfully decorated living room to find it covered with boxes, gym clothes, and a ninety-pound pit bull who may or may not have designs on my cat.

"Well, this is our life now," I whispered to Zelda who was glaring at me from the hallway. I should probably have put a little wine in her water bowl.

Bart was right. We didn't go to work the next day or the day after. Seattle shut down while we waited for the three snowplows to do their jobs and free us from our neighborhood. There's a fine line between "living" together and "stuck" together and we dashed across it.

"Be careful what you wish for," Judy reminded me on our daily phone call. "Or rather, agreed to."

"What I agreed to was an upgrade to my cable service and having someone to help take out the recycling, all while maintaining the freedom to do simple things like go outside, walk on a sidewalk. Stop at Safeway and get more wine!"

Judy sighed. "That's how it is in a big-girl relationship."

"Well, what if we need to get away from each other?" I asked. "There's nowhere to go. The living room, dining room, and kitchen are all one room!"

"You could go stand in the hallway, I guess."

"Oh, sure. That wouldn't look weird at all."

"Well, not as weird as you wearing one brown suede boot and sobbing in the bathtub."

I scoffed at the notion. "I was not in the bathtub."

Judy laughed. As bad as she felt about the incident, she still took Sadie and Bart's side. She didn't want *them* to feel bad.

"It's hard enough having to live with you," she said. "How could you make that little dog feel bad?"

"It's not easy for me, either," I whispered so Bart couldn't hear me. Although he was technically in another room, it was still only like seven feet away. "It's not like we subscribe to the same ideals when it comes to cleaning and organizing. There were dinner crumbs on the counter when I woke up today! They were there all night!"

"Awww," Judy mock pouted. "Don't you have a little wizard spell you could pull out of your book to make the crumbs disappear?"

Now that would be nice. Maybe some cantrips? But we were talking about mere mortals here.

We were out of work for two full days. Now, I know what you're thinking, a freak, paralyzing snowstorm when you're moving into a new place? What a brilliant stroke of good luck Mother Nature has gifted you. All those perfectly good bonus days you can use to get settled and unpacked in your new digs. If that were me, I'd have my clothes ironed, hung up, organized by color, season, and maybe even alphabetical by designer if the sun didn't come out soon. Alas, Bart took a more leisurely approach to settling in.

"These boxes aren't going to untape themselves," I said in attempt to be jovial.

My voice said *oh, ha ha!* My blood was seething *get rid of these godforsaken boxes before you end up living in one!* Perhaps I was feeling a bit . . . pardon the pun . . . boxed in.

"Do you need help?" I asked. "I'm very good at putting things away."

He took his earbuds out and smiled. "Oh. Yeah. The boxes. No, I'm good!"

"They don't bother you?"

"I guess I don't really notice them."

There are things I'm glad Bart doesn't notice. Maybe I've gained a few pounds. Maybe there's a massive zit on my chin. Maybe I've gone too long between eyebrow waxes and I'm starting to look like Bert from *Sesame Street*. But the thirteen cardboard boxes stashed in roughly 700 square feet? These are the things I kind of wish he paid a little mind to.

"Besides, I don't know where to put anything," he said.

"Well … things like clothes can go in the bedroom. Razors and toothbrushes generally go in the bathroom. I usually put books on bookshelves, but that's just me."

"Ha, ha," he laughed. "It would be nice to have a drawer. Maybe some closet space. But that's just me."

"Umm … I, and the seven black garbage bags full of clothes I brought to a consignment store, find that morally offensive." There is a perfectly good drawer in the bedroom just waiting for him to toss some socks and gym shorts in. What an ingrate!

"Okay," he smiled, putting his headphones on and returning to the blog he was reading. "In a bit."

"Well," Judy asked one week into our cohabitation. "Did he move out yet?"

"No, but if he wanted to it would be supereasy seeing as his boxes are still packed."

"Do you think his inability to get settled is his subconscious way of saying this was a terrible idea?"

I hadn't thought of that until now. "That's almost as terrible as my mother even suggesting it," I said. "Oh wait, did Dr. Phil say that? Because then I can totally dismiss it."

"I just mean," she continued, "that living with someone isn't easy. Especially your first time. You're a late bloomer. This should have been done in your twenties when you didn't have standards or the income to afford such a robust wardrobe."

"Yeah, sorry. I totally screwed up by buying my own home and investing in my future instead."

"There is a way to make the transition easier," she said in the same manner someone on Canal Street might approach you with a lead on tickets to Broadway's hottest show or this season's must-have Louis Vuitton bucket bag. "If you're interested."

"Not interested."

"It just takes seven easy steps."

"Stay away or I'll call the police."

"I'm telling you, Oprah's a believer. And look how long she and Steadman have been together!"

"*We're fine!*" But I couldn't mask the anxiety and pessimism I was feeling. I sounded like the flight attendant who got hip checked by the beverage cart and burst out crying on a very turbulent ride to Chicago.

"Well, I hope so," she said as she sighed. "This could be it for a while."

"What's that supposed to mean?" Oh, why do I bother?

"You know that old saying," she said. "About not buying the cow because the milk is so cheap?"

Yeah, I knew the saying. I hear it about four times a day now. Even heard it before I was old enough to live by myself let alone with a significant other. I chose to let it slide.

"Maybe I should just unpack the boxes," I suggested. "You know, as kind of a housewarming present?"

"Don't you dare! I mean, unless you want maidservant to be added to your resume. Once you pick up after him, he'll always expect you to."

"That's ridiculous! He doesn't expect nor want me to act like his nanny. He's a grown-up. He can take care of himself."

"Well, sure he *can*, but he probably doesn't want to. Your father and I went to Lake George for a vacation right after we were married and I made the mistake of picking up his wet bathing suit and hanging it on the doorknob. Do you know to this day he's never been able to pick a wet bathing suit up off the floor? It's like he's *physically unable* to."

"I'll keep that in mind," I said, hanging up.

Truthfully, I was worried. Sure, there were plenty of good reasons to move in together, but maybe we should have waited until we had a bigger place. I mean, 700 square feet isn't a lot of room when you're two adults and two pets. Maybe the reason we liked each other so much was because the novelty hadn't worn off yet. Was Judy right? Was I just cheap milk?

"Wasn't part of the reason you moved in together so that you could save money to get a bigger place?" Jodi asked on our way around Green Lake. Thankfully the snow and ice were gone and some of my regular routines could resume.

"It was, but that was before realizing I'm not able to cohabitate."

"Who said you're not able to cohabitate?" she asked. "Did Bart say that? I'll kill him!"

"No, Judy. And not so much said as implied. I'm too old for this crap. Too set in my ways. You know, a long time ago, before we were even dating, Bart mentioned an article he read about a married couple who lived in Manhattan. They both had their own apartments and didn't want to get rid of either so they lived separately during the week and together on weekends. We both thought that was a great idea and we *had* that! Why did we have to go and mess it up?"

"It's not messed up," Jodi said. "It's just *new*. You'll get used to each other."

"I know. I'm trying not to get on his case about every little thing but it makes me feel like those poor people who are still awake during surgery and can't make any sound or movement to let the doctors know. It's like *oh, look, he's using* my *towel again!* Shut up! Or *I'm pretty sure that old wok is going to leave a rust stain on my countertops!* Don't say anything! Just get a potted plant to cover it when guests come over!"

"You know what motivates me to come here and work out?" Jodi asked.

"The onion rings and peanut butter milkshakes we always get on our way home?"

"No. New gym clothes. I actually look forward to putting them on. And seeing as I refuse to be one of those people who think it's okay to run errands and go out to lunch in anything that contains more than 10% Spandex, I can only justify wearing them to work out."

"Sitting in my parked car on a dark cul-de-sac eating onion rings and chugging milkshakes doesn't count as going out to lunch, does it?"

"Please. Anyway, my point is maybe you could buy him some nice hangers or a new laundry basket to inspire him to pick up his clothes."

"Or he could get inspired by the ghost of Joan Crawford and use those hangers against me."

"True," she said. "In that case, get padded ones."

"What's wrong with my hangers?" Bart asked, pointing to the tubular ones that lay in a pile at his feet.

"I don't know, but I'm assuming something has to be. Otherwise you'd use them." Then I told him Judy's theory about me picking up after him and Jodi's about enticing him with nice things.

"Thank Jodi for looking out for me and tell Judy to quit worrying," he said. "I'm very happy we're living together."

"Aren't you eager to settle in? Stop living out of a suitcase like you're some washed-up country singer desperate to get a gig?"

Admittedly, I'm the same person who unpacks her suitcase in a hotel even if I'm only there for one night. I enjoy nesting. So sue me.

Bart studied the closet. "Doesn't matter what I hang my clothes on if there's no room to put them," he muttered.

"You have all this room right … here." I moved my clothes over to show him the space perfectly suitable for his possessions.

"That's it?" he asked. "That's my space? Oh sure, that'll work. If I were a Ken doll!"

"Very funny. You just need to use the right hangers. That's why I got you these!"

In case you are wondering, there are such things as the *right* hangers. They're the ones covered in that fake suede that grips your clothes without snagging them. They're way thinner than the tubular ones and therefore can grant you up to 13% more closet space. Try them and love them or I'll give you your money back. (Just kidding. Seriously. Please don't ask me for any money.)

Bart again looked at his discarded tubular hangers on the floor. "But what am I supposed to do with these?" he asked.

"I don't know," I said. "Maybe save them for our kids?"

It was 8:13 a.m., eight minutes out of the window of acceptable departure time to guarantee an on-time arrival at work (barring any accidents or blinding sunshine; Seattle drivers hate driving in the sun). We were running dangerously close to a guaranteed late arrival and yet I couldn't seem to leave.

"Ready, Buddy?" Bart asked.

"Almost," I said, brushing toast crumbs into the palm of my hand before shuttling them to their new home in the kitchen garbage can. Judy would disagree with this action, believing I have forever shut the door on Bart sweeping up his own toast crumbs, but I took my chances. It's not exactly hard work, which is why I can't for the life of me understand how *someone* totally ignores these crumbs day after day. That is if you count "adding to the pile" as ignoring. But I wasn't going to mention it.

"Just leave it," Bart said, which has become his motto.

"I can't," I told him, which has become mine. "Sadie will smell them and try to get on the table and knock over your computer and notebooks and dirty water glasses and little piles of papers. And what if glass gets on the floor and Zelda steps on it and gets her paws all cut up and needs a visit to the vet which of course will be after-hours so add on $500 right there and all of that could have been avoided if *you just cleaned up your toast crumbs.*"

I swear I wasn't going to mention it.

"Really?" he asked, his halfsmile contradicting the sarcasm in his voice. "A few scattered crumbs and we're out $500?"

"At least. That's just the after-hours fee."

"All because of my toast crumbs?"

That was ridiculous. Even I knew that.

"It's not just because of the toast crumbs. It's the water glasses. We only have ten glasses! Eight of them are on various end tables, nightstands, coffee tables, and bathroom sinks. Do you really need to take every sip of water out of a different glass?"

"I'll wash them. It's not a big deal."

"You're right. Washing them isn't a big deal. We have a dishwasher! But you're not washing them. You're leaving them everywhere! I had to use a measuring cup to swallow my vitamin today!"

He laughed. *Laughed!* "That's very resourceful. Now let's get going, or we'll be late for work."

"I don't want to be resourceful," I said, filling Zelda's and Sadie's water bowls. "I want to drink water out of a glass like a normal adult. Pretty soon I'll be sharing with these two."

"If you want to act like a normal adult then you should grab your lunch and go to work. Ready?"

"Yes. Wait. Is that a light on in the bedroom?"

"I don't know. Maybe," he said smiling.

"Is that your reading light?"

"Probably. Whatever. I'll get it later."

"Later is nine hours from now. Is anyone going to be reading while we're gone?" We look at Sadie and Zelda, who look at us like a couple of teenagers seconds away from an unsupervised weekend. I can just imagine Sadie rolling in a massive bully stick while Zelda speed dials her catnip connection. Nope. No reading going on here.

"Did you know 59% of electricity in the United States is wasted electricity?" I said, happy I happened to have glanced at the insert that came with our electric bill just so I could mouth off that impressive little tidbit.

"Nope."

"Do you hear that?" I asked. "It's the sound of Al Gore's heart breaking."

"I'll go turn it off," he said.

Later that day we had our D&D game.

"Did anyone pick up the eighth-level magic item you guys found in the chamber last week?" the DM asked. The Wyld Stallyns are notoriously bad about cashing in magic items.

"Well, I can pretty much guarantee that Holden didn't pick it up," I said, referring to Bart's character.

"He might have if Tabitha picked it up and put it on his pillow or stuffed it in his lunch bag," Bart suggested, perhaps in reference to the pile of junk mail that's been sitting on our dining room table for two weeks.

"Is Holden planning on getting new storm windows or at-home teeth whitening systems? I mean, clearly he is or else he would have tossed that once-in-a-lifetime offer for cement-based siding in the trash like a normal person," I told him.

"Maybe he *is* interested in those offers," Bart said. "Or maybe he just has nowhere to put things now because he doesn't have an office."

"Uh, guys?" the DM asked. "I just need to know who has the magic item."

"Oh, Holden should talk to Tabby about not having things!" I said. "She used to have a beautiful dining room table. And a cat that didn't pee on things! She can totally relate!"

"I think I have the magic item," Bertrand said. "Yeah. That's right. It's right here. Let's get this party moving."

"I hope it's an amulet of compromise," Jordan said. "Or we might be here awhile."

"We're role-playing!" we said, together on that at least.

"Maybe we could take an extended rest," Hilary, our usually quiet cleric suggested. "I think Tabby and Holden could use some sleep."

"You better make sure the contents of your rucksacks are unpacked and your crossbow bolts are organized by size or Tabitha won't be able to go to sleep."

"Tabitha likes order," I said. "Is that so wrong?"

"She likes control and, yes, it can be wrong."

"Well," Bertrand noted, "she is a controller, after all."

"That's not true!" I shouted and then remember who we're talking about. Wait. Who *are* we talking about? "Yes, Tabitha is a controller but she also is someone who wants to live in a filth-free home. A home where dust bunnies aren't glaring down on her. A home where the plastic on the bread bag isn't melted onto the toaster oven. A home where the bathroom walls aren't covered in toothpaste."

"*I have an electric toothbrush!*" he shouted. "It's messy! It sprays!"

"*I* have an electric toothbrush, too!" I shouted back. "Toothbrushes don't spray! Owners spray! We can't use cinnamon-flavored toothpaste anymore because every morning our bathroom looks like a scene from *Dexter!*"

"Well, why don't you use one of your *four* towels to clean it up?" he said as he sneered.

"Because my *four* towels all serve a purpose—hair, face, body, and postmoisturizer and predressing! And, oh yeah, because it's not my job to clean it up!"

"Uh-oh," Hilary said. "Not the towels."

Bart mumbled something under his breath that sounded like *it's stupid, but whatever.*

"What did you say?" I asked.

"I said, it's stupid but whatever."

"You're a big boy. You splatter it, you wipe it down with a Windex cleaning cloth conveniently located under the sink."

Jordan grabbed a handful of popcorn. "This is gonna get uglier than an orc in a prom dress."

"Your character is very bossy," Bart said.

"And your character is very messy," I said.

And we agreed our characters should work on these things and finally began the encounter.

★ ✲ ✳ ☆ ★

"Get him a little basket," Judy insisted.

Don't worry. I was confused, too, and I was *in* the conversation.

"What's Bart going to do with a little basket? Put it next to his bowl of curds and whey?"

"No," Judy said, sounding a tad impatient with my lack of vision. "He can keep all of his desk necessities in there. Then when you need to use the dining room table for something other than his office, you just put the little basket in the closet. There. Your home is in order."

"I see where you're going with this," I said. "But I don't understand why it has to be a little basket. I can't imagine him embracing a desk basket."

Judy sighed, a sure sign she had reached her patience threshold. "It doesn't have to be a basket. But you should check Pier One before you write me off. They have plenty of masculine looking baskets. They're brown."

"Oh, well, when it comes to 'little baskets' I think we're way beyond enfeeblement."

"Just go shopping after work," she said. "And get him something that's his own. It will make him feel less like a guest. It's his house, too, you know."

"Oh, I know it."

That may be true and all, but if Bart really felt like a guest in my home—our home—then wouldn't he try harder to be neat and tidy? I would never splatter toothpaste all over my host's bathroom mirror and leave it there. *For days.*

Regardless, I took what she said to heart. He is a stranger in my land. After we hung up, I went online and ordered Bart a gift subscription to a men's magazine. There. I'm sure he feels more at home already.

That night after work, we didn't talk much on the drive home. I called Judy so the quiet wouldn't be so obvious and uncomfortable.

"Why are you calling again?" she asked. "I know they don't let you watch reality television at work so whatever happened in the last eight hours can't be that important."

I wasn't about to tell her Bart and I were having growing pains and risk getting schooled in the seven easy ways to make sure your man never sees you enter or leave the bathroom.

"I heard one of the *Real Housewives of Miami* gets arrested for a DUI." It's a lie but a low-risk one. Someone on those shows is always getting arrested for drunk driving. You'd think they might want to focus less on the custom-designed fire pits and infinity pools and maybe put a little spare change in the taxi funds.

I could hear her clicking away on her keyboard. "Oh, which one? I'll Google it right now."

That bought me a good seven minutes but we were still about fifteen miles from home. I moved on to plan B.

"I'm supposed to bring dessert to Rachael and Lars's house next Saturday. What should I make?"

"Is Bart with you?"

Uh-oh. "Umm, yeah, why?"

"Well, shouldn't you be talking to him?"

This was weird, seeing as how he's with me every morning and yet she doesn't worry about etiquette then. Was it possible Judy was on to me?

"We talk all the time," I said. "Besides, you watch Food Network all day. You're a much better resource for these types of things."

"What does Bart want for dessert?"

"Oh, come on! Just give me a stupid Bundt cake recipe! I'll take anything!"

She was silent, but her fingers tapped away. Finally, she spoke. "Don't put anything in his name. And get his share of the bills in cash. Do you have a lease? Because you can get a template right online. Here. I'll send you a link."

"You're being ridiculous. I'm not doing any of that."

"This is your investment! You need to protect yourself!"

"Who says?"

"*The Good Girl's Guide to Living in Sin.* I'm paying extra to have it over-nighted. I should have thought of this sooner."

★ ✵ ✸ ☆ ★

The following week when our D&D group met, I had Tabitha trying out some new spells.

"I'd like to cast *fountain of flame,*" I said pointing to the area on the map where Tabby's zone would be. It's a daily power, but casting it right away seemed like a no-brainer. It creates a zone that lasts for the entire encounter and any enemy who enters the zone or ends their turn there will take five fire damage. Pretty strategic move for someone who either forgets to use her daily or tries to cast it three times in one turn.

"So that's where you want to put your burst?" our Dungeon Master asked.

"Yes, that's what I said, isn't it?" Jeesh. Why is he always repeating what I just said? When Bertrand shoots his bow or Jordan marks someone he doesn't make them triple confirm that's what they want to do.

"Are you sure that's the most opportune location for a burst?" Bertrand asked.

Jeez, Louise, is this contagious? But I can see why Bertrand's apprehensive. Tabitha accidentally scorched a few hairs on his bard's beard by miscalculating the burst radius of a fireball or two. Or six. Whatever. It happens.

"Yes, Bertrand, I'm sure. Tabitha's zone is right here." I showed them the clearly marked section on the playmat. "And don't worry. It only hits enemies." There. That ought to appease him.

"Okay, then," the DM said. "Tabitha has lit up this area here where there are no enemies within a good thirty feet."

Oh. "Well, no enemies *currently*," I pointed out. "But there will be."

"Considering we're standing over here and they came from there," Bertrand said, pointing to my clearly marked zone on the playmat, "maybe not."

"You don't know that, Bertrand."

The Dungeon Master did, though. When it was the kobolds' turn they pointed out Tabitha's magnificent wall of fire and ... laughed? Kobolds are such bitches.

"They easily walk around the flaming area," the Dungeon Master said. "And they throw their javelins at the wizard, assuming she's not bright enough to duck."

Tabby ducked but she hit her head on a low-hanging branch on the way down.

"That's fourteen damage," the DM said.

"I had a feeling...." Bertrand said.

After the game Bart and I walked back to his desk.

"Well, that wasn't my finest moment," I said.

He shrugged. "You didn't know where the kobolds were going to move next. It was rooted in good intentions."

"Bertrand laughed at me."

"Bertrand laughs at everyone," he said. "That's his role, just like you have your job and I have mine and the Dungeon Master has his. That's what makes a well-rounded party."

"What class is it that gets to laugh at people?" I ask. "Because I totally want to play one next time."

"Well, that's Bertrand's job outside of the party. He's actually a really good healer. But just because you play your character differently than he would doesn't mean it's the wrong way."

When we got home that night, Zelda's litter box was ransacked and what was left of the contents were scattered over the living room. Zelda glared at us from the couch while Sadie cowered in the corner of the dining room.

"Oh, look," Bart said. "Sadie is helping with the chores. She cleaned out Zelda's litter box."

"That's cool. Maybe next we could teach her to do laundry or empty the dishwasher?"

But the worst was waiting for me in the bedroom. There on my beloved duvet cover sat a blue towel. A towel that was presumably wet when it landed there this morning. A blue, presumably wet towel that has sat on my beloved duvet cover for more than nine hours. *Nine hours!*

What the hell? I mean, seriously? I've asked him how many times to simply hang up his towel when he's done with it. It isn't rocket science! It isn't curing cancer! It isn't ... a big deal? Standing there glaring down on the stupid towel I realized something monumental. The house was still standing. The animals were still alive (although one might have an upset stomach considering how much litter and kitty poo she ingested),

Everything I Need to Know I Learned from D&D
139

the duvet cover was fine, and most important, we were fine. Bart and I were *just fine*.

And then I had my second startling discovery in a four-second period of time. But this discovery was so alarming that even a toothpaste-splattered mirror couldn't hide what was in plain sight: *I am a controller*. A controlling, meddling displacer beast who makes big freakin' mountains out of potential mildew. And I made the people I loved feel bad in the process. *That*, I thought, was much worse than a wet towel on a duvet cover.

So, okay, we'll probably need to figure out a better place to keep Zelda's litter box and, yeah, Bart could use a brown basket or two and I have one less pair of shoes, but that's fine, too. I needed to make more room in the closet, anyway. And why bother having a pair of overpriced shoes that you only wear on special occasions? What's the fun in that? Sadie is a dog. Dogs do these things. Bart is a human being. A ridiculously patient, mellow and forgiving human, but still. And Zelda? Well, Zelda is a cat and there's not much you can do about that.

Instead of making Sadie a monster, I remembered the things she was really good at, like protecting me from that man in the electric wheelchair who tried to run me down in a crosswalk. And taking the rap for knocking over the glass of red wine on Bart's area rug. (She later peed on it, but it was still cool of her to cover for me.) She and I shared the best naps of our lives when it was twenty degrees *inside* last winter and we slept on Bart's cold leather couch wrapped up in my Snuggie.

Thinking back to our afternoon D&D game and what Bart said about all of us having our roles made me realize Tabitha and I had a lot in common. I, too, had the perfectly rounded out party: a striker (Zelda), defender (Sadie), leader (Bart), and controller (duh).

Bart came into the bedroom and found me zoning out, staring at the towel.

"Oh, no," He ran to the bed and grabbed the towel. "I'm so sorry. I can't believe I forgot that."

"I don't care anymore," I announced. "Not about the shoes or the towels or what hangers you use. I just want you to be happy here. I'm sorry I overreacted."

"It's okay, Buddy," he said. "And you have a right to be irritated. Your space is being invaded by two slobbery, sloppy, boundary-breaking beasts. There's an adjustment period for sure."

"I've been such a bitch," I lamented. "I can't believe you put up with me."

He laughed. "Honestly, I have nowhere to go."

The following Saturday, I woke up to find Sadie had knocked over Bart's laundry basket and his clothes had exploded from it like an alien embryo from its human host's belly. But that was five days ago. The pile was growing. I gathered up the clothes and tossed them back in the hamper.

"I'll start the laundry," I said.

Bart was having breakfast—two slices of extra crispy toast and a smoothie. "Don't use the shower yet," he said. "I just caulked it and need to hang some protective plastic so it doesn't get wet."

"Well, aren't you fancy?" I said, pointing to the martini glass he was drinking the smoothie from. "Are your friends from *Sex and the City* coming over for breakfast today?"

He laughed and looked sheepish. "We're out of glasses again."

"Oh, well," I said, filling up a bud vase with water and taking my daily vitamin.

HOME IS WHERE THE HALBERD IS

Well-rounded parties are worth their weight in gold coins. Well-rounded living situations are even more valuable. Can you imagine living with two controllers?

You hung your towel up wrong.

No, *you* hung your towel up wrong.

Yeah. No, thank you. Everyone knows there's only one right way to hang a towel. If you have trouble relating to your roommate, significant other or otherwise, maybe it would help to understand each other's roles and, subsequently, how to play nice with each other.

STRIKER: It's always the quiet ones....

You think you lucked out with this one, huh? They're sweet, seemingly accommodating, probably have an awesome DVD collection. They're usually peaceful and calm, clean up after themselves, and always pay the bills well in advance of their due dates. They probably still use actual checks instead of autopay. Charming, right?

Wrong. When a striker goes on the offense you never see it coming. They blow up faster than a helium balloon. You might think their freak-outs are out of the blue, but really they're calculated and targeted. Watch your back. And pretty much anything valuable you own.

Sample striker roommates: Jennifer Jason Leigh's character in Single White Female, cats.

LEADERS: In theory, leaders are nice people to have around as they spend much of their time trying to boost your confidence, make you look good, and tell you how incredibly awesome you are when you're down. What's bad about that? Well, imagine if your confidence is fine right where it is, you think you look fine, and you already know how awesome you are. Too bad! Leaders like to feel needed. If you don't have a problem they can fix they'll create one and presto! Now you have two problems. It's a vicious circle with these types.

Sample leader roommates: Dr. Phil, Judy, dogs.

DEFENDER: Ugh. I lived with a defender freshman year in college. She was a beautiful tomboy who showed up late on move-in day with a nanny whom she ordered around in German. She wore steel-toe boots and flannel shirts (so Seattle, yet so far away) and greeted the guys in our dorms with swift kicks to the groin. Can someone please tell me what question I answered incorrectly on my housing placement form for Ithaca College to think we were a good match?

Don't get me wrong, we had our fun, but our dorm room was not the room you wanted to hang out in. Defenders aren't exactly the welcoming committee. If you find yourself on the lease with one, feel free to throw out those barbeque tongs and plastic forks. You're probably not hosting the next bash.

Sample defender roommates: Mel Gibson, European football fans, soccer moms.

CONTROLLER: Oh, come on, controllers aren't that bad, are we? I mean, they?

Sure, they live up to their name and like to control their environments. Some do this with mass-affecting area bursts of acid, flames, or cucumber-scented bathroom cleaner. Some do this by insisting on using a specific type of hanger. Regardless, controllers have the unique ability to affect an entire room with their moods. If you find yourself sharing fridge space with a controller, do yourself a favor and delete shows off the DVR after you watch them and hang up your coat when you come home. Please?

Sample controller roommates: Gallagher, Sheldon from The Big Bang Theory, cats unhappy with their current living situation.

CHAPTER 7

DIAPERS & DRAGONS

ME: Something is wrong with Bart.

JUDY: Oh my GOD, WHAT? WHY ARE YOU CALLING me? CALL 911!

ME: No, no, not *emergency* room kind of wrong. It's much worse. I don't think I can talk about it.

JUDY: Then you SHOULD REALLY REFRAIN FROM CALLING people to TALK.

ME: I don't want to tell you because you'll take his side. Again. Like you always do.

JUDY: WHAT'D YOU DO this time? YELL AT him BECAUSE he CAN'T DO hospital CORNERS on the BED?

ME: You better be talking about the way to fold sheets and not some disgusting sexual position you learned from watching the Kardashians again.

JUDY: GOOGLE it.

me: Oh, like the last time you told me to do a Google search to find out what that white stuff was that came out of your salmon? I almost got sent to HR when my co-worker saw those pictures!

judy: You really need to loosen up. Come on, tell Mommy what's wrong.

me: It's awful. Possibly insurmountable.

judy: I wonder if it's too late to get those books back from Jodi....

me: We were out to dinner, having a perfectly nice time, when this family gets seated next to us. Why adults bring kids to restaurants is beyond me.

judy: So they can eat?

me: But they can eat at Subway or Red Robin or even Old Spaghetti Factory if it's a special occasion. Those places welcome kids. They even let them eat free sometimes. This was a nice Italian place. Tablecloths and everything!

judy: Seems almost too fancy for you two people who drink beer out of shoes, but go on.

me: It's called a boot, and it's German, and it's not an actual shoe. Google it.

judy: Dare I?

me: So these babies are like four and five.

judy: Babies?

me: And they start playing this game where the floor is water and their chairs are life rafts or something.

judy: Sounds right up your alley.

me: And the little girl baby is all "Helllllp meeeeeeeee, I'm falling in the waaaaaaaaaaaaattterrrrrrrrrrr!" and then she tumbles out of chair and starts screaming her face off.

judy: Was she hurt?

me: No! She was acting. Pretending to drown! First of all, what kind of game is that?

judy: Hmm, I seem to remember you and your brother playing Bonnie and Clyde. I'd say pretending to drown is on par with acting like mass-murdering bank robbers.

me: Whatever. But in a restaurant? So the brother starts screaming, too, and tries pulling the sister back on her chair.

judy: Admirable. Mike would have let you drown.

me: And the whole time the parents are just sitting there sharing a Caesar salad and sipping their Chianti and offering the occasional, whisper of, "Kids ... " I mean, really? Just a softly spoken "kids" as a means of discipline? As if reminding them of what they are will shock the a-hole behavior out of them?

judy: You can't call kids a-holes! They're kids!

me: Oh, please, you're as bad as Bart!

judy: Right. What was this horrible, insurmountable thing he did?

me: He laughed! Like it was *cute* or something.

judy: Unforgiveable!

me: These kids were downright annoying and clearly not being parented! And yes, I am turning into you because I caught myself doing those loud sighs you tend to do when you're irritated and want to passive-aggressively let the cause of your irritation know.

judy: I seldom get irritated anymore. I just let everything roll right off my back because I believe it's happening for a reason.

me: Please. I was on the phone with you when that "minivan-driving highway Nazi asshat" took your parking space.

judy: So Bart has more patience than you do. Big deal.

me: It is a big deal and here's why. Not only was he unfazed by the kids' unruly behavior but he said he wished he could play, too. He said, "Kids get to have the most fun. Anytime. Anywhere."

judy: That can't surprise you. You bought him Legos for Christmas.

me: That wasn't the surprising part. The look on his face was what surprised me. It was almost *wistful*. Like he enjoyed the noise and chaos of those kids.

judy: Not everyone breaks out in hives and develops stomach upset at the sight of Thomas the Train like you do.

me: So I have no choice but to ask him. 'Bart, do you actually *like* kids?' And he says ... Oh, God, it's too painful. I can't say it.

judy: *Tell me!*

me: He said, "Sure!" Turns out Bart fancies himself a dad someday.

judy: Yay, Bart! I like him more and more.

me: Please. You just like what he represents: The Holy Grailmother.

judy: Didn't you guys ever talk about having kids? I thought it might have come up somewhere between your third date and talking about moving in together.

me: Well, yeah, but in abstract terms. Like when we're both lying on our respective couches and too lazy to get up we say things like "If we had a kid, we could make him get us a couple of beers and a bag of chips right now."

judy: I think you'd be a wonderful mother. You learned from the best.

me: Did I? Hmm, I don't remember her. Maybe I could Google her sometime.

judy: You're an a-hole.

me: Hey! I thought we weren't supposed to call kids a-holes!

judy: I'm a mother. We make the rules and we can break the rules. You
      should try it sometime.

So okay, I don't have kids, and I think we established that I'm not their
biggest fan. Childless adults are actually pretty common these days,
especially in Seattle. Did you know there are more dogs than babies
living in my fair city? I know—it's the unmother ship, and I kind of love
Seattle even more because of it. Here's the weird thing: Judy apparently
doesn't know I don't have kids. How is this possible? I mean, I *know*
babies magically happen. I've seen their births reenacted on that television show where clueless women come out of Mexican restaurants
thinking they should have taken it easy on those chips and guac and
next thing you know they're hunkering down behind the dumpster
watching a baby head magically appear from beneath their miniskirt!
But that would never happen to me. I'm much too old for miniskirts.
(But I have been known to polish off a burrito the size of my thigh. Those
women on TV are wimps.)

It would appear that poor Judy is so blinded by Grandma Envy she has
taken another cue from her beloved book, *The Secret*, and acts like I either
have kids or am in the process of trying to get them. She sends me links
to articles about parenting strategies and hot trends.

Infant Stress Leads to Angry Adults!

What stress? Pooping, eating, and sleeping? Bring it on, you big babies!

Obese Women Have Less Sex but More Babies!

(See "burrito the size of my thigh.")

40+ Baby Boom on the Rise as Moms Decide to Wait on Parenthood!

I think this one speaks for itself.

I'm not quite forty, but I'm sure Judy is reassured by this random study
done by a small focus group somewhere off the coast of Suwarrow Island.
My usual response to these news items is firing back with a study conducted somewhere off the coast of my couch proving that mothers who
guilt their daughters into parenthood are ninety-seven times more likely
to end up in subpar assisted-living homes.

"Did you read the story about the girl who retaliated against her bullish
mother by publishing a tell-all memoir that included pictures of her mom
in a bathing suit?" I'd ask Judy.

"You wouldn't dare," she would snap.

"I have photos. And a scanner. Keep the baby books coming and see for yourself."

The spam usually stops. As much as I am terrified of not having contact solution (see Chapter 5), Judy lives in fear of someone other than those who were lucky enough to be sprung from her loins and the man who put them there (ew) ever seeing her in a bathing suit. But apparently her memory is as bad as mine and she'll be back to her old tricks in no time.

"The name Judith is making a comeback," she said one morning. "I'd be honored, thank you."

"Get a goldfish."

Here's the thing. I'm not against kids. I'm sure there are plenty of good ones out there. Some who will grow up to be the doctors who might cure my illness or go on to star in reality shows I'll obsess over in my golden years. Some of my friends have kids, and I like spending time with them for a few minutes here and there. I just never felt the pull to be a mom. At least not to a human.

Now show me a sad-eyed pit bull on a TV ad for the ASPCA and I'm in tears. I *do* feel the pull to adopt animals. As many as the city of Seattle and my homeowners association will allow me to. The other day I was watching a show called *When Vacations Attack* (don't ask—there really is no bar when it comes to what I'll watch on TV) and it showed amateur footage from that massive earthquake in Sichuan. It was chill-inducing. Totally awful. People were scattering in all directions, running for their lives. Mountains were literally exploding and tearing through towns ready to engulf those in their path. Tourists, locals, kids. Buildings collapsed like tindersticks. It was horrifying, to say the least.

"That sucks," I said to Bart. "How many faults is Seattle built on again?"

"Remember when the power went out at our hotel in Bellingham?" Bart asked. "And we were pissed because we couldn't chill our champagne in the minifridge? They should put that on this show."

I nodded, shoving another handful of Pirate's Booty into my mouth. "Amen."

Then I saw something truly tragic—a man running toward the camera, carrying a baby panda by its armpits. I totally lost it.

"Save the paaaaaaaaaaaaaaaaaaanda!!!!!!!!! How can they show this stuff on television? I'm calling Comcast right now!"

"You're sick," is what Judy would say about my reaction.

She is not an animal lover. Doesn't even like to see squirrels in her yard. Therefore she cannot fathom how one can experience heart-bursting joy watching a dog's paw move when she's dreaming. And that little sleep *woopf woopf woopf*. I die every time. But I can relate to Judy's animal apathy because I assume it's the same feeling mothers and fathers to human children must have that prevent them from vomiting into their diaper genies at the mere sight of Desitin.

With the exception of those that bear the same last name as my friends and loved ones, I don't like kids. I don't have an unfettered desire to hug a baby when it rolls by in its big pimped-out stroller. I don't even know how to properly hold a baby, which is why I have rules about being in the same room with babies:

1. Don't assume I want to hold your baby and toss it in my arms. I most likely do not want to hold your baby, and forcing me to is one step away from child abuse.
2. In the rare event that I do want to hold your baby, please don't leave the room. My urge is subject to change on a dime.
3. I will only hold babies while I am sitting down. Preferably on a couch. Preferably with a cushion to support my right arm. Babies get heavy really fast.
4. If the baby cries, squirms, passes gas, smells funny, or soils its diapers, please take it back immediately.
5. If the baby makes a poop face, he's yours. Hope you can catch. I. Don't. Do. Poop.

"But you have a box of poop in your living room," my friends kindly remind me, referring to Zelda's bathroom. I have nowhere else to put it, okay? And scooping litter is a lot different than digging green snot bubbles out of your offspring's nose—I can't even go there.

Ugh. I went there.

Maybe I'm not a baby person because I wasn't ever around them. My youngest cousins are only five and seven years my junior, so I was way too young to be trusted with their care. I only babysat once when I was twelve and that was for a toddler whose parents had MTV. I didn't do as much babysitting as Bon Jovi-watching and calling my twelve-year-old girlfriends at their babysitting jobs to make sure they were watching Bon Jovi, too. The sounds of babies crying and kids acting up make my spine rigid and my teeth clench. I can practically feel my ovaries shriveling up and moving to Boca Raton when I see or hear a kid having a meltdown. I know I should feel sorry for the parents. It's not their fault (I'm told) that their kids are acting like ... well, kids. But still, how dare there be an unhappy child in my radius? (I am immune to barking dogs, by the way. I know ... I know....)

"I think you'd be a really good mom," Bart said out of the blue one day.

"Why the hell would you say that?" I asked. I had a homemade apple crisp in the oven and was putting away laundry at the time so I sincerely hoped it wasn't some antiquated 1950s stereotype he was secretly harboring. Jeez. Maybe we do need to spend more time "getting to know" one another.

"You're very nurturing and generous," he said. "And you're good at putting Ikea furniture together. I think that would come in handy."

I generously toss Zelda off the couch and spread three months worth of magazines and catalogs out on the Ikea bedside tables. "Thanks. I guess." There are worse things he could have said to me, right?

But this conversation wasn't over. "And I think I would be a good dad."

"You'd be a playful one, for sure. But more important, do you want to be?"

There was a long pause before he answered quite simply, "Yes."

It's possible Bart's fatherhood fantasies involve always having someone to play D&D with and a reason to buy *Star Wars* action figures again. Not to dismiss his feelings, but I think there are parts of parenthood he glossed over. Like the part about "your freedom to do pretty much anything on a whim is O.V.E.R."

One night we were at a German bar around the corner.

"You know," I began after taking a long, hearty sip of my Spezial, "If we had a kid we couldn't just spontaneously decide to come out for a beer. These outings would have to be planned well in advance and likely cost us $10 an hour."

"Sure we could," he answered back. "We'd just put the baby to bed and bring the monitor here. Those things have insane ranges."

Please tell me he's not reading *Consumer Reports* for the latest in baby gear. "How do you know that?"

"They're the poor man's walkie-talkie," he answered. "Sean and I used them in our cars when we were moving his brother down to Eugene."

That made sense, but back to his initial statement. Even *I* knew there was something very wrong with bringing a baby monitor into a bar.

"Let me get this straight. You think it's okay to leave our baby home alone while we come to a bar a few doors down, prop the baby monitor on the bar, and proceed to get pie-eyed on Doppelbocks?"

"Why not? We'd hear her if she cried and the time it would take to get home is probably the same amount it would take to get to her room."

"Or maybe sooner, considering Child Protective Services would probably drive us."

Bart just laughed. "It's a great idea! But if you're worried what people would think, we could probably just stick the monitor in your purse."

After the beer-versus-baby monitor incident, we found ourselves at Crate & Barrel shopping for our friend's wedding gift.

"Check that out," Bart said, pointing to a wall-mounted tea light candle-holder. "Wouldn't that be the coolest kid nightlight ever?"

"You want to give a kid a wall of fire as a nightlight?" I asked.

He shrugged. "Why not? Sleeping by candlelight is very soothing."

"So is falling asleep to the sounds of your parents playing foosball and downing pints at the neighborhood bar, I guess."

Sometimes I think I have to have Bart's kid just to save her from her father.

"I think it might be slightly dangerous," I said.

Bart looked heartbroken. "Maybe when she's older," he said.

I made the mistake of telling Judy about both of these incidents. Maybe I was hoping she'd agree—we should not be responsible for the care and well-being of anything on two legs—but it had the opposite effect.

"He daydreams about nightlights and baby monitors? Oh, I just love him!"

"Nightlights made of *fire*, Judy! Can you get footed PJs made out of gypsum? Because she's going to need them!"

"Oh, he's just saying that now. Once he's a father he won't want to take any chances. He'll be a great father."

That I agree with. I *do* think he'd be a great father. Me, I'm not so sure about.

Everyone's a self-help expert when it comes to raising someone else's kids, imaginary or otherwise. Baby crying in a restaurant? Take him outside! Teenager stealing your Budweiser and Midol? Hello, Army! Toddler tossing a tantrum in the shoe department at Nordstrom? For the love of all things holy, teach that child to have some respect for culture! See? It's easy! And I don't even know how to change a diaper!

That Dr. Spock guy seems cool enough, but wow, did he open the door for "well-meaning" experts to offer up the unsolicited child-rearing advice. But maybe the number of advice books out there teaching people how not to raise rude, inconsiderate, SAT-failing jackasses is telltale that it's *not* easy to raise kids. Personally, I'd like to find the quack that encouraged mothers in the 1970s to take diet pills while preggers because they were "gaining too much weight."

Umm, Mom? You were growing a person inside you. A little weight gain is normal.

There's at least a common theme here. You don't want your kids to suck and neither do the rest of us. Poking around the bookshelves of my breeder friends, I noticed two things.

1. They have a lot of books on parenting.
2. I bought a lot of these books on parenting for them. What? They make great shower gifts.

Most of the books cover five basics: communication, involvement, education, discipline, and punishment. Once you master these, congratulations! Your kid can go outside now.

Is nothing left to instinct anymore? Look at how animal mothers protect their babies. I'm pretty sure they're not reading books.

Judy "Make Me a Grandma" Mazzanoble has another way of illustrating the joys of procreating. She tells me about how awesome other people's kids are.

"Little Hunter, the neighbor's daughter's best friend's godson?" Judy began, "was in his second cousin's wedding and burst out crying when he saw his tuxedo because he wanted to wear a red T-shirt like Winnie the Pooh! How cute is that?"

"Who wears a red T-shirt to a wedding?" I asked. "Unless you're a *Star Trek* security guard."

"He was a ring bearer!" she yelled. "Get it? bearer? *Bear*? Like Winnie the Pooh?"

"Oh."

"Oh, come on! You'd think it was funny if it was a dog!"

"Yeah," I agreed. "A dog who burst out crying because it was forced to wear a tuxedo instead of a red shirt like Winnie the Pooh? Anyone would find that funny. I'm laughing just thinking about it."

And then I got the whole why-are-you-so-heartless-and-cruel speech. Obviously I'm just torturing her by letting all that perfectly good DNA she passed on go to waste.

There are people who swear they didn't like kids until they had their own.

"You like them when they're yours," my friend Stacy told me. "But I still think other people's suck."

"But what if you don't like them *and* they're yours? It's not like there's a trial period." I like to remind Stacy of Joan Crawford, who clearly did not like kids, even ones she willingly adopted.

Another friend pointed out that you only notice kids who make themselves noticeable. How many sleeping, cuddly, quietly-playing-with-their-plastic-key-chain-set children do I walk by on a daily basis, unaware of their existence? Plenty, I'm sure. But I can't help notice the crying, pooping, flopping-around-on-the-cool-tile-floor-like-Ice-T-in-*Breakin'* babies. They, like Kim Kardashian's butt, are just begging to be noticed.

Those noticeable kids cross my path more times than I care to admit. Sometimes I wonder if we're all born with a super power and mine is the ability to unleash the inner demon of those three feet tall and under.

Take that rotten six-year-old who was in line behind me at Gorditos. There I was trying to decide between a fajita or a quesadilla when, *wham!*—I felt a thump on my right butt cheek.

"Excuse me," I said turning around to find a frowning little bastard with clenched fists. "Did you just punch me in the butt?"

He spun around to bury his face in his dad's crotch. Dad looked totally mortified, but I wasn't sure if that was because his kid just punched a stranger in the ass cheek or because his son's face was about a mile deep in his crotch.

"Did your son just punch me in the butt?" I asked the dad. "Because if he didn't, you did, and that's equally horrifying."

"I'm sorry!" the dad said. "He's sorry! I'm sure he is. Tyler tell the nice woman you're sorry!"

But Tyler refused to look at me, preferring the denim safety of his daddy's crotch. He wasn't sorry, and I was pretty sure neither was his dad. I know he couldn't wait to leave so he could get back in his Land Rover, stick a Bluetooth in his ear, and call everyone he knew on the way home to tell them about how little Tyler thumped an uptight, childless woman right in the ass. Probably trying to knock what eggs were left right out of my ovaries. "That'll teach her not to have kids!"

My pummeled butt cheek will be heralded across the land at Christmas parties, office functions, and Tyler's next thirty birthday parties. And Tyler, seeing the reaction random acts of assault garners from his daddy, will spend the next three decades whacking stranger's private parts. That's how it begins—one day you're bored, waiting for your chimichanga, and you suddenly lose patience with the entire world so *wham!* Hit a stranger in the butt. Pay it forward. You'll feel better.

Now conversely, I am no stranger to bad behavior exhibited by something under my care. My friends are terrified of my cat. Yes, she's been known to attach herself to a forearm or two and bunny kick the skin away like she's peeling a zucchini, but for the most part she just wants her head scratched. Don't get me wrong—I think cats are evil. But they usually give a warning before they attack. Their tails snap like a freshly laundered sheet in the wind, their ears point backward. But a kid? Nothing. No sign. No symptom. And clearly no provoking needed. No one is safe in the presence of children.

But similar to cats they can tell when you don't like them. You know how cats sidle on up to the one who's deathly allergic to them? Kids can sense that crap, too. You don't like them? Fine. Be a hater. But you'll pay for that negative attitude. Oh, you'll pay.

Shelly Mazzanoble

Big Wheel Hooligan is proof of that. I encountered him a few months after my ass cheek was assaulted. Bart and I were walking to a neighborhood restaurant for breakfast when we passed a kid on a Big Wheel.

"Big Wheel!" I said, remembering my old Wonder Woman wheels. I was so bad-ass on that thing, pedaling as fast and furious as I could down from the corner of Harrison to our driveway, four houses down. Four houses, on a Big Wheel, when you're six, is a lot of freakin' effort. It's the equivalent of traveling from Phoenix to the Badlands by foot. *In the dead of summer.* Just trust me, okay? And when I got to my driveway, I yanked up the little hand brake, causing me to do a donut and spin out in the foamy puddle of Dawn dish soap left behind from Dad washing the station wagon. See? Bad-ass.

I was smiling and thinking how cool it was that Big Wheels were still around as we passed the kid and fell deeper into nostalgia when I heard the telltale sound of Big Wheel tires on cement.

"Oh, the memories!" I said. "Doesn't that just sound like summer?"

And then I thought, hmm, that sounds like it's getting closer and closer. And then, weird. This sidewalk isn't that wide. If I didn't know better, I'd say it's almost as if this little boy on his Big Wheel is chasing us.

Just as I was about to mention this to Bart, the heel of my sneaker was torn from my ankle and a pair of handlebars rammed up against my calves.

"Owwwwwwww!" I shrieked, tripping over some shrubbery. "Watch where you're going! What's wrong with you? Texting while driving again?"

"Aw, come on," Bart encouraged. "He's just a kid. It's okay. He didn't mean it."

And then Kid Evil pedaled his Big Wheel in reverse, unramming the handlebars from my calves, surveyed the damage, decided it wasn't quite good enough, and came at me again.

"Stop it!" I yelled, hoping to get the attention of the pack of wolves that clearly raised this beast. "Get him off me! Go home, kid! Shoo! Beat it!"

He reversed again but he wasn't going home to atone for his sins. He was gathering momentum for a third attack.

"Bart! Do something!"

Bart practically dislocated a rib from laughing so hard. He fell on someone's lawn, grabbing his butt and guffawing like the true gentleman and hero that he is.

"Ahhh!" I yelled. "Someone get this little monster away from me!"

Kid Evil didn't speak. He just glared at me with these dead, gray eyes. I swear to God we fought something similar to his kind in D&D last week. If only I knew how to smite undead.

When he reversed a fourth time I ran for it, pulling Bart up by the wrist and running down the sidewalk. We ran for probably twenty blocks, way past the restaurant, until we felt secure enough to look behind us. The kid was nowhere in sight, but I wouldn't have been surprised to see him pop out from behind a dumpster or the back of a Volkswagen. I hadn't seen the last of that little hell on wheels, I was sure of it.

"Was that weird?" Bart asked, "Getting assaulted by a kid on a Big Wheel? That was weird, right?"

"I'd like to say it was," I said, "but given my history, it's actually pretty normal."

"Your history?" Bart asked, sounding a bit concerned. All this time I tried to shield him from the real me.

"Think of me as some kind of Cruella De Vil understudy and everyone younger than the age of ten are children of the corn hell-bent on taking me down."

"Maybe they sense your fear," he said. "Like dogs."

"I wish they were like dogs. I can handle dogs. Dogs listen to me."

Bart raised an eyebrow and smirked.

"Most listen to me. If I have a dog biscuit. But if we had kids, we'd have to donate them to science just days after they're born. Or give them to Judy."

He laughed. "That's not true! You're great with kids!"

Now I laughed. "Give me an example! When have you ever seen me interact with kids?"

He thought about this for a while before thoughtfully answering: "Just now?"

"See what I mean?"

"But wait," he interjected. "That's not true. Your friends have kids. You're nice to them."

"I send cards on their birthdays and make sure their moms get home safe when we go out drinking. Yep, I'm a regular Ronald McDonald."

"That's a terrible example," he said. "Ronald is creepy. No one likes that guy."

"Fine. I'm Angelina Jolie."

"Err . . . "

"Whatever. You get my point."

We walked a couple more blocks in silence before Bart piped up again. "You played D&D with that brother and sister at Gen Con! You were nice to them and they were nice to you!"

He's right, I did play with a seven- and a nine-year-old. Their father was playing in a delve and the kids were just sitting there looking a little lost. Bart and I had some spare time so we ran them through a very basic, scaled back adventure that involved a rabbit named "Chubbyfeet" and some very delicious macaroni. (We let them flavor the adventure Mad Libs style.)

"That doesn't count," I told him. "We were role-playing. They had imaginary heroes and ice picks. I wasn't going to mess with them."

Not to be deterred, Bart insisted the kids weren't playacting. "The little girl hugged you when she left. She clearly had fun with you."

I don't bother telling him my suspicions that her awkward, around-the-waist hug was a lame attempt to get at my wallet. Mission failed because I don't carry a wallet in my back pocket, but I never did find my dice after that. Besides, it wasn't me the kids liked. It was most likely Bart and the voices he gave Chubbyfeet and friends and the magical powers the game gave them. Who can compete with that?

Perhaps Little Tyler and the Big Wheeled Bandit could benefit from a little playmat action. Punch an orc in the butt, Tyler, not a nice lady. Run over a kobold with your Big Wheel, Little Demon. He's a bad, bad monster, not a girl looking to fulfill her craving for buckwheat pancakes. Even Judy is hard-pressed to deny D&D has its benefits for kids.

"I would have loved it if you and your brother played D&D," she said. "That means you would have had friends, right? Like human friends and not stuffed animals or the adulterers and hysterically pregnant residents of Pine Valley."

I don't bother reminding her that D&D is a game that requires use of your imagination, and therefore it was likely Mike and I would have figured out a way to play with Mr. Bunny Pants and Erica Kane.

The "friends" thing is true and I can't help but imagine I would have found a better group to pal around with than the mean little hens I tried desperately to fit in with.

In fifth grade I invited my "friend" Beth for lunch. She was a notorious two-timer who would be your friend until something better came along. On this particular upstate New York winter day, something better, in the form of the Evil Trio, came along. Beth and I were on one side of the street while the Evil Trio was on the other. The trio catcalled to us, encouraging Beth to ditch me (and Judy's famous liverwurst sandwiches; *that* was the real crime). Beth obviously believed in quantity over quality in her friendships. She whispered a half-assed "sorry" as she crossed the slush-filled street. They cheered her decision and continued yelling fifth-grade insults at me until I made a left on Matthews Street and they continued onto Park. I ate both liverwurst sandwiches listening to Judy explain to me all the reasons that Beth was a loser, anyway.

I didn't give Beth the boot after that. I took her back when she asked if she could come over after school a few days later to watch the *Magic Garden*. Apparently I subscribed to the quantity-over-quality belief, too. I thought if Beth and I had a "shared experience"—a stupid commercial, an after-school special, my brother's friend's first zit—our friendship would somehow become tangible. Or at least strong enough to keep her on my side of the street.

"Hey, Beth!" I would shout across the bustling lunchroom. "Remember that commercial we saw yesterday with the guy who was wearing those pants? What was up with those pants?"

Anything we could witness together and recap, with heads tossed back in laughter the next day at school, would prove to the Evil Trio and everyone else that we were cemented in friendship. Sadly, there was nothing up with that guy's pants. At least not enough for Beth and me to bond over.

"What guy?" she asked, with this silly, confused look on her face. Clearly she was taking great pleasure out of embarrassing me. "I have no idea what you're talking about."

Of course the other girls jumped on the Shelly's-talking-crazy bandwagon. After school, those bitches followed me to the corner of Matthews and Schubert Streets shouting vague, inane questions at each other.

"Terry, what was the color of that car?"

"Do you remember that hat, Beth?"

"What was up with the peanut butter, Molly?"

Oh, they were hysterical, they were. If only I had a fireball, I'd have blasted the whole lot of them. Instead I used the next best thing.

The next day after school I went up to Beth and punched her square in the jaw. The surprise knocked her off her feet, and instead of walking away (I had proven my point, after all) I couldn't resist her shocked, flailing horizontal body, and took it as an invitation to keep punching her. My fists of fury pummeled her until the crossing guard pulled me off and made Peter Winter's mom go inside the school to call Judy. Apparently I was a menace to the streets and couldn't be trusted to roam alone.

When Judy and her green Cordoba rolled up to the crosswalk, the crossing guard stuck his head inside the driver's side window.

"Shelly took a couple of cheap shots," he said. "But that girl deserved it." Then he winked at me.

"Wait until your father hears about this," Judy said, pulling away from the scene of my crime.

I couldn't wait. He's the one who taught me those cheap shots.

I knew what a shared experience felt like in theory, but didn't realize these things have to happen organically. Just like they do in a D&D game.

If you play, you know what I mean. Those moments you can't stop talking about. The new catchphrase that springs from them. The song you'll never be able to hear again without thinking of your bard. The diversions and tangents and made-up words that will be part of your vernacular forever.

How many times have you wished you could go back in time to the ten-year-old-you and offer some advice? I'd tell the little Shelly she needs to quit making fun of those boys who draw dragons and castles in the margins of their notebooks and befriend them immediately! Judy would be thrilled to make liverwurst sandwiches for your Wednesday D&D group.

The following Friday after work, I headed off to Gig Harbor to see my friend Des. We have been trying to get together for months. She's a mom of two, works part-time, and now lives nearly an hour outside of Seattle. Our days of running into each other while stocking up on Red Hook and blue corn chips at Fred Meyer are over. If we want to have quality time it needs to be scheduled around dentist appointments, day care schedules, and Nordstrom Anniversary Sales months in advance. Thanks to her work-from-home schedule and my half-day Fridays, we finally found a date that worked.

Des opened the door to find me laden down with gift-wrapped packages and homemade cookies. I missed a lot of birthdays and holidays since the last time I saw her.

"I'm here for my play date," I told her, throwing myself into her arms.

Des led me into the family room where Gabe, her five-year-old, and Ruby, her three-year-old, were sitting quietly in front of the television watching one of the few kid cartoons I know.

"Hey, that's *Dora the Explorer!*" I announced.

Des laughed. "How do *you* know who that is?"

"The kid I sponsored for the Giving Tree three years ago was into her."

Des stood in front of the television. "Don't you guys want to say hello to our guest?"

Gabe eyed the wrapped packages I was carrying. Sorry, Dora. You're good but you've got nothing on a stranger with gifts and cookies. Gabe and Ruby crept closer to me.

Ruby looked at me with a modicum of skepticism because she's not entirely sure who I am, but her mom and brother seem to think I'm okay. Gabe remembered me and broke into a wide grin. "Hellooooooooo, Shelleeeeeeee!"

His enthusiasm is warranted. He's the reason behind Rule #5 about poop and takes great pride in that. I may never forgive him or Des for that time he filled his diaper when I was holding him. I saw the face, heard the sounds, even felt the pureed fruits of his labors pressing against my arm.

Everything I Need to Know I Learned from D&D
159

"He's pooping on my arm!" I shrieked. "Ahhhhhh! Get him off me before it gets on me!"

But Des couldn't do a thing about it because she was crumpled up on the kitchen floor in a fit of laughter. Nice. At least when Zelda attacks my guests, I help them apply Neosporin and *act* contrite. A few years later I reminded Gabe of that incident. His response?

"I know."

"Really?" I asked him. "You know? You were four months old."

"I remember," he said. "It was so funny!"

So funny that he spent the rest of that visit wearing nothing but his Underoos and trying to get on my lap for a repeat performance. We need a new tradition before the kid turns sixteen.

I should be able to hang with Gabe because he's really not a kid. I mean he is, he's six, but he's a very *adult* six. This was true even when he was born. For one thing, his feet were so big they didn't even fit on the birth certificate. He didn't bother with the goo goo gaga gaga warm-up chatter like other babies. He went right into making complete sentences. When he was a year and a half old he greeted me at the front door wearing his Alex P. Keaton button-down and baby Dockers and said, "Welcome, Shelly. Would you like a kiwi? How about some bottled water?"

What kid knows what a kiwi is? He even corrects my grammar. If he weren't so cute he'd be annoying.

"Yeah!" Gabe continued with his cheer. "I'm gonna poop on you!"

Here we go again.

I gave them their presents: a baby doll and play make-up for Ruby and an X-Men inflatable punching bag for Gabe. He was appeased for the moment, way more interested in hitting his sister with the punching bag than pooping on my arm.

Des pulled a bottle of red wine from the cabinet. It's weird having friends who live in houses not just with kids but with wine *cabinets*. It's nice and all, but to me it's just another barrier to getting to it. Before she can finish filling the glasses her phone rings.

"It's my boss," she said. "Better take this now rather than after a few of these." She took her wine glass into her office.

"Shelly! Look at this!" Gabe called from the living room.

He positioned Ruby and her baby so that when he punched the bag, it hit them both on the head.

"That's awesome, Gabe," I said, filling my glass to the rim.

Gabe hit her again. "Look!"

Not really paying attention, I tried to change up my reaction to make it look like I am. "Yikes! Ow! Ruby is so tough."

Ruby, who has been patiently taking the hits, decided she's not that tough after all and should really be wailing her face off.

Des poked her head out of the office, and I shrugged my shoulders. "I didn't do it."

She made a motion with her free hand that points from the living room to the phone in her other hand.

"You want me to bring the kids to you?" I asked.

She violently shook her head and pointed at the living room and then me.

"You want me to go into the living room? With a full glass of wine? I don't know if that's such a good idea."

"*Mommy!*"

Next Des was pointing from me to Ruby and then making little *shoo* motions with the back of her hand.

Her boss must be on some kind of tirade because it looks like she's trying to tell me to get in there and calm her kids down. Ha! That's crazy talk. What does she think I am? Super Nanny?

"Get in there and calm them down," Des hissed at me.

Huh. I was right.

She put her hand over the mouthpiece. "Please? I've got a small crisis here. I'll be done in a minute."

"Um, okay. I guess."

Maybe I could call Judy and ask her how to quiet a screaming three-year-old.

"Hey, you guys," I said in a voice so sweet I'm giving myself a brain freeze. "You want to maybe stop crying and, um, take naps or something?"

Ruby responded by screeching even louder. My goodness, that kid has pipes.

"Oh, please don't do that. Your mommy is on the phone and I don't want her to think I'm hurting you."

Little red-faced Ruby pointed at Gabe and sobbed harder. Gabe stared at Ruby with a look that read partially contrite and somewhat disdainful.

I sat near Ruby. Should I touch her? Offer a hug? Or would that backfire and bring back painful memories of getting clobbered in the face by an inflatable Wolverine? I've seen enough movies starring Valerie Bertinelli to know this is a distinct possibility.

"I have a big brother, too, you know," I told her. "Sometimes he would hit me, sometimes by accident, and I would cry my face off. Kind of like you."

Ruby sniveled at the thought. "You can cry your face off?"

"Sure," I said, believing this will encourage her to stop crying. "If you cry hard enough or long enough it will just melt right off."

"No, I don't wanna cry off my face!"

Oops. Might have had the opposite effect here. Man, kids are gullible. Des poked her head out of the office again.

"It's all good," I shouted. "Nothing to see here!"

"Ruby, it's okay. You can't really cry your face off. That will never happen."

"You lied?" she asked, looking more traumatized than she did back when she believed her face was in danger of disappearing.

"Not lied," I said. "I was kidding. There's a difference." Why do I have explain this? Doesn't Dora teach them anything?

"Did your brother ever poop on you?" Gabe wanted to know.

"Nope, he didn't, thank you very much."

This set Gabe off again and I think I saw the beginning of a smile on Ruby's face.

"What did he do to you?" she asked between sobs.

"Well, he would sometimes sneak up and then tickle me until I called 'uncle!'" With that I lunged at Gabe's belly and started tickling him, having no idea if this was appropriate behavior or not. Ruby thought so as she gleefully joined in.

When Gabe had had enough, he yelled *uncle* and we helped him stand up.

Des joined us, looking more frantic than when she was trying to get me to care for her kids using gestures and finger pointing.

"What's up?" I asked.

"I'm so sorry," she said, looking like she's about to cry. "My boss needs me to run a report right now. It's really important, otherwise I'd say it could wait until Monday. Would you give me a half hour to do it? You could just hang out here with the kids?"

She said this last part the same way I'd say to someone, "Maybe you could use this disposable razor to cut off your right arm and proceed to whip yourself across the face with it?"

"Me? Hang with the kids?"

"For a half hour. Maybe forty-five minutes? Okay, an hour tops!"

Wow. I think I'll take the use-my-right-arm-to-beat-myself-in-the-face option, please. "Is there a neighbor who could come over? I'm willing to pay."

"I'm sorry," she said, shutting her office door. "I'll be as fast as I can."

Clearly she was in a bind and felt bad. This wasn't how either of us planned to spend our Friday afternoon. Besides, I see her kids maybe once a year. Is it really the worst thing to actually get to know them?

"There's markers and construction paper in the cabinet under the television," Des shouted from the other side of the door. "And feel free to put in a movie! A *kids'* movie, please!"

Gabe and Ruby were quiet. They stopped all movement and looked at me. The quiet they exhibited unsettled me. The calm before the storm. The stillness of the water before the shark attacks. The showdown in a western movie where the hero meets the bad guy. We are face to face (to face) in our stance, guns twirling at our hips, waiting for the other person to make a move.

"So," I said.

"So," they said.

"Who wants to watch a movie?"

Gabe shook his head. "Nah. We've seen movies."

"No movie!" Ruby screamed in agreement.

I rustled through the kitchen cabinets. "How about an all-natural peanut butter sandwich with some sugar-free, organic jelly? On gluten-free bread, of course. Yum, yum, doesn't that sound good?"

"Gross," said Gabe.

"Ew!" Ruby bellowed.

"Okay, how about we draw some pictures."

Again Gabe vetoed my suggestion. "I drew pictures yesterday in school."

"Me, too!" Ruby said.

Gabe pushed her. "No, you didn't! You don't go to school!"

Getting called out like that set Ruby off again. She wailed like a Midwest siren during tornado season. Obviously I couldn't let Des be bothered by this commotion. I'm an adult with two generally well-behaved kids I outweigh by at least sixty pounds. I could handle this.

"Okay, okay. Let's play a game!" I said, trying to make those four words sound like the most awesome idea ever to pass through their budding eardrums. "Doesn't that sound fun?"

I hoped they wouldn't be turned off by the creepy, singsong, reeking-of-panic, psychotic manner in which I was talking to them. Why do people take on such weird vocal inflections when talking to kids? Other people do this, right?

The potential game was interesting enough to Ruby to get her to stop screaming but not enough to stop the waterworks and runny nose. I handed her a tissue.

"You might want to take care of that," I said, pointing to her nasal area. Seriously, bubbling kid snot gives me an immediate gag reflex.

"How about charades?" I jumped up and started pantomiming something that could be a combination of jazz hands and "girl being held up by chorus members from West Side Story."

"No!"

"Hide and Seek?"

VITAMIN D&D

Whether you play D&D with your kids or raise your future kids with the same attention to detail and compassion as you would your PC, D&D can be as much a positive influence on kids as Vitamin C, a good night's sleep, and Big Bird. Why? Because kids love to pretend, as evidenced by my Nemesis 1 and Nemesis 2. (I'm going to pretend Tyler thought I was The Joker and he was doing our fellow patrons of Gorditos a favor by attacking me because otherwise I can't bear the thought of living in the same zip code with that goon.) And kids love fantasy. You probably did, too, when you were growing up. But what do I know? I work in Marketing. And . . . I've never conducted any studies off any coast of anywhere and kids don't even like me. But you would trust a librarian, right? And I know plenty of librarians who will back me up.

I've had the pleasure of meeting several librarians as part of my job. Every year, Wizards packs up the Old English Bookshop-themed booth and deposits it on the floor of the American Librarian Association. Let me tell you, librarians are some of the nicest people on the planet. (And OMG, they sure like the wine!) I feel really bad for how poorly I treated Miss Roach, my elementary school librarian. Miss Roach, if you're reading this, I'm sorry. I was loud and obnoxious and I made fun of your name and your weird haircut and your slouchy bathrobe-like cardigans. The thought of you traipsing through the Anaheim Convention Center with your Vera Bradley satchel full of books and pamphlets and stickers all geared toward making me a lifelong reader makes me feel rather guilty. I do love reading, and if you want to take the credit for it, that's cool. (Never learned to spell, though. You don't have to take credit for that.)

Anyway, these librarians, maybe even Miss Roach, will agree—kids love reading about magic and dragons and mysterious worlds. They eat up ettin, devour doppelgangers, and strive to become sorcerers. And when they find one book that interests them, they want more books just like it. Guess what? D&D has all that and lots more like reading, writing, math, social and analytical skills, and cooperation, just to name a few. What better way to teach kids all of the above, then, when they don't know they're learning?

"No!"

I was about to suggest we do what I did at about their age and find a nice little daytime drama on television when I heard Judy's voice.

I would have loved it if you and your brother played D&D.

"Er ... how about Dungeons & Dragons?" I asked.

"What's that?" Gabe asked.

"It's a game about make-believe," I said. "You two are mighty heroes with magical powers and weapons on a quest where you'll encounter all sorts of treasure and adventure and the occasional bad guy."

"Yeah for treasure!" Ruby cheered.

"Yeah for weapons!" Gabe cheered. "I want to be Wolverine!"

"I'm Cinderella!"

Gabe rolled his eyes. "Cinderella isn't a hero! She's a dumb old princess!"

I saw Ruby's lip begin to quiver so I jumped in.

"She can be Cinderella! Or better yet, she can be a magical princess wizard. Would you like that, Ruby?"

She beamed. "Yes!"

"And you, Gabe, can be a brave human fighter. That sounds fun, right?"

He is the same guy who keeps smacking his sister in the face with a shmoo, after all.

"Yeah!"

I had them both cheering at this point.

"Oh, okay, let's bust out the Doritos and Mountain Dew!" I shouted, knowing full well if Des heard this she'd probably smack *me* upside the head with an inflatable punching bag. Offering her kids Doritos and full-sugar soda is like suggesting we walk down to the Kwik Fill and score ourselves some black tar heroin.

We went in search of every board game they owned that uses dice. Good thing I happen to have a d20 in my purse. (Who doesn't?)

I excused myself to find the second computer in the house—the one the kids use to play alphabet bingo and take math quizzes for fun. I download a copy of *Heroes of Hesiod*—a kid-friendly adventure R&D created for the sole purpose of giving babysitters something to do with kids on Dora overload. And teach them the principles of D&D. I printed out a copy of the adventure and all the necessary accoutrements. I worked on my character voices in Gabe and Ruby's Jack-and-Jill bathroom. Chubbyfeet I'm not, but I can do a pretty good Count Chocula.

Next, I somehow managed to convince Gabe and Ruby that celery and peanut butter is just as good as Doritos. The raisins they insisted on dotting the peanut butter with will work for the monster hit points.

After cutting out the tokens that will represent the monsters and the heroes I suggested we look over their character sheets. I was already losing Ruby, who was much more interested in putting the character tokens in her mouth than on the playmat.

"Maybe Ruby should play the monster," I suggested, while retrieving the slobbery tokens with about forty-nine pounds of paper towels. "Monsters eat the players, too."

"Ew," Gabe said. "I don't want to get eaten by a monster!"

"Exactly," I told him. "That's the whole point of the game. Try not to get eaten by the monsters."

Ruby stopped chewing on the tokens long enough to look at me with big, watery eyes.

"I don't wanna get eaten," she whimpered.

"You won't," I said. "But even if you do, nothing happens. You just live in the monster's belly until someone tickles it and lets you out."

"Like throw up?" Gabe asked.

"Um, kind of. But not that gross. More like a big sneeze."

That made them giggle.

"I wanna get in the monster's belly!" Gabe declared, making me think he and Bart would have a great time playing D&D together.

"So guys, here's the deal. You are friends who are in training to be monster hunters. Doesn't that sound exciting?"

"I wanna be a robot!" Gabe exclaimed.

"Me, too!" said Ruby.

"Well, today we're going to be monster hunters, okay?" These kids are too young to bully me. "A princess wizard and a big boy human fighter."

"Why?" they asked.

Good lord. Why must kids ask so many questions? Here's one: whose dumb idea was this?

"Because I said so." Hey, look at that! I *do* have some motherly instincts!

Technically we're short two people, but we solved that problem with me playing the DM and a hero and letting one of Ruby's "babies" round out the party. I laid out the playmat and the character tokens and explained a little bit about each one. Ruby immediately put the shaman in her mouth.

"Remind me to tell your mom to get you some fiber supplements or something."

Gabe practiced his "fighting" by popping his little sister in the bicep.

"Yay!" he exclaimed. "I'm a fighter!"

"You're not that kind of fighter. You're a fighter for good things. And your sister is on your team. You're supposed to work together."

Ruby got all watery eyed again and I tossed a handful of tissues in her direction as a preemptive strike. I don't do poop *or* snot. "How about you play a barbarian princess," I suggested. "Then you can be a big, tough girl, too."

Sold! I played the wizard and Ruby's baby played the rogue. I started the story about the gang being sent to monster-hunting training grounds and left to fend for themselves as various monsters are sprung from their cages.

"Scawee monsters?" Ruby asked. "Or monsters that want to play with us?"

"Umm, no," I said. "Not really." What kind of Dungeon Master would I be if I encouraged these kids to beat up monsters who want to play with them? "They're scary to most people, but not to you! You're big, strong adventurers! And this is your test. You have to defeat the monsters with your special powers."

Ruby chomped away on the barbarian. Gabe asked me where the robots were.

"Let's keep playing and maybe we'll find one, okay?"

They put their tokens on the playmat. Ruby's was covered in spit.

Partial to beholders, I brought one out of his cage onto the playmat. It moved three squares toward my wizard so I could show them what to do on a turn.

"Can you count how many squares away from the wizard this monster is?" I asked Ruby and Gabe. Not being a kid person, I was sincerely asking. I had no idea if kids can count at their ages.

"Three," Gabe answered, all *duh, what a stupid adult you are.*

"Well, unfortunately for the wizard, this monster's evil eyestalk can hit any creature within *six* squares. Looks like that'll hit. Who wants to roll the die to see what the effect will be?"

Rolling dice is apparently a highly sought-after kid activity because both Ruby and Gabe practically fell over themselves trying to get to the d20.

"Okay, okay, you can roll to see who gets to roll for the effect." More rolling of dice equals more fun, right?

Ruby won and rolled a six, *evil eye*, which meant the beholder switches places with the hero. Now he was standing adjacent to Gabe's fighter.

"Uh-oh!" he said. "The monster's next to me!" To illustrate the danger this presented, Gabe tried to strangle his sister.

"And all of his eyeballs are staring right at you!" I made big buggy eyes at him. "You need both hands free to block your face!"

He giggled, which made Ruby giggle, which in turn made me giggle.

Ruby's baby got to go next, but given she doesn't have fingers, Ruby rolled for her.

"Now remember," I said, "You want to attack the *monster*." Just in case she had any ideas about retaliating on her brother. "And you can move six squares. I'm sure Gabe will help you count."

"One, two, three, four, five, and six!" Ruby was overjoyed at her ability to count to six. I'm quite impressed myself, not sure if this is normal for a kid her age or if I've just inadvertently discovered her hidden genius. But she can't read, so maybe "genius-in-training" is more like it. It's pure luck that she moves her rogue to a flanking position with her brother.

"That's really good!" I told her. "Now if you hit, you'll do two points of damage instead of just one."

I handed her the die, which she promptly whacked against the glass table.

"What was that?" Des yelled from her office. "Everything okay?"

"Mommy, I killed a bad man!" Ruby responded.

"Not really, Des," I called after. "We're just playing!"

"What number is that?" I asked Ruby, directing her attention back to the battle.

"Eleven?" she asked, not entirely confident with her competence in double digits.

"That's right!" I squealed. Honestly, I have no idea if this normal or if I'm unleashing a beautiful mind. Regardless, I was happy to be in such close proximity to a kid who wasn't punching, crying, or running me over with a Big Wheel. Then again, there's still time.

"You hit the monster!" I announced. "You do two points of damage." I slid two raisins across the table to her, one of which her brother plopped in his mouth. Ruby was so delighted by hitting the monster, she didn't notice.

Next it should have been Ruby's turn but seeing as though she just rolled for her baby and I could sense Gabe's impatience, I let him go next.

Although Gabe is a much more advanced reader, I still had to help him read what was on his character sheet. I explained that because he's standing right next to the monster he can just reach out and cleave him.

"I cleave him!" Gabe announced. "For four raisins!"

As much as I appreciated his enthusiasm, I went over the rules.

"You need to roll the big, round die to see if you hit. If your number is higher than the monster's number, you can cleave him."

Gabe chucked the die on the table and again Des called out from her office.

"That noise better not be from something hitting my table."

"It's not!" the three of us called back.

"I got a twelve," Gabe said, leaning over the die.

Wow, these kids have some serious dice juju.

"That's great," I told him. "And you get to add four to that. So what do you get?"

Gabe pondered this for a minute and wiggled his fingers. "Sixteen!"

"You hit him!"

Next, Ruby's barbarian went.

"Make sure you hit him too, Ruby," Gabe instructed.

She rolled the dice but only got a six. Technically it was a miss, but I couldn't stand to see a three-year-old get booed by her brother.

"You hit him, Ruby!" I handed her two more raisins.

We went a couple more rounds with my wizard and Ruby's baby all taking damage. Gabe delighted in the idea that his fancy footwork shirked the beholder's *chains of ice*. The monster is down to two hit points, thanks mostly to Gabe and Ruby's baby's expert flanking.

"If you manage to hit him two more times," I explained to Ruby, "you're going to win!" I avoided saying, "kill." She is three, after all.

"Ruby!" Gabe commanded. "Get over here by me so we can *fank* the monster!"

"Good idea, Gabe," I said. "*Fanking* is very strategic."

He was so excited by his tactical thinking I didn't bother correcting his pronunciation or noting the fact that Ruby's barbarian can't flank. Only the rogue has that ability. It's a Dungeon Master's prerogative and by "prerogative" I mean, "desire to not make your best friend's kids cry."

Ruby carefully counted out five spaces and moved to a *fanking* position. She tossed the d20 on the glass table and rolled an eight.

"Not enough?" she asked, her bottom lip poking out.

"Do you get to add anything special to your eight?" I asked.

Gabe looked over her shoulder.

"You do!" Gabe exclaimed. "You can add five! Ruby, what is eight plus five?"

She thought about this for a minute. Those are some serious double digits for a three-year-old. If she got this, I was going to call the nearest Montessori school and pack her bags for Harvard.

She held her hand in front of her.

"Nine, ten," she began. "Can Gabe help?"

Gabe was chomping at the bit. And he'd already peeked over my shoulder so he knew exactly what it took to beat the beholder.

"Well, this is supposed to be a cooperative game so I guess it would be okay."

"Thirteen!" Gabe yelled. "You hit! We win!"

There were cheers all around. Even Des lets out a whoop from the office.

"Whatever you just won sounds very exciting!" she said.

To celebrate we finished off the box of raisins. I cut out the badges proclaiming them Heroes of Hesiod and Scotch-taped them to their collars.

"Your mom can make them stick better," I said. No way am I going near kids with safety pins. Three minutes later they were on the couch fighting over Gabe's Nintendo DS.

"What did you do to my kids?" Des asked, heading into the living room with a full glass of wine. "It sounded like they were having fun."

I couldn't tell if she was being polite or if she was just surprised I spent nearly an hour alone with kids and no one (most of all me) was crying.

"Oh, you know," I said, brushing her off. "Just hanging out."

Sure beats a punch in the ass.

Des called a few days later. I could hear Gabe and Ruby giggling in the background.

"Seriously," Des asked. "What have you done to my kids?"

Uh-oh, I think. They're having nightmares, or they're *fanking* the neighbors and clobbering them for raisins, or worse—they've destroyed Des's beautiful glass table with the d20 I left for them.

"I'm really sorry, Des," I said. "I really thought they were enjoying it. And I never used the word *kill*."

"I don't care if you did!" she yelled. "They won't leave each other's side! They have chores, easy stuff because you know they're just kids, but still I keep finding them doing things together. Ruby and Gabe were both

LEVELING UP THE
NEXT GENERATION

When I was little, my dad and I bonded over sneaker shopping (in the kickball days: I had to have the same sneakers that he did) and cassette-tape shopping. Such a thrill to come home, kick off my red Nikes with the white swoosh, and listen to my coveted Bananarama tape for the next seventeen hours.

These days geeky parents are finding creative ways to introduce their offspring to their beloved geeky pastimes. Inspire geek culture in the young adventurers in your life with these reads by some of Wired.com/geekdad's contributors:

★ Collect All 21! Memoirs of a Star Wars Geek—The First 30 Years, by John Booth

★ Geek Dad: Awesomely Geeky Projects and Activities for Dads and Kids to Share, by Ken Denmead

★ The Geek Dad's Guide to Weekend Fun: Cool Hacks, Cutting-Edge Games, and More Awesome Projects for the Whole Family, by Ken Denmead

★ World Myths and Legends: 25 Projects You Can Build Yourself (Build It Yourself Series), by Kathryn Ceceri

★ Around the World Crafts: Great Activities for Kids Who Like History, Math, Art, Science And More! by Kathryn Ceceri

holding the hose to water the garden, they help each other clean their rooms, they carried the dinner dishes to the dishwasher together. Like each one held one side of each dish!"

Wow, talk about lazy. I didn't like doing dishes either but I could certainly carry my own dish to the machine that washed it for me.

"I asked them what they were doing," she continued, "and they said they had to work together, *as a team*, so they could win some treasure."

"I don't know, Des, I mean, it sounds pretty normal for your kids," I said. "I have to admit you're doing something right because even I liked hanging out with them."

She hesitated. "I don't know. They keep talking about a monster that will give them raisins if they defeat it. Do you think they're calling me a monster?"

"They're much too young to think you're a monster," I told her. Someday they will, but I didn't tell her that. Instead, I let her bask in the glow of her new, improved kids.

"And they want to know when they'll see you again. You're suddenly their favorite friend."

"Me?" I asked. "They liked me?"

"Liked? They loved you! I don't know what you did but they can't stop talking about how much fun you were and how funny you are. You're right up there with Dave and the Giant Pickle."

Not to get all Sally Field on her, but I couldn't get past them actually liking me. Not just *tolerated* or *used as a vehicle for evil doings* but apparently enjoyed my company. And dare I say, I kind of enjoyed them? I was alone with them for nearly an hour and we all survived. I don't provoke an innate urge to hit, punch, or run over in *all* kids, at least.

Then I had the strangest vision. It was of my red CB ski jacket. The most coveted possession a twelve-year-old could own. All the kids at West Middle School had CB ski jackets. For good reason, too—they skied. Not me. In fact, I barely went outside if it was below 40 degrees but I *had* to have a CB jacket. Had. To. Simply could not survive another day without one. Only problem was, those suckers were expensive. Like hundreds of dollars. A pretty steep investment for a hobby I had no intention of ever participating in.

"Absolutely not," Judy said over and over. "You don't need a fancy ski jacket to walk from the front door to the driveway in."

"But I need a warm coat!" I pleaded. "It's every child's right!"

"You have a warm coat. It's fine. Get over it."

I would never "get over it," as Judy suggested. At least, not really. But I could do the next best thing—stage a loud, vocal, aggressive smear campaign against CB jackets.

"Look how puffy Heather's coat is," I said to Mary and Kristina at lunchtime.

"Do you smell that?" I asked Peter, when we were waiting for the crossing guard to give us the go-ahead. "It's coming from Sean's CB. I hear they use the feathers of birds that died from disease and murder for those jackets."

It was a noble effort but the only person I was fooling was myself. If I couldn't have the one thing I lusted after, the only thing I believed would make a preteen me happy (next to Bon Jovi playing at my thirteenth birthday party), then I pretended I didn't want it.

I'm not picking out names or picking out running strollers at Babies"R"Us but ... could it be possible? Could kids be ski jackets to women in their late '30s who have spent the majority of our lives single?

"I hope you don't mind," I said to Des. "But I'd like to make plans with Gabe and Ruby again. Maybe they could come to Seattle and Bart and I could take them to the zoo or the aquarium or, I know! The Science Center. Bart has been dying to go there."

"They would love that!" she shouted. "And I'd love a little time in the city to myself." Then she added, "Are you sure Bart wouldn't mind?"

"He'd love it," I said with confidence. "I'm sure he and Gabe will be best buds."

She sighed. "You're so lucky to be with someone who is good with kids. I hope you know that."

"I know," I said, realizing for the first time in, well ... ever, that was true. "But if you tell Judy I hung out with your kids—and liked it—your glass table gets it."

CHAPTER 8

LAIR OF THE HARPY

ADVENTURE OVERVIEW

Nestled inside the Pacific Northwest's fabled Ring of Fire, between the evergreens and hilly one-way streets untouched by salt trucks or snowplows, lies Seattle's twelfth-most-popular neighborhood. Potholed streets, an embarrassing lack of sidewalks, a plethora of bodegas offering piñatas and Jarritos soda (which the party should definitely stop in and try), and one delicious tap house are all hallmark's of Seattle's twelfth-most-popular neighborhood. Well, those hallmarks and the one they seldom discuss: the vicious harpy and her familiar—a dire feline—who live complacently in a condo, which may or may not be under a massive assessment at this time.

THE TAP HOUSE

The party, parched from a day of dodging potholes and walking single-file down streets in the bike lane, stops by the tap house made famous by the Harpy. She loves not just the twenty-four rotating beers on tap but their creative use of vegetarian Field Roast in their menu offerings. You half expect to see her here, but alas, it's a Wednesday. The Harpy never goes out on Wednesdays.

The townsfolk of Seattle's twelfth-most-popular neighborhood are in a tizzy, believing the Harpy has taken a brave, albeit somewhat lackadaisical, adventurer as her hostage.

"It will take a mighty band of warriors to bring him back safely," the barkeeper says. "Danger is inevitable, but the rewards are great."

"What are the rewards?" the party asks, sampling a delicious array of IPAs from Seattle's more popular neighborhoods.

"Justice," the barkeep says, staring you right in the eyes. "And free beer."

The party gathers up their belongings and heads out in the sidewalk-less night.

HISTORY

The party arrives at an old, stucco, multi-unit dwelling, which may or may not have water damage. This is the home of the Harpy, where she has lived for nearly thirteen years, alone mostly, with the exception of various visiting hell-hounds and her evil familiar. Only few have dared to enter the Harpy's lair and usually come armed with pad thai, groceries, or boxes too big to fit inside the USPS-approved pigeonhole.

THE OUTSIDE AREA

Although this is a secured-entry doorway, the Harpy's neighbors are careless when entering and leaving and sometimes don't close the door all the way or (heaven forbid) leave the door propped open while they carry in the groceries they actually go out and purchase themselves or move out busted-up Ikea coffee tables and rust-laden shower caddies. Much to the Harpy's dismay, you have no trouble getting into this building.

There is a flight of stairs covered in threadbare commercial carpet that looks like it's been long traveled by deliverymen and logistics service coordinators in brown uniforms. You come across a spot on the carpet near the elevator.

Perception Check DC 17: The spot is likely the result of a senior, arthritic dog with diarrhea who couldn't get out of the building quickly enough.

You take the stairs. On the second floor, you come across the unit rumored to be the lair of the Harpy. The door is brown and thick and pocked with indents that may be the result of your predecessors' failed attempts at entry, or perhaps the Harpy's failed attempts at nailing a hook to her door to hang the red-and-green-feathered wreath she got at Nordstrom. No matter.

Perception Check DC 4: The lock on the door appears weak, and again to the Harpy's dismay, looks like you could pick it with a credit card, barrette, even the corner of a takeout menu.

Thievery Check DC 6: The lock gives in with some minor fidgeting.

THE INTERIOR AREA

You notice a very lived-in space with designer paint on the walls and comfy, oversized couches that dip and sag in such a way, you'd surmise the Harpy loves her television. The welcoming feeling that overtakes you is surprising. That couch looks *very* comfortable. You can see why the Harpy spends a lot of time here. Oh, how you'd like to snuggle into it with that chenille blanket over you and watch several, commercial-free episodes of *Say Yes to the Dress* on her DVR. You move a few large, cardboard, sealed-up boxes out of the way to get a better view of the couch.

Perception Check DC 15: The couch is in fact a trap.

The remains of a pizza and Caesar salad dinner are left on the coffee table, along with cloth napkins dotted with sauce, empty wine glasses ringed with cheap cabernet (that's going to be a bitch to get off), the burned-down nubs of decorative candles, and several empty water glasses. Judging by the hard pellets of sauce on the plates, you surmise those dishes have been left out overnight.

Perception Check DC 3: You hear snoring coming from the living room and notice a large, lazy pit bull sleeping on a pile of dog beds. She is unfazed by your arrival.

The bedside tables look brand new. You stop and admire them before continuing into the kitchen/dining room, adjacent to the living room.

There is an empty pizza box on the dining room table, along with piles of papers, books, and torn-open envelopes. A brown, decorative basket sits next to the laptop computer.

Perception Check DC 2: The brown, decorative basket is empty.

The kitchen looks as if a team of novice caterers have just completed service for 150. Olive oil, that appears to be much too expensive for such haphazard treatment, is uncapped and left out. An empty wine bottle sits in the sink, approximately three and a half feet from the recycling bin. The once-pristine stainless steel countertops are marred with a large rusty circle approximately the same circumference of the filthy wok you notice on the shelf above the stove. A colander with three cherry tomatoes sits in the sink along with—*gasp!*—more dirty dishes. From all you have heard about the uptight, controlling, stuck-in-a-routine Harpy, you are suddenly not sure this is her lair after all.

Perception Check DC 8: It is. You see pictures all over the refrigerator of her with some guy.

Perception Check DC 18: The guy looks very similar to the brave adventurer who has gone missing.

The party follows a trail of toast crumbs into what appears to be the washroom. Definitely something wicked has transpired in here as evidenced by the red, sticky globules all over the basin.

Perception check DC 5: Blood!

Perception Check DC 15: Nope. It's just cinnamon toothpaste.

The mirror above the washbasin is speckled with white dots, making it difficult to see your reflection. The white porcelain sink is dotted with tiny black dots.

Perception Check DC 8: Those black dots are hairs from a freshly shorn chin.

A tub of Clorox wipes sits in the corner of the basin.

Perception Check DC 5: The Clorox wipes have not been opened. Not ever. Which probably explains the chin hairs.

The shower curtain is falling off the hooks and barely conceals the disgusting mess of a tub behind it. What the heck is that along the rim of the tub, anyway?

Perception Check DC 7: This tub was caulked recently.

Perception Check DC 14: The tub needs a professional to caulk it.

The drain of the shower is covered in something dark and fuzzy.

Perception Check DC 2: Ew! It's hair! It's the Harpy's hair! And she thinks the toothpaste is bad? Why is it so hard to clean the drain out after every shower?

This room is creepy and gives the party a sense of the willies. You leave the area and continue into what appears to be the Harpy's boudoir.

Perception Check DC 26: The dreaded dire feline is asleep on the bed. She does not appear to hear you.

The party treads lightly so as not to wake the feline.

There are two closets and two dressers in this space. You peek inside the larger of the two closets and notice something odd. Six hangers appear to be holding men's clothing. You also notice two pairs of jeans that look oddly out of place.

Perception Check DC 7: Relaxed fit. From what you know of the Harpy she favors boot cut or skinny leg jeans. These definitely belong to someone else.

Several pairs of men's shoes litter the floor but you don't see any women's shoes except those in boxes on the top shelf of the closet or slung in clear plastic pockets over the back of both doors.

Perception Check DC 2: The Harpy has a lot of shoes. You find this ridiculous.

The bed is unmade. You don't know what hospital corners are but are pretty sure they are not on this bed. The duvet cover looks expensive and goes perfectly with the gray paint and yellow and white accents. Perhaps the most shocking thing you encounter is what lies next to the dire feline on the bed: A towel!

Perception Check DC 12: The towel is still damp!

Again the party is filled with suspicion that perhaps the Harpy no longer takes residence here. Has the brave adventurer slain the Harpy? Has her infamous mother finally crushed her daughter's soul under the weight of a thousand paperbacks? Has the Harpy's attempts to untangle herself from her obsessive, stagnant, mired ways driven her mad?

Could be.

But then, her familiar is still alive. And seemingly healthy. Even though that cat is a jerk, the Harpy is a notorious animal lover. No matter how many scars or bouts with Cat Scratch Fever, or pleas from friends and pad thai delivery men, the Harpy wouldn't abandon the stupid cat. Plus the Harpy's clothes are here. There are way too many lovingly folded, hung, and organized by color to assume she could leave these behind. Besides, everyone knows the Harpy couldn't pack her most precious belongings into a backpack.

Just as you saw on the refrigerator, here there are more pictures of the Harpy and the assumed brave adventurer. They stand sunburned and sweaty in front of the Parthenon; perch overlooking Puget Sound with a magnificent picnic spread out before them; and pose steins in hands, in cheap, polyester Bavarian costumes. They smile, heads bent temple to temple in every photo. It's almost hard to believe the smiling, relaxed woman in the pictures is the same woman who could make a grown man cry for putting wine glasses in the bottom rack of the dishwasher.

Perception Check DC 4: Yep. You fully believe these are photos of a happy-looking couple.

The party passes by a bookshelf crammed with books. You see the shiny domed heads and round glasses-wearing faces of Today's Top Self-Help Experts next to tomes full of tentacled monsters with eyestalk-sporting heads. Books about heroes and dangerous lands and handbooks and compendiums are side-by-side with hardback readers promising to unleash the power of the universe. Some of these books, especially the ones with the strange-looking experts' headshots on them, look very scary.

Perception Check DC 9: The spines on the scary-looking books show zero signs of wear and tear. These books have never been opened.

As you look around, the dire feline yawns and stretches on the expensive duvet cover. It's hard to imagine the Harpy would allow the furry, shedding, dander-ridden beast to lounge on her bed and yet freak out over some dirty gym clothes. On second thought, dirty gym clothes *are* pretty gross. The dire feline has beautiful blue eyes, you notice, then you quickly avert your gaze lest you be turned into a pile of catnip. It is then you spot another book lying on the bed. This book is facedown and opened. The spine is crackled and creased. The pages appear to be dog-eared and marked with sticky notes. There is what appears to be a woman in white on the cover holding a bouquet of purple flowers.

Perception Check DC 5: Unlike the scary books on the shelf, this book has been read. A lot.

A neon orange Post-it Note arbitrarily stuck to the front covers some of the book's title.

Perception Check DC 9: You can make out the words planning, guide, and fabulous.

You can't be entirely sure what the handwritten note says because no one in the party wants to get that close to the dire feline, but you're pretty confident you can make out the words love, mom.

Perception Check DC 21: You can also read the words see chapter 5, buffet, reception, and don't worry about budget.

A chill runs down your spine as you realize what this means. There is not much time. You must leave the Harpy's lair and return to town. This is much worse than anyone thought. The townspeople of Seattle's twelfth-most-popular neighborhood and beyond must be warned. No caterer, DJ, or florist uninformed.

The Harpy and her mother have a new project. And for once, it looks like mother and daughter are on the same page.

ABOUT THE AUTHOR

SHELLY MAZZANOBLE is the author of the ENnie Award-winning *Confessions of a Part-Time Sorceress: A Girl's Guide to the DUNGEONS & DRAGONS® Game,* and she writes a monthly column for *Dragon* online. Her short stories and essays have appeared in the *Seattle Times, Carve, Whetstone, Skirt!,* and SomeOtherMagazine.com. In a fit of narcissism, she has appeared in her own work, sometimes casting herself as the lead in her plays, which have been produced in Seattle's Mae West Fest and Manhattan Theatre Source's Estrogenius Festival. Originally from upstate New York and a graduate of Ithaca College, she now lives in Seattle with a bipolar cat, a dog who may or may not have murdered a cat, and a guy who sometimes leaves wet towels on her expensive duvet cover. Visit her online at shellymazzanoble.com.

VIE FOR GLORY

NEVERWINTER™

GAUNTLGRYM
Neverwinter Saga, Book I
R.A. SALVATORE

NEVERWINTER
Neverwinter Saga, Book II
R.A. SALVATORE

BRIMSTONE ANGELS
Legends of Neverwinter
ERIN M. EVANS
November 2011

NEVERWINTER
RPG for PC
Coming in 2011

NEVERWINTER CAMPAIGN SETTING
For the D&D® Roleplaying Game
August 2011

THE LEGEND OF DRIZZT
Neverwinter Tales
Comic Books Written by R.A. Salvatore & Geno Salvatore
August 2011

THE LEGEND OF DRIZZT™
Cooperative Board Game
October 2011

Find these great products at your favorite bookseller or game shop.
DungeonsandDragons.com

CONTINUE YOUR ADVENTURE

The Dungeons & Dragons® Fantasy Roleplaying Game Starter Set has everything you need for you and your friends to start playing. Explore infinite universes, create bold heroes and prepare to begin– or rediscover– the game that started it all.

Watch Videos
Read Sample Chapters
Get product previews
Learn more about D&D® products
at
DungeonsandDragons.com

Get More Out of Your D&D® Experience.

Add more to your characters and campaigns with a constantly growing source of new and exclusive tools and online applications like:

D&D Character Builder
D&D Compendium
D&D Adventure Tools

Plus articles, art, maps, galleries, and other exclusive content.

Level up your game at DungeonsandDragons.com